ABDUCTED FOR THE PACK

CELESTIAL CLAIM, BOOK ONE

NATALIA PRIM

Created with Vellum

CONTENTS

Content Warning   5
Preface   7

Chapter 1   13
Chapter 2   19
Chapter 3   41
Chapter 4   56
Chapter 5   68
Chapter 6   75
Chapter 7   88
Chapter 8   95
Chapter 9   108
Chapter 10   129
Chapter 11   134
Chapter 12   146
Chapter 13   153
Chapter 14   162
Chapter 15   172
Chapter 16   178
Chapter 17   186
Chapter 18   193
Chapter 19   206
Chapter 20   216
Chapter 21   225
Chapter 22   229
Chapter 23   238
Chapter 24   246
Chapter 25   252
Chapter 26   260
Chapter 27   266

Chapter 28   271

Chapter 29   285

Chapter 30   300

Chapter 31   306

Chapter 32   313

Chapter 33   323

Hunted for the Pack Blurb   331

Want more??   333

About Natalia Prim   335

Guide to The Glade   337

⚠ YO, READER! ⚠

Please visit www.nataliaprim.com for the full content
warning!!!
THIS IS YOUR FINAL CHANCE.

TRUST ME, YOU WANNA KNOW WHAT'S IN HERE!

Someone actually read my dedication in the last book, totally wrecking my theory! So, perhaps you're reading this, hoping for something pithy, something that will make your mind explode in fairy jizz and butterflies.

No dice. There's a sm^ttastic, plot-filled, paranormal werewolf mate-fest with a robust cast of characters, each with secrets and agendas starting in just a few pages. I bled digital ink into these beautiful, horny idiots, and I've got nothing left for this lil' block.

I hope like heckfire you've read the content warning. It's go time.

Monsters are real... and I'm in love with them.

I've always been the quiet wallflower. Invisible. Unremarkable. No friends, and no memories worth having. Coasting through my last year of college, I take a chance on a frat party, and wake up later surrounded by monsters. What follows is an encounter I couldn't scrub from my brain if I tried. Worst of all, I don't want to.

I'm tossed into their world, where any hope of escape is wrecked by the filthy-mouthed alpha, and his pack's obsession with me. They show me pleasure—and pain—like I never thought possible. Even love.

But our fledgling bonds are tested too soon, as we're pitted against rival packs, ancient foes, warring factions, crazy zealots, and an illusion of choice which could leave me irreversibly changed.

Contains:
_____

✓ Multi-pov ✓ Inter-pack relationships

✓ Unique world-building ✓ A veritable buffet of pairings

⚠ Head to nataliaprim.com for all the content warnings ⚠

#LetTheGuysKiss #LoveIsLove

#IfYouClutchedYourPearlsThisAintTheBookForYou

Hey Reader! You've been warned. The story is about to begin. If you haven't read the content alerts and you still plow forward, don't attack me via ratings if you come up on something you don't like! If you have specific content questions, PLEASE reach out. I know what being triggered feels like, and if you're worried, I'm more than happy to help! #knowledgeispower

REANNE

Collage is nothing like I hoped it would be. This is my last year, and I'm still lost, still friendless, still an outsider. I sit at the front of every class, keep my head down, study, and do what I'm supposed to, which never earned me social points growing up, so I don't know why I thought that would change.

True, I'm not here for that reason, not really, but it would be fun to hang out. Party a little, I guess. Have the promised 'college experience.' Even my dorm is boring and lonely. My roommate stays with her boyfriend nearly all the time, and even when she is here, we don't speak. Don't even acknowledge each other. There's no tangible animosity, just one of those situations where you don't mesh with someone. I've wondered more than once if she even realizes I'm still here most of the time.

So, it's just me. And that's fine. I've had to look out for myself basically since I was born, like every other kid who grew up in the system, bounced from house to house. No brothers, no sisters, no parents...

Normally, it doesn't bother me much, but there's something in the air today, an itch of loneliness I can't scratch. I stroll through the courtyard, lost in thought, weaving through other students as they rush to their next class.

A bright orange flyer appears under my face, shocking me.

"Full moon kegger tonight at the Zeta Lambda house. See you there, gorgeous?"

I scoff a laugh on reflex before I glance up. The guy is cute, sure, but I can't tell if he's mocking me for his own amusement, or if his friends are nearby, recording the conversation. Either way, I know I'm not gorgeous. Normal? Sure. But absolutely unremarkable in every way. Brown hair, brown eyes, not particularly curvy, average height, average features, quiet. I'm one of those girls who blends into any background in any gathering, ignored by everyone.

"Nah, I don't think so. Thanks, though."

I step around him, but he blocks my path, waggling the flyer. "At least take it. I've gotta hand all these things out. Maybe you'll change your mind."

When I don't grab it, he shoves it down my open purse, smiles and stops the next girl who passes, repeating the same line, only replacing 'gorgeous' with 'love.'

Whatever. I have my own fun-filled Friday night planned, chock full of nothing.

But I think about the flyer my entire drive back to the dorm. I think about it while I shower. While I eat dinner. While I stare at the TV, pretending to watch it. The crumpled orange corner juts out of the top of my purse like a beacon, until I finally storm over and snatch it out.

Hmm. It's nothing special, just a mixer, but it does promise music, drinks, and games. And it's not that far from here, I could walk it. It's only been going for thirty minutes, too, so I wouldn't be all that late. I suppose there's no harm in going. It might even be fun. Maybe.

I get ready, not doing anything fancy at all. Dark jeans, loose grey blouse, white canvas shoes, hair back in a low ponytail. No sense dressing extra nice or over-doing makeup for a bunch of guys who won't see me anyway. It's not like I expect to get laid. They won't even notice me.

Would sex be nice? Hell yes. I love it. I've had a couple of very short-term boyfriends in my life, some one-night stands, and enough time with my right hand to teach a class. It's probably how I'll end tonight, in fact. Fantasizing about all manner of dark, devious things no one would expect a quiet girl to know or want.

Heat crawls through my stomach, and the flame doesn't die the whole walk there. The itch of loneliness grows, melding with the heat, turning into a deep longing for... some undefinable thing. I haven't felt this before, and I don't particularly like it. The moon is gorgeous, at least. Big, full, casting a warm white glow over everything. My heart pangs, and I stall. What the heck is going on?

I almost turn around, but thumping bass echoes down the street, followed by cheers. Right. The idea is to have fun with other people.

There's movement out of the corner of my eye, behind one of the houses, but I don't see anything when I look. I swallow down the anxiety. Cat, just a cat.

I walk faster, cresting a small hill, and spot the Zeta Lambda frat house, lit up like it's daytime. A crowd of guys and gals mill around, pawing at each other, drinking, laughing, and dancing. It does look fun. There are lights strung through the trees, corn hole boards, beer pong on a fold out table, several kegs, and—

Movement at my other side this time. I whip my head, but there's still nothing. My pulse pounds, and I trot toward the group. It's probably just...night animals.

A guy holds out a red plastic cup as soon as I reach the first table, but he doesn't even glance my way, chatting to some girl in a string bikini top and cut-off jeans.

"Thanks," I mutter to the watered-down beer.

As usual, no one notices me as I make my way through the crowd. I stand next to the beer pong table and cheer, moving with the group when they swap to corn hole. When it should be my turn, they leave, like I was invisible the whole time. I grip the cup between my knees and toss the bean bags in the hole, one right after the other.

"See, I would have been good for the team," I say to no one, and down the rest of the beer.

Warmth hits my back, seeping through my shirt like someone's looming over me. I gasp and turn, but there's no one. I take a few steps backward, watching, and bump into a hard, hot body.

"Oh! I'm s..." I turn, but again, there's no one. "Okayyyy, what the hell is going on?"

I run toward the house and slip inside, between a guy and girl leaning in to kiss. They don't notice.

The air in here is thick, smokey, and weird. Another red cup is held out to me, and I take it without question, downing it quickly. I'm on edge and it's stupid. The booze has to help, otherwise I'll freak myself out and go home. Then what would have been the point in coming at all?

Air brushes my neck, like an inhale, and I yelp, stepping to the side as I turn, but again—no one.

Women giggle on the stairs, guys cheer in the kitchen, and the music gets louder the further in I go.

Another obvious inhale along my neck raises gooseflesh, and I turn to find nothing. What the hell?! When I whip back around, the shadowed guy is gone.

I can barely breathe through the fear. I might be in a crowd of people, but I've never felt more singled out in my life.

"Okay," I whisper. "I think that's enough fun for one night."

I take a step back and bump into a hard body again, but this time when I turn someone *is* there. The hoodie guy. Wow, he's tall. How did he get here so fast? He doesn't move, other than a smirk forming on his full lips. I can make out the edge of a large scar running down the side of his neck, and tanned skin, but that's it.

"S-sorry, didn't see you."

"Let's get out of here and you can make it up to me."

I blink several times and laugh. I see. It makes sense the only reason I'd be singled out is to be made fun of.

"Uh. No thanks." I step to the side and suck in a gasp as something brushes the back of my arm. I grab the spot and glance back, met with just the empty hallway. A bug...maybe?

Hoodie guy doesn't move, but the smirk fades, replaced by a sneer. "Did you say no?"

I start to reply, but clamp my jaw shut, make a wide circle around him and trot toward the door.

The night air feels much better on my skin, and I take a

deep breath. Maybe too deep. I stumble a bit and shake the dizziness from my head. Probably shouldn't have had those beers so fast. Nothing I can't sleep off.

The guy chatting up bikini top girl holds out another red cup as I approach, but I brush it away and hit the sidewalk with quick steps.

The moon is brighter, hazier. I blink several times, but the haze doesn't clear. My skin feels too tight, buzzing like I'm loaded with static. The first three times I see movement in my peripheral, I try to track it, but each whip of my head makes me dizzier.

There's nothing but the pound of my own heartbeat in my ears as I force my feet to move, each step getting harder to control.

Something growls nearby, and I scream, stumbling as the sound reverberates through my skull. The dorm. I just need to make it to the dorm. It can't be that far away, and it's nearly a straight shot.

I trudge forward, my legs heavy like they're stuck in wet sand. Is it an allergic reaction to the bug bite? Was there something in the beer? Everyone else seemed fine.

Another step, another, and that's all I can do. I sway, my hands on my head, until my knees give, and I drop.

REANNE

I wake up outside on the damp ground in the pitch dark, my head spinning. I can't make my body respond at first. Slowly, feeling comes back in a dull wave through my extremities, and I try to sit up, but can't.

My neck is held in place by a large collar. No matter how hard I struggle, it doesn't budge. My hands and ankles are secured by heavy bands attached to something, while my knees are open, chains looped around them.

And I'm... Oh, God. Why am I naked? How did I get here? Where is here?

I clench my legs together, but they don't close. There's no give on the chains at all, only a slight rattle. A sound that apparently riles up someone, or something. The rustling grows in volume, and I realize it's not dark, I'm blindfolded.

Fear rips through me as I jerk and kick, screaming for help.

A heavy hand presses down hard on my mouth.

"Told you we should have gagged her."

"Shut up, Chris. She was unconscious. I didn't expect her to wake up so soon."

"Should have put more stuff in those drinks."

Wait...I fight with my hazy memories. I...was at a party. That's right. Zeta Lambda. Full moon something.

This must be the guy who handed me the drink when I walked in the house. I can't...I can't remember anything else. If I get out of this, I'm definitely telling the Dean. Utterly terrified, I scream once more for good measure, but my throat aches.

"Yeah, well, too late for that now. You got the knife?"

"It's too pretty to use for something like this," the other one mutters. "Looks old. What if it breaks?"

"Who cares? Aim for the heart, like he said."

My blood turns to ice. Before I can gather the air to scream again, my knees are wrenched wider, exposing more of my tender flesh. I fight to close them again, but there's still no give, leaving me completely vulnerable.

"Mason, what are you doing?"

I distinctly hear a belt buckle. "She's right here. Might as well make use of her. Don't tell me you didn't think it."

"Jesus," the other guy mutters under his breath. "Can't we just do what the freaky guy asked us to do and get back to the party? Layla is waiting for me upstairs."

I give everything, every ounce of power I have, to struggling in my restraints, screaming words no one can understand.

I don't want to die, I don't want to be 'made use of.'

"We'll still kill her, chillax." He drops down between my legs, bumping into my inner thighs, lining up even as I struggle to get away. "Nothing saying we can't have fun fir—"

There's a vicious growl out of nowhere, barely covering a sick squelch and the guy is gone, leaving a rush of cool air

20

against my leg. The other two men scream, and all I can hear are sounds of flesh being ripped, bones cracking, things falling to the leaves around me. I'm splattered with warm droplets, over and over, as my mind blanks in terror.

This is it. I'll die out here, in this fucked up position. Eaten by wild animals I can't see. Hopefully they don't leave enough of me behind to identify. Not that anyone would care.

Everything stops, except several distinct somethings breathing heavily, laced with low growls.

One steps a bit closer, crunching the leaves near my head, and I suck in air to scream, but stop.

There's a weird feeling in my stomach, curling around my heart. Tugging, warmth...heat? No way. Why in the whole damn world would I be feeling that right now?

I finally get enough oxygen through my constricted throat to call out.

"Help! Anyone, please!"

There're only low broken rumbles. Leaves crunching louder all around me in no discernible rhythm. Feet. It must be. Lots of feet. Heavy steps and heavier breathing.

Something touches my waist, and I yelp, twisting my torso as far as I can, but that's barely at all. Coarse fur and a clawed hand brush my outer thigh, and keep brushing it, as whatever it is travels the length of my leg. Wait...a hand? How could...what kind of thing has claws and fur and a hand? I don't want to find out.

"Please, please, please," I cry. "Somebody!"

The creature laps my knee with a hot, rough tongue, near the chains, shocking my system. It growls, and terror slides down my back. A tiger...or...or a bear? Huge, whatever it is. There's a snapping, deep snarl from nearby and I suck in breath after breath.

This has to be a nightmare. That's the best explanation. Stuff like this doesn't happen, things like this don't exist. I passed out on the sidewalk and that's where I'm still at.

Something licks my calf.

"No, no, no, no." I try to kick when it licks my ankle, but my foot is firmly pinned. "Stupid...whatever you are, stop!"

It snorts, in what I swear to God sounds like indignation. Deep growls that border on laughs sound nearby, but I must be imagining it. Monsters like this can't laugh, can they? That's when I realize I was right. I'm dreaming. There are *really* no such things as intelligent monsters.

Despite knowing I must still be knocked out, I scream when a long tongue slides across my stomach, a giant body pushing against my legs to make room. Shocking heat pools in my core, my heart beating a bizarre rhythm, aching like I've just been broken up with. Or something. I can't really explain it.

A different tongue laves my nipple, another one licking the side of that breast, the two working together until they've canvased the whole thing. My nipples harden with the contact, and the creatures apparently enjoy that. They nip at my peaks, lapping and biting, while the other keeps bathing my lower stomach with long, hot licks. One takes my whole breast in his maw and mouths it, not hard, but firm enough that there's still pleasure.

No. How could I possibly *think* that word right now?

They move to the other one, licking and nipping, twangs of excitement shooting to my clit. I jerk in the chains, breaths coming faster. This is not okay. No matter...how hot it's making me.

"St-stop," it's too breathy to be a real command, my body completely betraying me. "No!"

There's a rumble father off to my left, almost like a chuckle, but it's so deep I can barely make it out. Is there another one?!

The one at my stomach moves to the inside of my thigh, long slow licks along my chill-bump-covered skin. Maybe he's tasting me, trying to decide if I'm a suitable meal.

That jerks me out of my growing arousal haze, and I scream again, ending on a sob as I jerk in the chains.

A huge, clawed hand covers my mouth, and I expected to smell animal, but there's only an undercurrent of...ocean? What in the—Nothing makes sense. I can't figure out what's going on, which only scares me more.

Sharp teeth graze my inner thigh and I clench on reflex, but still can't escape, can't close off or protect myself.

Tongues. Tongues and teeth and claws and hot panting breaths everywhere but where I want it most.

NO! I don't want anything to happen there.

But everyone and their neighbor could tell you that was a lie by the wicked moan that escapes me next. As if he read my mind, the one between my legs runs his teeth down, and settles his muzzle square on my slit. I gasp behind the hand, on fire everywhere. He draws a long inhale, sniffing me from top to bottom, exhaling a monstrous growl that vibrates my teeth, his hot breath fanning over me. The sensation drives me absolutely wild.

The other two pause, and the air around me changes.

A rumble from one, a chuff from the other, and an

23

answering growl from off to my left. Okay, definitely another one. Great. Wait, are...are they...talking?

Maybe I'm not asleep, or dreaming, but I've clearly lost my mind if I'm considering that.

The one between my legs snarls, and launches forward, bracing on the ground by my waist, covering me with heat. The other two rear back, my mouth freed for a moment.

Okay, he's obviously in charge, or at least higher rank. And that shouldn't excite me, but it does. The weird tug in my belly gets stronger as he slowly returns to his position, but it almost feels like it's tugging a different direction. To my...left.

I can't focus on that right now, as I whimper, tremble in anticipation, and the other two crowd me again, resuming their tongue assault. One is licking my arm, the other snuffling my ear, licking my jaw and neck. It tickles, and I squeal on reflex.

It's all so overwhelming. It's wrong and I shouldn't be as aroused as I am, but I'm practically moaning here in the dirt.

My thighs are jostled as he settles his muzzle again and laps in one long, slow, hot, rough motion, from bottom to top sliding along every inch of my core with his wide tongue. He pulls back a little at the top, barely touching my clit. Just enough that I'm shaking from need.

"Oh, God!"

Clearly, they forgot my mouth was uncovered. I forgot, too. Forgot to call out for help, because...I can't even admit it.

The ocean-scented one fixes it immediately by running his huge tongue across my lips over and over. The only way to keep him out is to clamp my jaw shut and press my mouth closed. Way more effective than a hand.

My pussy is laved again. And again. Another. Faster. I don't even bother hiding how turned on I am, whimpering and keening.

The other one still relentlessly licks my body, shifting positions, swapping breasts, dipping into my belly button, grazing my hips. Their fur pricks, their teeth are sharp, their claws dig.

It all feels amazing. I don't want to come from this. I don't want to enjoy this. But I do. I do both. One more fast lick and I explode, shuddering in my restraints but unable to cry out. I refuse for my mouth to be invaded by a gigantic tongue.

My orgasm changes the game for them. I'm surrounded now by low growls. The one at my mouth shifts his body until something hot and hard ruts against the faint crook of my elbow. The monster lapping me becomes ravenous. He licks my dripping juices with huffing breaths, snout mashed against my folds, his massive body touching my knees on both sides.

The one at my stomach moves back to my breasts, nipping my hardened peaks. The rutting on my elbow goes faster, harder. Claws scratch my sides, my arms. Teeth bare down on my clit next, sending me into a shocked muffled scream as the licks against my mouth push harder. I jerk at the chains on my knees as he nibbles, over and over, but I can't escape, my poor nub utterly helpless to the pleasure.

I'm so turned on and so ashamed it burns. I come again, shuddering, convulsing, but they don't let up. I swear I hear another low chuckle from my left, but the other growls and my own thumping pulse drown out any chance to be sure.

My clit aches, tender from the constant attention, but he just keeps going. There's a brief pause in the assault against my mouth, followed by huffed breaths and a massive load of hot cum on my arm. He leans back with an obviously satisfied growl, and I take a quick deep breath, sure I'm safe, but my mouth is attacked immediately. Only, it's not a tongue that invades, it's something bigger. Much bigger.

The cock that thrusts in isn't like any I've ever had near me, but the skin feels...human. My brain fights with this information, because it doesn't make any sense.

I choke when it hits my throat. Now might be my only chance to fight back, so, I bite down, but there's a matching bite down on my breast. I let out a muffled scream and release the pressure, and the pressure lets up on my breast.

That's the rule of it, then. I want to avoid as much damage to my body as I can, which means I let the monster fuck my mouth. My clit is finally released, and the lack of sensation is almost more painful.

"Did I say stop?"

It's such a shock to hear the deep, angry voice, I jump, shaking all my restraints. I try to talk around the cock, to shout for help, but it keeps pistoning. Tears prick my eyes from the shame of someone seeing me this way and the cock slapping my throat.

There's an answering growl, as he lowers his head back down. My mind reels. These things answer to a man? And he's telling them to—

A guttural groan escapes as that wide tongue dives deep,

twisting inside me. God, it all feels so good. So wrong. I roll my hips in encouragement.

"Dirty little slut. I knew you'd like it."

Shame floods my system, and I battle the moan that wants to escape as I'm tongue fucked even harder, but I can't. It comes out, broken by the downward pressure of the cock in my throat.

"Just can't get enough, can you? Where's that 'no' now?"

His words slice me open, but I can't stop the ecstasy spreading through me, the way I buck against the massive, furry body between my legs, hitting all the right spots, or the way I scream around the bulbous cock. It's hot having my mouth used like this, my body at their mercy. I don't know what's wrong with me.

I struggle to place the voice, through the haze of building orgasm, but all my attention is brought back to my mouth as that cock thrusts deeper and spills cum down my throat. I choke, gag, on sheer stubborn principle, not because of the taste. In fact, it has a subtle sweetness. When he finally pulls out, I spit the excess on the ground, coughing, surrounded by more growling.

"Please," I whisper. "Help."

"What do you think we're doing, slut? Those bricks of shit were going to kill you."

I open my mouth to ask what fucking me stupid has to do with that, but the ocean-scented hand covers it, only there's no fur this time, it's just a normal, wide, hot hand. Lips press to my ear—human lips—and he whispers, *"Better not, it'll only make him angrier."*

The heat from his breath and the timber of his voice twist my insides. How does he smell the same as the monster? Tears spring up, partly from exhaustion, but mostly confusion. He kisses them away, shushing me. "Aw sweetheart, no need for that."

The one between my legs pulls his tongue out slowly, and resumes the assault on my clit, wrenching a scream from my tired throat. Even though it's muffled by a hand, it's still loud.

"Keep her quiet." The leader is closer, but still distant.

"Gladly." The bearded one gives my ear a nip and whispers, "Open wide, sweetheart."

I don't want to, but what choice do I have? I don't want to find out what'll happen if I fight it. I whimper and let my mouth fall open, craning my head to the side as my legs shake and the creature keeps flicking my clit.

"Look at that, how could you not want to fuck such a pretty mouth?" A large, definitely human cock bounces off my bottom lip several times before diving in deep.

A different set of rough male fingers tweak my sore nipple, before molding my breast in his palm. "Damn, I couldn't wait to feel this myself. Her skin is so tasty."

Yet another new voice, this one smooth toned. I'm trembling from head to toe, my thighs shaking, fighting the building orgasm. The hand slides along my torso, and the monster pulls back, making room. The hand ghosts over my mound, and two fingers slip inside.

He plays, fingering fast and slow. Despite not wanting to, I scream through another orgasm, around the cock thrusting along my tongue. My hips buck, all my muscles quake.

"Nice." The smooth-toned one fingers me harder,

curling up, hitting my spot, and tweaks my nipple at the same time.

I chase his hand, eager for another release, but I honestly don't think I can.

"Fuck, she's actually sucking." The rough voiced one moans, humping my face harder. He's not wrong, I love cock, when it's human. "Yeah, take it sweetheart."

"Why hasn't she come again?" A hard slap hits the back of my thigh, and I jerk, yelping. "You getting lazy on me, slut?"

The guy fingering me picks up his speed, and I moan, but just can't come.

"I think she needs something else, Cyan," he slows before sliding his fingers up over my clit, which the monster has left.

Cyan must be the angry one. I wish I knew what I did to make him so mad.

"Finish him off. I've got what you need."

I'm pretty sure I don't want whatever this asshole has to offer, but I suck hard, and the guy above me shudders, before pushing in deep to the back of my throat. He lets out a loud moan and pumps his nut into me, but his I hungrily swallow down. He pulls out slowly and gives me a kiss on the cheek. "Nice work, sweetheart. That was outstanding."

I can't decide how to feel about that.

"You two, get the fuck out of here. Tell the others we'll be back soon."

Sounds of feet retreating fill the silence around my labored breathing.

There are still hands molding my breasts, and finally a

human mouth lands there. I moan again. I can't help it, I shouldn't like this, but I love it all.

Bare human thighs press against my legs. Hands fiddle with the shackles around my ankles until they're freed. I'm relieved until they're gripped in a rough hold and lifted in the air.

"Bite those little nipples, Aeon, make her squirm."

He does, and I do. I do more than squirm, I whimper, begging. Cyan slaps his cock against my slit several times, the sensation making me twitch.

"Damn. You really are a slut. Tell me you don't want me to fuck you."

"I don't." My smile gives me away, all my willpower gone. "I don't want that. Please don't."

He chuckles. "What a filthy fucking liar you are."

His hips slam against my ass as he thrusts all the way into me in one move. I shout as he bottoms out.

Aeon tongues my nipple, rubbing slow circles on my clit with his finger.

"You know how we punish liars?"

Cyan is relentless, violent as he pounds me, and Aeon's light touch is almost as violent in its contrast. My neck is rubbed raw from the shackle, but there's so much pleasure I don't care. There's a growl from above me, and Cyan's cock swells. I gasp, stretched like I've never been before, and it's fantastic.

It doesn't stop swelling as he grinds into me. His hands turn to claws and his grip tightens.

"They get fucked like the lying dogs they are." His voice is animalistic now, deep and growling, otherworldly. "Fucked until they can't talk and fucked some more."

Aeon keeps featherlight contact with my clit, guiding me to the edge until Cyan rams me right over it.

"Yes! Oh, God. Yes, please, just like that." I moan and shout as the orgasm wrecks me.

He pistons so hard I can feel the bruises forming on the backs of my thighs, but I don't care. He lets out a terrifying growl and thrusts a final time. Something big at the base of his cock, a bulbous harder spot, stretches me further, the slight burn finally giving away to unreal pleasure as it pushes in with a dull pop.

My body jerks, convulsing in ecstasy as Cyan shouts, the sound aimed at the sky. He pumps rope after rope of cum, bathing my insides, filling me. Weird possessiveness hits me from nowhere, and I become desperate to keep it all in, hooking my heels around his thighs as he falls forward and braces on the ground by my chest.

The blindfold is ripped off, and I blink rapidly, focusing in the low light. Finally. Now I can see—Oh. My stomach dips at the gorgeous face hovering above mine. Sun-tanned skin with short, dark hair framing defined, angry features with a heavy low brow. There's a deep, gnarled scar buckling in the side of his corded neck, which leads to sculpted muscles and tendons that flex, holding his weight.

Wait. I do know him. Hoodie guy.

"You," I pant. "From the party."

He thrusts, pushing the swollen part deeper and I gasp, both at the feeling and how insanely hot he looks doing it. A snarl tugs at his thick lip. "Yeah, and you turned me down, slut. Nobody says no to me. Period."

I laugh at the sheer absurdity, high on adrenaline. "I

thought you were making fun of me. No one ever asks me out."

"That's a nice sound," Aeon murmurs. "And your males are useless," he says, giving my nipple a lick. "Especially the college ones." I still don't know what he looks like, but his voice really is nice.

"Aren't you frat guys?"

Cyan rams into me harder, and another wave of pleasure swims over me, forcing a moan out.

"We look like those fucking college punks to you?"

I stare at him, the strange wildness his eyes.

"No, I guess not. But, then why were—"

"Those parties are great places to find a quick fuck. Almost always one on our night to party, too." Aeon flicks his tongue the whole time he talks, it's amazing, even though my nipple aches.

Cyan growls. "I let the guys pick, we have our fun, then it's back to The Glade before sunrise. But then you showed up, and for some fucking reason," he slams into me again and Aeon bites my nipple, causing a needy gasp, "everyone kept saying you were who they wanted, were all they could smell. I buried my face in some girl's tits, and her scent made me sick. You fucking broke us."

It's a lot to take in, especially in this position, with my brain scrambling from mini orgasms. The thought, the sound of it is so bizarre I can hardly process. They not only noticed me, they wanted me. Had to have me.

"Were you the...things following me while I was walking to the frat house?"

Cy stills. "Before you showed up? Nope, we were camped inside." His gaze turns deadly. "Probably those dumbasses who grabbed you," he cuts himself off with snarl so deadly I shake inside.

I guess that makes sense, and it's not like I could see to identify them.

Aeon hums against my skin. "It's a good thing we were here."

It is. It really is. Not just because they saved my life.

"T-thank you."

Cyan grunts, rolling his hips, and Aeon pops into my line of sight.

My stomach flips again. He's just as gorgeous, but with much kinder features, soft brown eyes which match his hair, and a cute smile in a faintly stubbled face. Unnh, these guys are dangerous.

"You're welcome. Whatever they gave you should be out of your system soon. No aftereffects." The cute smile morphs into something dirty as he gives my nipple a tug. "At least, not from the drug."

His expression sends a thrill through me, and if I get out of this, I will absolutely need therapy to figure out why I don't want to get out of this at all.

"You're one lucky slut." Cyan gives me a punishing thrust again, threatening to pull the swollen area out, and I clench, desperate to keep it in. He smirks and rams it deeper. "We've never fucked a human in shifted form. And you loved it, like the dirty whore you are." He repeats the threat of retreat and thrust again until I crash through another orgasm, trembling around him, gaze torn between the way Aeon watches and the way Cyan loses himself.

"God damn, I can't get enough of that," Cyan throws back his head and grunts, coming in me again.

33

Me either, and that nearly comes tumbling out of my mouth, before I bite my lip, holding it in. No reason to show my hand so soon.

"I can't wait to mount her," Aeon groans around my over sensitized nipple.

I want that, too, even though I shouldn't. I like every bit of this. The claiming, the roughness, the wrongness of it all. How can I ever be normal again?

"Guys, please. Let me out. I won't run. Or fight back."

Cyan full-on smiles, predatory, gorgeous. "I know. You won't be running anywhere with my knot in you. Even when I'm out, you'll never get away. Or maybe I should let you try, huh? Plug your little hole, watch you run, my seed sloshing around in there...fuck!" A shudder ripples his muscles as he closes his eyes, his cock twitching. Another blast of arousal hits me at the thought, too. It's so dirty.

"I think we'll all be sore come morning," Aeon chuckles around my nipple. "Dunno how we'll have the strength to eat."

"What a fucking way to die." Cyan thrusts into me again and lowers himself along my body, rolling his hips erotically as he bites my collarbone. "Why the hell do you feel so good?" It's almost like he's asking himself, instead of me.

"You're s-so hot," I whisper, more shocked than anything that someone, multiple someones, who look like wet-dreams are using my body, enjoying me. I feel like I'm going to wake up any moment.

He chuckles against my skin, licking and nibbling, rolling his hips again. "Wait 'till you see my beast."

My mind reels. "Your beast? You...you guys were...the things from before?"

"Werewolves. Not the fluffy four-legged kind you humans like to imagine." Aeon runs his tongue along my cleavage, lapping at a line of sweat before returning to my nipple. "Damn, every part of you tastes amazing."

"I don't...I don't understand."

"All you need to know is I only took you half shifted this time. Next time, I'll destroy you." Cyan shoves into me deeper, growling. "And you'll love it, slut."

God, there really must be something wrong with me. That idea has my body lighting with heat again. I nod, because I probably will. So much for keeping my cards hidden.

His face hovers above mine again, closer. "Yeah? You like that idea? You think you'll like being our little toy? Taking dick for the rest of your life?" He thrusts into me again. "That abused little kitty of yours dripping all the ti—damn it! I'm never getting out of here!" His head rolls back again, and I feel another pump of hot cum hit my insides, the swollen part pulsating.

If it's possible to die from pleasure, it'll happen tonight. Every cell in my body is wired.

Aeon growls and grips my stomach hard, his teeth clamped around my nipple even harder.

"I'm about to come on the damn ground, Cy."

"Fuck." Cy thrusts again, groaning. "Jam your dick in her mouth. That's her job now anyway."

I'm more than ready to help.

"Unhook me and I'll...take care of that."

Aeon's gaze snaps to mine, then to Cyan's. Cyan snarls, grinding into me. "Go ahead. Like I said, our little slut's not going anywhere. Girl can take a straight up pack bang and

35

ask for more. Even if you weren't special, you'd be ours forever."

I don't quite know what he means, but I can't control the twisted burst of emotions the simple word "forever" causes. Fear and excitement, mostly, but my life-long ache of loneliness lessens as well. I've never been anyone's long-term anything, let alone someone's forever.

He moves in me the whole time Aeon undoes my neck and wrists. Small thrusts like he can't help himself, pushing that thicker part against my swollen core, and it's amazing. He was right, I did need it.

Finally free from the waist up, I twist and cup a hand under Aeon's balls as he lines up his cock.

"Damn," he moans, letting his head fall back, and thrusting into my waiting mouth.

"Yeah, suck it, slut." Cyan's hips roll in micro-movements, too thick to make headway either way, and drags his fingers down my chest.

I can't stop staring at Aeon's body as he bucks. He may be slender, but he's incredibly toned with a long torso. His defined abs twitch, the visible veins throbbing. He grips the sides of my face and loses himself as I swirl my tongue around his tip. It's so unbelievably sexy, heat crawls through my lower stomach again.

"Felt that, you dirty little whore," Cyan whispers with a chuckle.

Aeon arches back and gently grips my clit, rolling it in his fingers. I moan around his cock, willing the orgasm to come, but it won't, my poor muscles used more than ever before. Cyan grips both my breasts, hard, digging his fingers into the flesh as he rocks against me. The unexpected pain sends lighting through my bloodstream.

"You better come, bitch." He squeezes even harder, and Aeon shoves his cock all the way in. "Milk this fucking knot."

God, it shouldn't work, the way he degrades and bruises, but it does. The swell of shame and heat and submission crashes over me in an instant.

I explode into a thousand pieces, tremors wracking my spent body as I scream and struggle for air around Aeon. He thrusts nonstop through it until he stills and releases with a loud growl, shooting down my throat. He tastes better than I expected, and it's nearly a treat to swallow. He pulls out and descends on my neck, licking and nipping.

Cyan shivers, drawing that thick bottom lip in under his teeth as he rolls his hips again. "Fuuuuck, yeah." He lets out a loud, deep moan, head lolled back. "Yessss." His shoulders bunch, rolling forward as another spurt of cum bathes my insides. "God damn," he whispers and lets out a quiet laugh, releasing my breasts and pitching forward to rest his cheek against my collarbone.

It's startlingly intimate. Right up until he collapses, his weight fully on me, forcing my air out in a rush. Aeon pushes him over a little so I can catch my breath.

"Is he dead?" I turn wild eyes to Aeon, who laughs.

"Nope. But this is a very good sign."

His gaze is affectionate and almost...reverent. I can't stop trembling, but it's not from the cold. And I can't stop my shaking fingers from finding their way slowly through Cyan's slightly damp hair, or from tracing Aeon's jaw when he presses a tender kiss to my cheek.

"Don't tell him I said this, and he'll never admit it," he says low, to my ear, "but I think he might not hate you. That's kind of a big deal. He can't stand humans."

I don't know what to say, so I say nothing. Now that the afterglow is gone and flurry of activity is over, all that's left is the reality of what happened and a swollen cock stuck inside me. I feel sick. Ashamed to a degree that physically hurts. My heart skips and races.

They're monsters. They may be insanely hot at the moment, but they're still monsters. I don't even know what they look like shifted. I was just fucked by who knows how many of them, and apparently, they're going to keep me for exactly that reason. What about my future?

"Hey." Aeon lays beside me and curls his arm under my head, sliding close. "What's got you so worked up?"

I almost laugh and stare up into his eyes. What I see shocks all the thoughts out of my head. He's so content, gazing down at me with concern and...no, it can't be. There's no way anyone can like anyone this fast, let alone me, but it's there, that glow.

"I...I'm scared," I whisper. "I have plans for my life. They aren't great plans, I know, but still."

He shrugs a shoulder and kisses my nose. "Plans change."

"No, I don't think you understand. You guys are—and then you—this can't happen. It's not normal to fuck monsters."

He draws his cheek back in chagrin. "Yeah. I probably shouldn't tell you this, but fucking you shifted wasn't part of the plan. We were chuffed after killing, so we couldn't shift back yet, and were just cleaning off the blood. But you got excited." He bounces his brows. "Really excited. And... you were there for the rest." He winks, biting his lip and I swear on my life he's the cutest guy I've ever seen. But I'm still upset, and he can tell. He frowns and strokes my stomach. "What else is wrong?"

"I don't want to live the rest of my life as a-a sex slave."

Oh, but damn does my body disagree. Cyan stirs, and I hold my breath, willing the arousal away.

Aeon chuckles and nips my cheekbone, in a surprisingly sweet, yet possessive way. "You really are a little liar, aren't you? But don't worry about that sex slave thing. That's just Cy being ...well, Cy. You're way more to us than that." He moves to my mouth next, pressing teasing kisses there as he talks. "What's your name?"

"Re...Reanne."

He grins against my lips. "Hi, ReeRee."

I've always liked that nickname, though hardly anyone uses it.

"I probably shouldn't tell you this, either, but I guess it can't hurt. You're an Aruna. Every pack needs one, but they're rare. Been searching for a really long time. Never thought we'd find one. You're our missing piece. I can't wait to spend every day with you."

The words are too heady. I've never felt so seen or wanted or satisfied or scared, but when his tongue dances along the seam of my mouth, I open for him. The kiss deepens, slowly, stealing my breath and my fear. He threads his hand through my hair, cupping my head, and I give in. I've never been kissed this way, so sweet and hot, and full of so many promises. It's intoxicating, consuming. I don't know what an Aruna is, or what's going to happen in the next few minutes, the next hour, or the next week, but I know I don't want him to stop.

Cyan mumbles something against my skin, his hips bucking. I gasp into Aeon's mouth, wincing, and we both still.

He chuckles and leans back. "Sorry. You're just so sexy, it's hard to control myself. I suppose that's a preview of what's coming, huh?"

Me? Me. He thinks I'm...

"We're stuck here until he releases and wakes up. Never seen him so relaxed. Hang on."

He grunts and stands. In a matter of moments, the chains are gone and blood rushes back to my knees, my hips screaming from the release. I bite my lip hard to keep in the pained groans, while he rubs the joints, wrinkling his nose.

"Yeah, that's not gonna feel good for a while. But it will, eventually." His gaze shifts to my swollen sex, where Cyan and I are joined, and he pauses. Hunger sweeps his features, but he shakes his head and comes back to my side, pulling me against him again.

"I know it's not comfortable, but I'll keep you warm. Best doze while you can. Once he's out, it's a long, sticky walk home, and, well, probably not much sleep after that."

It's a terrifying and arousing concept all rolled into one. But sleep comes quick, wrapped in his arms and covered with Cyan's weight.

REANNE

Cyan's cock slips out, waking me way before I want to. I don't know how long it's been, but it's still night, the forest illuminated by the fat moon. I'm in basically the same position as when I passed out. Tucked against Aeon's side with Cyan's weight along my other, and all three of us still quite naked. I'm sticky in some places and covered with dried semen in the rest.

I'm also a bit achy all over, but honestly, it's not half as bad as I expected.

Aeon stirs with a stretch and palms my breast as he nuzzles my ear. "Time to move, ReeRee." More butterflies spring to life, and I can't help my smile.

Cyan wakes next and is quick to jump to his feet. "Let's go. We're running out of time."

"For what?" I groggily push up to my elbows, gaze trailing the faint outline of his muscular body.

"Don't recall telling you to ask questions, bitch."

Ah, right. How could I have forgotten what an ass he is? Aeon stands and offers me his hand but Cyan slaps it away with a scowl, crossing his arms.

"She can get her damn self off the ground. She'll have to put up with way more than that."

I'm more taken aback than Aeon is, who mimics his posture.

"If you want to make it before The Glade closes, she might need help."

"Here you go with the coddling." Cyan turns toward the forest and back again. "She's not a damn pup. All she needs is proper motivation. Watch." He focuses his scowl on me. "Get the fuck up or I'll chain you to a tree and leave you for the ants. When they're done, I'll come back and gnaw on your bones."

It's so oddly specific, it shocks the hell out of me. Plus, he still manages to look dirty sexy while saying it, even though I want to punch him in the throat. I would have gotten up without the threat, but I can't be sure he wouldn't do it just to prove a point.

I grunt and whimper, pushing up to my feet with only a slight sway. I catch Aeon's apologetic gaze, but it quickly morphs to lust as he scans my body. His cock swells and bobs, but he makes no comment about it or attempt to hide it. I still can't wrap my brain around the fact they find me so attractive.

I almost don't want to see if Cyan's hard, but I can't help it. I glance at him and heat flares in me again. He's not only hard, he's stroking himself, long and slow. But he couldn't look less pleased about it if he tried.

"You either walk or keep staring with those fuck me eyes and spend another night chained to the ground with my dick in you. Your call, slut."

"O-okay. Sorry." I lower my gaze, but flick it back up after a second. Thankfully, he's looking at Aeon.

"Get moving."

Aeon strolls up beside me and curls his fingers around my waist as he whispers in my ear. *"Don't worry. We can't be out another night anyway. By the by, you look amazing with our marks all over you. I can't wait to be in that tight slit. Also, keep up with me, or he'll catch you."*

He walks past, leaving me breathless, aroused, and scared. Honestly, I can't decide which scenario is more exciting. But ultimately, even though my body is keyed up at both prospects, I follow.

"Fuuuuck...you...Aeon," Cyan growls behind me, grunting. "What the fuck did you say to her?"

Aeon doesn't stop walking, but he does chuckle. "Oh, nothing."

"Unnh. Hold still, bitch."

I freeze, because if I've learned anything so far, it's listen.

He grips my hip with one hand, pushing his fingers in to the flesh, and shoves my upper back. "Bend over."

I want to argue, to remind him we are apparently running out of time, but I really don't want to make him even angrier, so I put my fingertips on the ground for stability.

"God damn," he whispers. Instead of the harsh ramming I expect, he palms and molds my left cheek, spreading me wide. I glance around my leg and lust flies through me again. He's jacking off, just looking at me.

I can't stop watching. He's so unbelievably hot, the way his muscles roll, the tendons and veins in his hands and forearms, the twitches in his thick thighs, the angry pleasure sweeping his face.

He's transfixed, stroking faster until he lets out a quiet groan and shoots all over my ass. I bite my lip, stifling a moan. That may have been the sexiest thing I've ever seen or felt, and I'm including what happened earlier. But then he runs his fingers through the cum and smears it. I gasp when he shoves his thumb past the ring of muscles over and over, pushing his load inside.

I have no idea why he's doing it, but it's hitting pleasure spots I didn't know were there. I close my eyes and rock back against him, seeking more, trying to imagine how it would feel with him fully shifted like he said.

He freezes. Claws extend from the fingers on my hip, threatening to pierce my skin, and a deep, ominous growl sounds behind me.

Aeon practically teleports in front of me and crouches, resting my forehead on his shoulder. He holds it in place by a warm hand on the back of my neck as he whispers, *"Don't move, Aruna. Be perfectly still."*

"Wh-what's wrong?"

His scent hits me, and I breathe deep. Earth and salt, woody, like the entire forest. I really like it. From my vantage point, his cock stands fully at attention, the head glistening. I want to taste it again, so bad. What's going on with me? I've been horny before, sure, but never like this.

He sighs. *"I shouldn't have egged him on by making you excited. Didn't think it would trigger his beast. This is new for all of us. I mean, it's not a bad thing. Just, not such a good thing when we're not at home. Hold still."*

I have no idea what he's talking about, but my legs start to tremble from the weird position.

"That's hard, my legs are so weak."

"I know, but you're doing really great," he whispers back, giving my cheek a gentle kiss.

My heart flips, butterflies dancing in my stomach again. He seems like such an amazing guy, why does he have to be part monster?

"Miiiinnne," Cyan growls, even louder, and coarse hair springs up on the hand attached to me. Before I can react, he plants his mouth on my hip and bears down, but not hard enough to cut. Yet. I yelp, but other than shaking more, I stay motionless.

"Alpha." Aeon's voice is so loud by my ear, so commanding, it rattles me. "You're not thinking straight. You know you can't mate her outside of The Glade."

Cyan snarls, vicious, hot breaths against my skin. His teeth bear down even more, and I wince. There'll be a serious bruise, if he doesn't actually bite. I don't know what they consider mating, but I feel like we did a whole hell of a lot already.

"Alpha," Aeon's tone shifts lower, rumbling deep in his chest. "Aside from the obvious, the rest of the pack also needs to accept her. Dawn is an hour away. We have to go. Now."

I can't see it, but I can feel the standoff happening above and behind me. There's a palpable energy, like the moment before lighting strikes. I'm not sure what Aeon could really do, if Cyan just went ahead and bit me, but there's obviously something giving him pause.

But maybe not pause enough. Cyan's growls sharpen,

45

his claws press even harder, and his teeth are one more push from tearing into me. Pain radiates in small waves from the spot, but I breathe through it.

Aeon jumps to his feet, supporting me by my shoulder instead. "If we all die out here, that puts Agnar as Alpha, and no Aruna for them ever, because the only one for SteelTooth Pack will be dead. That what you want?"

"Wait, what? Why would I die?" I really want to jump away, but I struggle to stay calm. Aeon squeezes my shoulder.

"Our magic isn't the same out here. A mate bite would poison you, Cy, and all the werewolves under him not protected by the barrier. Right now, that's me. Seriously nasty stuff. We can fuck whoever out here, anything we want, except mate. That can only be done in the protection of a pack's territory, with the Alpha being the final mate." He raises his voice. "All of which the Alpha knows, and he clearly doesn't want to us to die. Right?"

When Cyan's growls fade, he opens his mouth, running his tongue along the hurt area. Blood rushes to the spot.

He rumbles a despondent, "Right," against my skin, dragging his tongue again. Chills pop up.

"You should lead, anyway," Aeon mutters, sounding a bit embarrassed as he glances around.

Cyan huffs and straightens. I assume he's going to move, but he drags some of his nut down my slit. I hold my breath, screaming at my brain to not make a single sound or twitch, but it feels so deliciously dirty.

I guess my skin reaches a satisfactory level of semen-paint, as he gives my ass a hard, stinging slap. Rather than fall forward, thanks to Aeon's hand, I straighten and twist away, yelping.

"Walk," Cyan growl-barks it at me, and doesn't even look back as he takes the lead. "And you better keep up, Aeon. Don't have time for you to get lost again."

I can't breathe, can't move. The moonlight breaking through the trees outlines his retreating form with near perfect clarity. His left arm is huge, black, hairy, and home to a terrifying set of claws. My God, how didn't they shred me to ribbons? With each step, the arm shrinks, until it's exactly the same as his other, a perfectly human arm. My heart thunders, and I stumble backward.

"Easy," Aeon purrs over my shoulder as he wraps his arms under my breasts. "Slow breaths or he'll get worked up again."

I know they told me, and I know what I heard and felt, but seeing it is an entirely different thing.

"He...He's a..."

A low chuckle warms my neck, followed by a gentle nip. "We all are, little snack. Seriously, though. We have to move, both before his scent dries up and he has to cover you again, and before sunrise."

He bumps his hip against mine, urging me forward.

"Is that what he was doing with the, his, you know?"

Aeon takes my hand, threading our fingers, and tugs me along at a faster pace.

"Yep. Mostly for protection, but it's territorial, too. Plus, he likes it. I, for one, can't wait to do almost exac—sorry. Sorry. Ignore that. Think unsexy thoughts."

I laugh uncomfortably and shrug, willing my brain to do exactly that. "Okay. So, how does that protect me?"

"We're not the only werewolf pack. By far. And not every werewolf who visits the humans has good intentions." There's something sad in his tone as he casts his glance to the treeline. It's gone by the next sentence, "This way, you won't smell like such a tasty, wet treat to them." He nibbles my knuckle as we walk, sending sharp little thrills through me. "Though, I swear you could be buried two feet underground, covered head to toe in mud, and I'd still scent you out." His shoulders shake as he lets our joined hands drop. "Which is another reason we have to hurry."

I track Cyan's movements, oddly flustered that he took the time to make sure I'd be safe, even though what he really wanted was to pound me into oblivion. Who the hell am I kidding? That's what we both wanted.

There's a weird tug in my stomach, like a string dragging behind Cyan, connected to me. He glances back when it thrums hardest, and scowls before refocusing ahead. Did he feel it too? No, that's stupid.

"What does mating mean?"

"The fuck you think it means?"

I almost can't find the energy to be irritated at his attitude. Almost.

"Well, if I knew I wouldn't be asking. I'm not an idiot, you know. This is all brand new to me. Plus, I'm tired, hungry, thirsty, sore, scared, and being taken prisoner, in case you've forgotten how my evening went."

He doesn't respond. Tears drip, but I swipe them away as Aeon rubs his thumb over mine.

"Mating is when we share a part of ourselves with the individual we choose to be our partner for life."

"Like marriage?"

"Sort of and not really. It's a lot deeper than that. Means more. It can't be undone."

The tug in my stomach happens again and I stare at Cyan's outline.

Mated to him. To all of them. Stuck with them until I die. I try to muster up the sorrow I know I should feel, but there's this weird happiness, deep inside. That lonely feeling I've had my whole life is fading. I'm not sure who I am without that, to be honest.

Aeon's palm is nearly scalding hot, and even though I try to focus on that, I keep having fear spikes, or sadness dips. Each time I feel anything at all, he squeezes my hand, or brings it up to his mouth again. I don't know how I could deny there's a literal connection between at least me and Aeon, but I can't imagine connecting with a whole pack. It's a really nerve-wracking prospect.

They seem to have no trouble with it but traipsing through dim woods barefoot and nude is pretty uncomfortable. Being home on the couch without a bra is one thing. Small twigs snap against my arches, brambles and leaves give way, and Cyan's steps are louder even than mine. Is he doing that to draw attention to himself? To scare other critters away?

"There's so much I don't know or understand." I mean it more as a quiet complaint to myself, but it's evidently quite loud.

"You'll learn fast or die trying." Cyan's somber voice cuts through the woods and straight into my gut. "Don't worry. Your new BFF there will make sure you're set," he grumbles.

Aeon squeezes my hand, but I don't feel reassured. Cyan's jealous. I don't have to be a werewolf or have super

49

senses to pick up on that. It's his own damn fault I'm holding Aeon's hand and not his, though!

"And if he fucks it up, there's four other needy shits for you to choose from."

"Woah." My steps falter. "Your pack has six people?" I thought four at most.

"Seven now." Aeon kisses my hand again and tugs me back into motion.

Dawn colors the edge of the sky, dusting it pink along the horizon. We walk a few more minutes in silence while I process before the trees ahead of us shimmer, a milky iridescent flicker of light.

Cyan stills, and Aeon covers my mouth, moving us both into a crouch. Adrenaline shoots through me, and I grip his knee.

Leaves crunch in the distance. One, maybe two sets of feet. I can guess, based on their reactions, it's not any of their pack members.

Massive upright shadows outlined by the moonlight weave between the trees, low, quiet huffs filling the silence.

There's a deep, slow rumble in Cyan's chest. Aeon grips my mouth tighter, wrapping his other arm around my head as he turns it toward his shoulder. I fight it, because my imagination is always way worse than reality, until Cyan lets out a terrible growl, shocking me immobile. He explodes away from us, in a rush of snarls and destroyed underbrush. I both wish I could see him fully shifted and am really glad I can't.

The sounds are horrific. He's clearly attacking whatever or whoever it is. Aeon tenses with each growl, yelp, and snarl. His muscles twitch in time with certain sounds. I can't tell if it's a reaction to blows Cyan's taking and giving, or a desire to be in the battle himself.

One of the other creatures retreats, footsteps broken like its breathing, but Cyan is still locked in battle. God, I wish I could see! Though, it's too dark to make out any real details.

Finally, a clearly triumphant howl rings out, and the other werewolf limps away, each step followed by a dragging sound. Step, drag, step, drag. I keep waiting for Aeon to let me go, but he doesn't. He tenses even more, straightening his spine.

"This isn't over," the retreating monster growls.

I whimper against Aeon's palm, but he dashes away in a burst. I don't know what compels me to follow him, maybe fear at being left alone, maybe worry that something would happen to him, but I strain my ears, listening for his footfalls. I trip on a root but manage to keep going.

His sounds stop before I reach him, but I can hear Cyan's harsh breaths now, labored, mixed with obvious grunts of pain. I can see his outline shrink from the large, inky black mass to muscular human. I stop beside him and suck in a breath. He's seriously hurt. His forearm is bent at an unnatural angle, his shoulder too low and pitched forward, his stomach covered in bleeding gashes.

"That was fucking amazing, Cy. I've never seen you fight so hard. It was also stupid. They hadn't done anything yet."

Aeon hooks his arm around him and urges him forward.

"Too close. To home." He groans, stumbling. "Couldn't risk..."

"Do you think they saw her?"

Cyan shakes his head, wincing.

"That voice sounded familiar, was it—"

"I think so."

"What were they doing at our entrance? Shouldn't they cross closer to their territory? Do you think they wanted the Aruna too? Could they have been the ones following her?"

"I don't fuckin' know, Aeon." Cyan sneers, drawing in a sharp breath. "God damn it, this hurts."

"Sorry, sorry." Aeon concentrates and there's a spark, a sort of static in the air, and Cyan takes an easier breath.

"Are...are you going to be..." My lip trembles, and a tear slips out, landing silently on the underbrush. I shouldn't care, shouldn't be this upset over someone I don't know, especially Cyan, but he did help rescue me, and he's in so much pain it practically vibrates through the air, bleeding into me.

His eyes open enough to allow a sliver of glowing gold to shine out, aimed straight at me. My breath catches. They're so beautiful and mesmerizing. I hadn't seen this before. Is it just because he's in pain?

I ease my hand toward his stubbly cheek. As soon as my fingers make contact, all his muscles shiver, stopping him in his tracks. He doesn't lean into my touch, but he doesn't pull away. Stress lines on his face smooth, and his eyelids droop, such a look of contentment. I'm lost in the moment, too many feelings swirling around to make sense of.

Holding my gaze, he tilts his head toward my hand and snags the side of my palm in his teeth. A zing shoots up my arm. It's not entirely comfortable, but doesn't hurt. It's possessive, in an oddly sweet way. What passes for sweet from Cyan I'd imagine, anyway.

He jerks his face away the next second and sneers, trudging forward out of Aeon's supportive embrace.

"I'll be fine. Walk, God damnit."

Annnd moment gone. Though, I have to admit, he does seem to be moving slightly better.

I pass a glance to Aeon, who aims a small smile at me and winks as he catches up, holding Cyan's waist again without asking.

"Wait, shouldn't we give him time to heal?" I trot a few steps, sucking in a breath as a twig pokes my arch. "What if moving makes him worse?"

"We need to get home. They might come back."

That's a sobering thought.

Something else occurs to me, as we amble toward the shimmering line. "If you show up injured like this, won't someone just finish you off? Take the Alpha spot?"

Aeon could have already done it, many times over. I don't say that, though.

"Nah," Aeon grunts, shifting Cyan's good arm around his neck. "Werewolves don't operate like regular wolf packs. Cy has the right to lead by blood, and our loyalty by sacrifice and honor. He has to die of natural causes. Even then, none of us are Alphas, so we'd just be packless. Besides, we love his cantankerous ass. Be lost without him."

Cyan grumbles, grimacing with each step, while my mind races.

"What would have happened if those two had killed him?"

Any amusement vanishes, both their faces going grim.

"You ask too many fucking questions. And you," he elbows Aeon, who grunts, "talk too fucking much. Next time a mouth opens, I'm nailing it to a tree with my dick, understand?"

I blink several times, irritation, fear, and excitement warring in me. Aeon seems particularly excited by the idea.

The threat works however, and we're both silent shadows for the next few hundred feet.

We reach the shimmer, and before I can get myself in trouble by asking what comes next, Cyan grips my upper arm and shoves me through.

The forest brightens abruptly, like we've lost several hours. It's different here. Colors are more vibrant, and the air is cloyingly sweet, so clean it disorients my system. The world is tilted, I'm tilted. Dizziness creeps in, and even though I'm breathing normally, it feels like I'm getting too much oxygen. All the spots branded by dried or sticky cum tingle, the nerves coming alive. I rub, scratch at the places, more and more aggressively, but it doesn't stop. My vision hazes, all the colors merging into a muddy blur. Two upright blobs appear beside me at the peak of my lightheadedness, and one of them catches me by the elbows when my knees give out.

"What the fuck?" Cyan's growl hitches with what sounds suspiciously like fear. I let out a rush of air when our skin touches and all the tingling stops. Home. He feels like home. He grunts in pain, adjusting his hold on me.

Aeon drops to a crouch beside me and examines the fresh scratches on my arms and thighs. He picks up my lolling head, and the shift in position turns my stomach. I gag, but nothing comes out.

He gently lets my chin go and runs his fingers through my hair. "This isn't good."

"No shit, genius. Fix her."

"I can't." Aeon stands, keeping light contact on my head

while my awareness circles. "She just needs time to acclimate. I hope. Nothing strenuous or her system might overload. That means no f—"

"You hope?!"

"I don't know for sure, okay? We weren't exactly prepared to find her. Plus, I haven't dealt with this before. She's the first Aruna I've ever seen and she's human, I didn't even know that was possible. Cut me some slack. She probably needs rest, some of our food, and water. Also, it'd be better if everyone didn't come at her at the same time."

I dip into unconsciousness, coming to as Cyan shifts me in his arms.

"Not a word, Aeon, or I'll throat fuck you until you pass out, too."

Aeon's light chuckle is drowned out by Cyan's strained grunt as he adjusts his grip. He shouldn't be carrying me, especially with a hurt arm and shoulder, but I'm in no position to argue. Plus, it's nice being so close to him. No... it's more than nice. It's right. I slip in and out of consciousness as he walks, blurry trees bleeding into a gurgling river and eventually blurry buildings until finally —nothing.

CYAN

This bitch is already too much trouble, even if she tastes and feels like literal perfection. I bite back my grunt, adjusting my hold again. Should probably let Aeon carry her, but I'm the Alpha. Besides... feels good to hold her. Better than good. The endless fucking razorblades that swim under my skin all the time are almost gone, leaving just a warm buzz. It happened in the frat house, too, when she bumped into me, but my dumb ass didn't make the connection. If I had, I'd have never let her leave. Her being special is just icing on the cake, she would have been mine anyway.

Can't believe I fell asleep in her, but it'd been so long since I hadn't hurt, my body just gave up. Like a fucking chump. I've felt different since we woke up, though, and I don't like it.

"I'll have to check with Agnar, too. See what he knows."

Aeon and his damn mouth. I don't need to hear more about how I have to wait even longer to mate her. Before Aeon said she was the Aruna, I formed a plan of having everyone tear into her at once so I could bury myself in her for the rest of eternity, finally free of this miserable agony.

Now that's shot to hell. Now, I have to be patient. Share. When the fuck have I ever been patient?

"I like her. I think everyone else will, too."

"Literally don't give a shit if they like her or not. They just have to mate her."

"I know, I know. But it'll be, you know, nice. For everyone to be happy. And she's an Aruna, they're built to match. Besides that, she seems like a sweet girl. I bet she'll even find something to like about Veikko."

I snort. "That would be a god damn miracle."

"Right?" He holds out his arms. "Want me to take—"

"No!" I snap my jaws at him and swing her out of his reach, wincing.

He eyes me sideways and gives me a weird look with his stupid smile. "Mmkay."

Without another word—fucking finally—he walks a few steps ahead of me. I glance down at her unconscious face and feel things that scare the ever-loving shit out of me.

No. Hell to the no. Rage sweeps me and I catch up to Aeon. "Here, take the whore." I don't even wait for him to be ready. If he catches her, great, if not, then maybe I won't have to lose control of myself to some stupid, gorgeous woman who showed up at our god damn fuck fest and ruined everything by making me better.

"Whoa, hey!"

I don't even look back to see. I don't care. I can't care. Fucking Aruna bullshit. I'm the Alpha. More than enough by myself. We didn't need her. I don't need her.

A snarl hooks my lip as I rub the ache in my chest. That's what I know. The pain is good. Keeps me strong. I don't need to be distracted with—

She lets out a small sound and my body thrums to life, all my cells pulling me backward, toward her. What the fuck? I gnash my teeth, forcing myself to keep walking.

"I think we need to clean her up."

"Couldn't care less. Figure it out on your own."

"O...kay. Well, whose house should she—"

"Mine," I growl and clamp my lips closed, wincing. Fucking beast taking over.

"That's a bad idea."

I finally twist and eye him. My heart flips as soon as I see the curve of her hip and the bruise forming from my teeth. That's exactly where I'll mark her. Or right above her sexy little pussy, so anyone who goes down there will see it. Ugh, damnit. I scowl harder. "Why's that?"

"Well, I'd been afraid you'd mate her early, but now I'm afraid you'll hurt her."

I grumble, but I can't argue with the fact I feel both those extremes. Maybe I'll mate her to death.

My eyes widen, stomach turning. What the actual fuck is wrong with me? Is this because I'm denying myself? Not touching her? I'm less in control by the second. If I was holding her right now, I'd be in her, unconscious or not, and that's even scarier. Yeah, I can't be near her right now.

"I'll sleep somewhere else." I face front again and storm ahead. "My cabin's the nicest, she needs rest. It's a fucking no brainer, Aeon. I thought you were smart."

My shoulder resets itself with a snap and I grunt, finally able to rotate the joint. This is way faster than I've ever healed before. Is it...because of her?

Handy trick, if she doesn't die. I'll be even more glad we

snatched her if it means the guys will stop whining for so long when they get injured.

Our little log cabin village comes into view, and I'm greeted by welcoming energy as the guys move toward the fire pit. Fucking love this part, honestly. I can feel it in my whole body. There may not be many of us, and they may get on my last damn nerve sometimes, but I love being their Alpha. Love having this family. Not that I'd ever tell them that.

Showing love is a weakness, point blank. That's how dad ran BriarMaw, and it fucking worked. It was the strongest pack around, even after mom was...killed. And just because I kicked off and started my own pack after he died, didn't mean I needed to change what worked.

Aeon smiles down at my little slut, and lifts her higher, grabbing a leaf from her hair with his teeth and blowing it to the ground.

I frown and roll out my shoulder. She likes him better. He's good with all that niceness and shit, where I'm just as cold and fucked up as dear old dad. He never treated mom any different than he treated the rest of the pack, so. That's how it's gotta be, obviously. If he'd found the Aruna, I bet he'd have been just as much of a jackass to her, too. Right? Or are you supposed to treat them different? Hmm.

Whatever, she responds to me like I am now. My balls grow heavy, smirk tugging my lip. It didn't matter how fucked up a scenario I threw at her, she was hot for it, which is hot all by itself.

"Ugh." I shake out my skin. Pain explodes in my chest again, spiderwebbing through my limbs, and I double over, the world turning shades of pale as the beast takes control out of nowhere.

Her. I need her. Can't wait. It hurts. She can fix.

I whirl on Aeon, and he stops short, brow lowering as he clutches her tighter, even though I tower over him. "Alpha. You can't yet."

Beta wants me to hurt.

"That's not true. There are rules." He glances behind me. "Just breathe, Alpha. Shift back and we can get her—"

Give me. My mate.

"I can't do that."

The pack descends on me, pulling me away with teeth and claws. I don't want to hurt them, but I need her.

"Mine," I snarl, and manage to get a claw around her heel.

As soon as we touch, the pain stops. My beast retreats, sated. I let out a whoosh of air, collapsing under a pile of werewolves and we all shift back, huffing. Veikko and Agnar lift me to my feet, while Korey helps Aeon get her to safety.

My heart aches. Safety. To them, it looked like I was attacking her. Fuck. Maybe I was. What would I have done if I'd gotten her? Just another example of how my fucking control is gone, thanks to her. I'm confused, horny, and I officially hate this.

I jerk my arm out of Veikko's vice-grip and glare up at him. "You got something to say?"

I know he doesn't. He might have a solid three feet on me and be built like a Viking war lord who ate his ship, complete with that annoying long hair, but it ain't the size of the man that makes a killer. It's the monster that lives inside. And mine's the biggest killer of all.

He scans me with his unscarred eye, lips drawn unimpressed, but doesn't say anything, as usual. *Yeah, fuck you too, buddy.*

I know he didn't hear me, the bastard refuses to talk in link. I don't think anyone's heard him speak at all, actually. He just guards the perimeter, tends his fucking herb garden, and carves skulls into decorations. Beats all I've ever seen. He wasn't one of the ones I invited to form SteelTooth Pack, but where Agnar goes, Veikko goes, even though they don't like each other. Life debt or something like that.

Agnar steps in front of me and crosses his arms. "He might not, but I do."

My cells hum again, and I lean toward the cabins, stumbling a few steps to the side before steadying myself. God damnit that's really pissing me off. This is my body. No one else should have that sort of pull on me. Veikko gives me a parting glare and heads back toward the cabins.

Agnar's angry expression doesn't falter. "You could have been killed."

I blink.

"We all heard the fight, but it was over too quick for us to get to you."

Oh, the stupid BriarMaw fucks. "Pff. That wasn't even a fight. Thought you were gonna bitch about—"

"That's next. But do you know who you fought?"

I know what he's really asking. And unfortunately, yeah, Fen was one of them, but I know it'd hurt him like hell to know that. They might not see eye to eye on anything, and blood is still blood, but pack is stronger. Pack is chosen family.

61

"It was too quick." I shrug. "Couldn't tell. Plus, I was keyed up from having her so close."

"To that point," he lowers his voice, even though it's just us here, "you need to get your shit together. That stunning creature holds the power to make us stronger or rip us apart but that all depends on you. It's your job as Alpha to make the tough choices, the ones that are in everyone's best interest, not your own. You could have lone-wolfed it, but you brought us with you. Don't make us regret all these years by tearing this family to pieces."

"Don't tell me what my fucking job is, Agnar. And you don't think I know that? You don't think I'm trying? I could have mated her back there, said 'fuck you' to all of you and gone about my life. But I didn't. We're here, and you're all gonna mate her, and la di da, fucking happy ever after."

He narrows his eyes. "Why does that make you so angry?"

"I'm not angry, I'm scared!" I whisper-shout it, clearing my throat of the leftover emotion. Agnar's the only one who's ever seen this side of me. He was there when I... when dad died. He was the only one who knew what I went through before then, too. Was there for me more than anyone else.

"What about?"

"Just." I scrub my face and link my hands behind my neck as I stare at the clouds. "I'm losing control. I guess I'm worried it'll get worse, and I'll kill her like—"

"Like your dad did your mom. I see. Look, Cy, you're different than he was in all the ways that matter. If I'd thought you were gonna be just like him, I never would have followed you. Yeah, your beast runs hotter, but that's the whole point of that woman in there. If you do this right, if you're patient a little longer, you'll be something he never was."

I chew my lip in thought and cut my eyes to him. "What?"

"Complete. Happy. A good Alpha."

"Dad was a good Alpha, what the fuck are you talking about?"

"No. He ruled by fear and fear alone. Yes, everyone was in line, but he wasn't a 'good' anything. In fact, everyone that was tolerable in that pack is in this pack now. Just be patient, son." He pats my shoulder and smiles.

It feels weird to have him call me that, since he's only a few years older than me, but I also don't want to kill him for it, so I guess that's something. Hell, even my own dad didn't call me that.

There's nothing left to say, really, so we head toward the fire. Neo is busy cooking, Veikko is down by his personal farm, Korey stands guard outside my cabin, and I assume Aeon's inside with her which is the only place my body wants to go. Even though I try to steer toward Neo, I wind up at the window, watching Aeon watch her sleep. This need to be by her, on her, in her, is fucking suffocating. I really don't like it.

He looks way more concerned than he let on before, hand curled around his chin, brows knitted. I try to focus on that, on being worried, but she just looks so god damned beautiful laying there. Like a fucking princess or something, waiting on my big bad wolf to come eat her up.

Fuck. This is ridiculous.

"Food's ready!" Neo turns a smile toward us and adjusts

his glasses. My stomach rumbles and the urge to rip the walls down and take her fades. Thank fuck. I crack my neck and fight to pull back my Alpha wave to basically nothing. I can tell when it's enough, because Neo's posture relaxes. I give his upper arm a gentle squeeze and his shoulder a soft kiss as I grab a plate. He gets different energy from me than the others do, because he needs it. Perk of being one of my partners. Besides, he can't handle me at even close to my roughest. Not like Aeon can.

We each take a seat just as Aeon slowly emerges, expression still sad.

He eases the door closed and takes his time crossing to the table. Worry pours off his body, so thick we all stop chewing.

I swallow my bite of rabbit. "What's the verdict?"

"Hard to say." He exhales and stares at his empty plate. "Her breathing is really weird. She's lost almost all her color. And if you want my honest opinion..."

He trails off and shakes his head, grabbing several hunks of whatever other meat Neo cooked.

"Well, I don't want you to lie to me, so let's fucking have it."

"I'm not sure she'll make it."

Nobody moves. The only sound is Veikko's trudging footsteps coming up from his farm. We all turn, eying his tray of herbs, a bucket dangling from his hand and a bunch of other shit stuffed inside it. I expected him to come here, grab a plate and leave like he always does, but instead he goes straight to the cabin, ducking as he waltzes through my door like it's his.

He's never been in there. In fact, he's never been in

anyone's cabin. The guys and I exchange glances, none of us really sure what the fuck is going on.

I can only hold out a few more seconds before I set my plate down and rush back to the window, followed quickly by the rest of them. It's not that I don't trust him, I just still don't know a damn thing about him. I know what the Alpha link tells me, which is he's not trouble, he follows commands with no real problems, and he's always on guard to protect the village, which is all I ask for. But I don't know him as a person. He makes damn sure of that.

What I see shocks me more than if he broke out in song and tap danced on a goat. He's smiling. It's a tiny curve on his lips, but I didn't think he knew how to do it. Plus, he's got all those herbs and flowers laid around her on my bed and is mixing something in his hand.

I glance at Agnar on my one side and Aeon on the other, who both shrug.

Veikko smears a line of his mixture down the center of her chest with his thumb. Next, he wipes a swath of it across her forehead, and around the base of her neck like a collar.

It starts to steam, releasing a super flowery scent laced with peppermint. We're all transfixed, watching him do his little ritual. He's mouthing words, yet somehow not thinking a damn thing in the link. I swear, I dunno how he does that.

The steam stops at the same time he closes his eyes, and immediately her color comes back. She doesn't wake up, but she does take a nice, steady breath. Feels like ten thousand pounds of weight off my chest to see it happen.

It all slams back into place when he picks her up. I make a move for the door, but all four guys stop me.

"I don't think he's gonna hurt her," Neo murmurs. "Why would he go to all that trouble? Let's just see what he's gonna do."

That's the last thing I want, but I also don't want to do something that might make her worse again, so I shake them all off. I glance back in time to see him set her in the soaker tub in my small bathroom.

He fills the whole damn room almost. He's so gentle with her, supporting her head while he carefully cleans every inch with a rag and water from his bucket. Makes me almost happy to see her being taken care of, even though I'm jealous. I shouldn't be, it's not like I couldn't have done the same damn thing, or can't in the future, but I want to be touching her so bad my bones ache.

I don't know why we all stand here, watching the entire thing like we have nothing better to do with our night, but it's sort of calming. The last thing he cleans off is the excess mixture that hasn't soaked in, before he carefully dries her off, and carries her back to the bed. She looks so small next to him. I like the visual. He's so methodical, too, like this is just as calming to him. And he hasn't done anything remotely sexual. Yeah, he cleaned all of her, but I was watching, it was nothing but caring and clinical.

Maybe he's a good dude under all that damn silence and brooding.

Once he starts picking up the flowers around her, the guys head back toward the fire in silence. But I don't. It's almost impossible to make my feet move. She's clean and looks healthier and all I want to do is go in there and fucking ruin her.

How are they all so calm? Damn it, I hate this.

Angry again, I storm back to my plate and dive in.

"She still might not make it, but whatever he did helped her pain level." Aeon talks around a bite of food. "Who knew he was into medicines or...whatever that actually was."

Great. Now I'm back to worried she'll die again. But am I worried she'll die before I can mate her, or worried she'll die because I'll miss the hell out of her?

I'm not sure which and that worries me even more.

Aeon senses my unease and shoots out a Beta wave, calming my nerves. I give him a wink, which has his ears turning pink. He's a helluva lot easier to be with than Neo, but I wouldn't trade either of them for all the females in the world.

Veikko comes out and doesn't even glance at us as he plods his way back to his sanctuary. I don't know if it'll matter, but I say it anyway.

"Vik. Thanks."

His steps stall for just a second, then he resumes his path in silence.

5

VEIKKO

I finish my clean-up and toss a crow skull into the river, dropping to my seat with a huff. These young shifters don't know what they've stolen, what they've set into motion and undone by bringing her here. Their facts are terribly wrong. She is powerful, yes. Beautiful, yes. But dangerous. Too dangerous, like a vicious cobra, poised to strike.

She is not an ordinary Aruna, which are rare enough. No, these foolish few brought the Aruna Rigdus. Who, among other equally deadly things, can become Queen of the werewolves. One is born every two hundred years, and though I didn't know where, or who she would be, I knew it fell within this generation, and I should have been on guard. But in choosing to avoid the full moon freedom we are granted once a month, I instead chose to allow chaos to bleed into our world.

A human. Never before has the Rigdis appeared on the other side of the barrier. I hoped my herbs would tell me I was wrong, but they confirmed. Even knowing what she is, what I should have done...I couldn't. She is perfect, and her scent is the stuff of dreams. My decrepit heart knows it is to be hers just as sure as I sit on this rock. So, I did my best to mask her, instead. Protect her. In the span of a breath, I became a traitor.

Forgive me, brothers.

A breeze carries whippoorwill song across the gurgling water as I hang my head.

The Sentinels, my ancient guardian tribesmen, have never once failed to keep an Aruna Rigdus from rising and seizing power, in the whole stretch of time. Yet...here I sit. A failure.

She's not only in The Glade, but the magic is also already fusing with her blood. She commands Cyan's wolf with nothing but a whim. A feeling. She's not even aware of it and he thinks he's broken.

He could not be more wrong. Cyan carries the mark of High Alpha in his blood. His destiny, his only reason for being alive now, is to mate the Aruna Ridgis, fulfill the ancient prophecy, and there is not a more dangerous outcome then the two of them meeting.

I rub my temples, willing the dark memories away.

I've failed my calling. Failed to protect the secret of her existence, then failed to wipe her from it to protect our kind. My whole life's work, my sacrifice, my diligence, the oath I made...thrown away. I could still save us. Simply walk in there and snap her neck.

But I will not. All for the hope of being in her thrall, feeling love, real love, which is a bond I swore I'd never take from anyone, let alone her. It would be less painful to kill Cyan at this point, yet another thing I'll never do.

I'm shaken to my foundation. If it is so easy to break the one tenant I've held onto so hard all these years, what other things might I do. Will I open my mind to Cyan and his motley pack? Break my vow of silence? Reveal my deepest secrets and my clandestine mission?

Will I fight my own brethren when they come for her? Kill them to keep her safe, while damning myself and the rest of Werewolf kind in the same swing? A chill settles on my heart. The answer...is yes.

Movement by the back of Cy's cabin catches my eye. I twist, but not in time to see who slipped inside. Simple enough to deduce by who's still sitting—

A twig crunches behind me, and I whirl, claws at the ready and poised to slice.

"Hello, Veikko."

My breath stutters as my eyes widen. Darkness manifest. Fen. How the hell... My perimeter alarms should have gone off, or any of my traps. I thought—hoped—I would never see his calculating expression again. His black hair falls the same, swept off to the side, his black eyes, rimmed with gold still burrow through my armor, that damn mouth, kicked up in a smirk.

His gaze travels my body, hungry, and everything feels painfully familiar again, like I never left, never broke free of his prison. I can't stand the way he reads me, never could.

"Oh, don't look so surprised. Who knows your little tricks and traps better than me?" He brushes my arm away and steps into my space, staring up at me with his cocky expression. "I was near. Wanted see how you've been doing."

After all this time? It's been years, more than a few. I'm considerably larger than most everyone, but he has this way of cutting me into bite size pieces. It's a vulnerability I hoped I'd never have to feel again. At least, not with him.

"Oh, I've missed how you never talk back." He rests his hand on my stomach and my dick jumps. "How you never say no. You're a hard possession to replace."

I scowl, irritated how my body still reacts to him, as I shove him away and glance over my shoulder. They're all so close, but too busy chattering. Agnar has his back to us, oblivious. I've never regretted avoiding the pack link until now. At least he won't be able to smell the Aruna. I'll do what must be done to keep him in the dark about her.

He follows my line of sight, closing right back in on me like I didn't do a thing. "Business before pleasure it is. How is my brother?"

Dread runs through me. I'm not interested in his pleasure, but I answer with a shrug and nod.

"And Cyan?"

My eyes roll on their own. Fen couldn't care less about Cyan or anyone other than Agnar and me. Bit of an obsession, really, which is why Agnar was quick to leave with me.

The two couldn't be more different. Fen was an insufferable, possessive, twisted ass before we left BriarMaw. I can't imagine the hell he's put everyone through since.

He chuckles, one shoulder lifting in indifference. "You know me too well, Vik. Just like I know you." He trails his fingers a bit lower and my heart thunders. "Know what you like. Tell me." His voice dips along with his hand, inside my shorts before I can react. I dig my fingers into his shoulders, willing my body to push him away, but he tenderly strokes my cock, and I can't. I know his touch more than I know my own. Know it and hate it as much as I crave it.

"What was he doing outside The Glade, hmm?"

My jaw clenches and I sway to his rhythm, chasing what I loathe the most.

"You should know, I almost killed him earlier. Almost had you back."

I grow harder against my will, and he grins as turmoil eats me alive. I haven't been with anyone since I left. He was the last one, even though I never wanted him. I still don't, but the unhealthy longing roots in my chest.

I've endured a lot in my long life, but there's no memory so sharp and painful as Fen.

He eyes me, moving quicker, but lightly, his teasing brand of torture too familiar. "But he fought different. Harder. Like he had something to lose for the first time in his ridiculous life."

Pleasure builds, stealing my breath. It's been so long. My grip hardens but it's to keep him from leaving.

"Would that be," he stills, "because you're his now?"

I buck my hips, growling low in my throat and shake my head.

His smile eats at my soul. "How sweet. You've been saving yourself for me." I shake my head again, but a groan slips out as he runs his thumb along my tip, dragging my excitement.

"My favorite part about you, Vik," he shoves his other hand in my shorts, thumb still teasing, "is how easily you fall apart for me. How you're such a big, strong werewolf, deadlier than anyone knows." He grabs my balls and tugs, sending a twinge of pain, fear, and arousal through me. "But you'll always be my little object, so eager to hit your knees and give me what I want."

I wish I could say it's not true. And if he hadn't shown up tonight, I would have continued my internal lie that I've moved past it. That I've healed. Agnar and I would have continued to avoid the topic and pretend like nothing happened by pretending to hate each other. But Fen's right. It's impossible to forget a decade of training to be someone's unwilling slave.

"Well," he murmurs. "Go on. I'll leave right after. And you can get back to your chores."

He's dismissive as ever, but there's no hesitation as I fall right back into line, our old pattern disgustingly comforting. My knees press into the damp moss. It's over quick, and he leaves as promised, with no other words. The unreleased ache in my cock is a necessary penance for being so weak, for being his victim when I could kill him just as easily. Exactly as it was all those years. The whole incident could be another waking nightmare, one of countless, if not for the fact his sweet taste lingers this time.

Though, I begin to question that, too, as seconds tick by and still no traps trigger, no trip lines twang, nothing to indicate the slightest disturbance.

I grip my neck and wince. No. No, he was here. I don't know how he got in, or...why, but he was real. I refuse the tears, sending them back to the hell from which they came. I won't cry. Not for the loss. Not for the torment. Not at the way I hate myself for missing him. Not for the question of my sanity.

The only saving grace is he didn't find out about her, whether now or earlier when he attacked Cy.

Instead of dwelling any longer, I set about doubling the protections around my sanctuary first. The rest of the night I'll focus on different traps for the main camp.

Reanne

The next time I'm fully aware, I'm on a soft surface with a warm, hulking, naked body pressed against my back, and a heavy arm draped over me. Someone's cleaned me. I don't smell a soap I'm familiar with, but there is a soft floral scent in the air, and I'm not sticky anymore. It's a huge relief, though being bathed while unconscious is...different. Not that I gave them much choice.

My head still swims, but it's better. Guess Aeon was at least partially right, rest helped. I remind myself to breathe slowly as I orient. It's dark again and I'm dying of thirst. Did I sleep an entire day? Something small and delicate shifts in my palm, and I carefully investigate with my thumb. Oh! It's a flower. I slowly bring it to my nose and inhale, grinning. Such a sweet gesture.

The longer I lay here awake, tracing shadows with my eyes, the odder I feel. But when the body behind me shifts, my skin tightens, burns. My insides turn all fluttery. I need...something.

Lips press to my ear, barely whispered words sending

chills over me while a beard tickles my jaw. *"Don't move, don't say anything, sweetheart."*

Sweetheart? My heart kicks into overdrive. Is it the one from before, who...who...

I can't help the shiver of desire that screams through my body.

He chuckles, grinding his growing erection against my ass, the hand that had been resting calmly on my stomach now playing with my nipple. *"You remember. Name's Korey. I'm not supposed to be in here, but I couldn't stay away. Couldn't pass up a chance to hold you. Cy will be in as soon as he knows you're awake, so be a good girl and keep quiet a bit longer, hmm?"*

This doesn't feel right, but it also feels so good.

Every tug he does on my nipple twangs through my whole body. Maybe it's the weird air, but my senses are alive on a level I've never experienced.

He hooks his heel around my calf and pulls my legs apart, abandoning my breast in favor of lightly toying with my clit.

I buck at the contact, gasping. The pleasure jolt is frighteningly intense, but levels out as he continues. He does a twist maneuver with his upper body, and I'm lying on top of him, my feet planted by his hips, his other hand covering my mouth. His chest is covered in soft hair, and he's broader than Cyan, dwarfing me while he continues tormenting my ear.

"Poor thing, all twisted up inside. You want me to make you come, sweetheart?"

He works his finger faster, circles still teasing and light. I moan, muffled, as pressure builds. *"I can't fuck that pretty*

76

mouth of yours right now, but I can make this little clit sing, as long as you're quiet. What do you say?"

He doesn't stop, so I can't tell if he's really asking for my permission or just giving me the illusion that if I say no it'll change anything. I don't plan on testing the theory.

"Shh, there we go." He holds my mouth harder, craning my head back over his shoulder as my legs tremble. *"Mmm, look at that. So gorgeous. That's a good girl, keep those knees apart."*

I can't handle the sensation overload. His beard tickling, his words heating my ear, his fingers dipping in and swirling gently in contrast to the harsh way he holds my head in place. I soar toward an explosion in near record time, just a few more strokes from release.

"You're so sexy but play time's over until it's officially my turn." He gives my inner thigh a farewell pat, and I whimper, clenching helplessly, on fire everywhere. *"See you soon, sweetheart."*

He kisses my cheek and dead lifts me up, plopping me on the bed beside him.

He's gone before I can muster the energy to lift up on my elbows, panting.

Holy hell! That was so hot. But my insides are scalding now, throbbing and swollen, yet hopelessly empty. Maybe I took more damage yesterday than I realized. I drop back down to the pillow and slip my hand between my legs. Won't take me anytime at all to finish.

"Who the fuck said you could touch yourself?"

Cyan's voice booms through whatever small building this is, lighting my stomach on fire. I snatch my hand away and push to a seated position in time to see him close a door behind himself, blocking the view of a roaring campfire in the distance. Darkness envelops us again, heightening my awareness.

"I... no one. But—"

"I'm out there for hours, thinking you might die, and you're in here, doing that. The fuck kind of thanks is that?"

I don't really have a good answer. I'm not sure what will happen if I tell him the truth. I think I like Korey, so if he'd get hurt, that's the last thing I want.

Cyan clears the room while I'm lost in thought and grabs a handful of my hair, tugging me to my feet. Despite the rough treatment, I'm happy he's here.

"If you didn't need to drink and rest, you'd be on your fucking knees, right now."

I yelp as he thrusts a canteen at my chest, but he doesn't let my hair go. I'm too thirsty to argue, or care, and manage to empty it with only a little overflow. With a relieved exhale, I toss the canteen over the other side of the bed.

"Thank you."

He grunts, but that's it. My body still burns, but with Cyan here, touching me, it's deeper. Stronger. Way too strong, in fact. My stomach rolls, bunching with need, and I flail my hand in the dark, colliding with his hard chest. I let my fingers trail down his soft hairs, panting. Who *am* I right now?

He groans and pulls my body against his, craning my head farther, exposing my throat. His cock is hard as steel, nearly bruising my tender flesh as he grinds it against me. The skin on my scalp stings, but the rest of me sizzles where we touch.

"Such a little slut," he murmurs, drawing a heavy inhale along my skin. "You want something from me?"

"Please," I whisper. *"Please, please."*

He bites my throat, my jaw, my chin, my ear, my cheek, and finally my bottom lip so hard it throbs, but all that does is make the rest of me throb harder.

"What are you begging for? Huh?" His palm collides with my pussy, shocking me into a loud, needy gasp. I blink wide eyes at the darkness. I've never been hit there before, in fact, I didn't know that was a thing people did. I don't hate it.

His chuckle is dark and full as he hits it a few more times, sending waves of pleasurable pain through me.

The next second, he jerks my ear to his mouth as he volleys slap after slap. I moan and whine, holding onto his wrist, as I twist, escaping the overwhelming sensations but chasing them when they stop.

He snarls, lips grazing my ear, *"I think I could step on you, and you'd ask me to do it again."* He drives two fingers inside, and my body shudders. I'm in a lust overdrive, sizzling everywhere, hardly able to breathe. *"Because you know you're nothing but my dirty little whore."* He pistons with frightening speed and force, ripping the orgasm from my body like it was his all along and I stole it. I scream in blissful ecstasy while he growls, *"Fuck. Why you gotta be so god damn perfect?"*

I can't help but think the same thing, as screwed up as that is.

He slows and I'm still riding the aftershocks when his snarl against my ear turns to a lighter brush of skin. He lets my hair go and grips the back of my neck instead. *"Still burning?"*

My legs are weak, and I gulp this oversaturated air by the lungful as I stare at him. "H-how did you know?"

"Answer the fucking question." His tone is low, deep and soothing despite the harsh sentiment, twisting my heart up. His fingers are still buried to the hilt, my juices coating his hand. At some point, my other hand had found his cock and I'm still stroking lightly.

"Only a little." I swallow, letting him go, taking stock of my less achy insides. "It's not as...as bad."

He grunts in response, before easing his fingers free and cupping my sex. The heat from his palm is better than any water bottle or heating pad I've ever used.

But it's the startlingly tender kiss he gives me that knocks me over. He flicks his tongue at the corners of my mouth before pulling back.

"If I catch you touching my property again, you won't come for a month."

It takes my addled brain a moment to catch up, but when it does, I lose all the air I'd managed to find.

"You need this kitty stroked, you come find me. I don't care what I'm doing. And if you can't get to me, you get one of the guys, but don't you ever," he tightens his grip painfully, curling his lip in anger as I gasp and clutch his wrist, "ever try that shit again. Are we fucking clear?"

I whimper, nodding repeatedly as my poor skin stings. "I didn't know, I'm sorry! I won't, I won't."

He lets me go and I stumble back, dropping onto the bed. There's a weird silence. I can tell he's still in front of me by his breathing, but it's more than that. I can feel him there.

Without any warning, he sits beside me, dipping the mattress so I tilt toward him. Our sides press and he gives the inside of my thigh a firm squeeze. I can't explain the way I react to him, but I'm hungry for his touch. It lights me up like fireworks. I'm afraid he might be right, that he could do anything he wanted, and I'd beg for more.

"It's an Aruna thing. If Aeon wasn't busy, the mouthy fuck would explain better than me." It almost sounds like that bothers him, though, he's hard to read. I don't know what there is to explain, but I feel compelled to soothe his ego.

"It's okay, I'm...I'm glad it's...you."

"That right?" His growly whisper is so hot.

"Yes."

"Careful," he murmurs, "might think you like me."

Out of everything I've felt since waking up, the tiny butterfly that appears in my stomach is the least expected.

"Well...maybe I do."

I find his clenched hand in the dark and work his fingers loose, winding mine with them. It's a scarier thing to do when I can't see him. I have no clue how he'll react. I brace for the worst, but he simply lets it happen, resting our hands on his thigh. He takes a deep, slow breath, giving my hand a squeeze as we share the quiet, and I even lay my head on his shoulder.

"No idea why you would."

I don't know if it's the insane buzz I'm getting from touching so much of him, or if I've finally lost my mind, but I decide to be playful.

"Honestly? Me either. You're kind of a dick."

He lets out a shocked laugh and bumps my shoulder with his. "You're funny. And not wrong."

"Don't tell anyone, but I...think it's kind of hot."

He chuckles and smooths the pad of his thumb along mine as he squeezes my hand again. "I know."

I get the feeling this is a rare side of Cyan. Maybe it's the relative secrecy of darkness, I don't know, but I feel a little lucky.

"I'm not supposed to be with you while you acclimate or whatever the hell he said."

Cyan shifts on the bed, rubbing his bare leg against mine. My thoughts race, filled with images of sucking him off, us tangled together, and everything feels hot again. Tight and achy all the way to my fingernails.

"Then why did you come in?" My words are clipped, breathy. I'm so embarrassed at my stupid body.

"I could smell you. You needed me."

So matter of fact and cocky in a way that only makes me hotter. He flings my hand away and scrapes his fingers up my inner leg. "You already need me again."

He doesn't phrase it as a question, his voice thrumming my insides. A whine hangs in my throat. He pushes my other leg out of the way with the tip of one long finger, opening me up to whatever he plans to do. I'm almost high on the air I'm gulping in.

"Can't give you the dick again, though, little whore. Not until you've had everyone else. And apparently, that won't be safe until you're better."

I can't even begin to understand the rules here while I'm

so horny, so weirdly hazy. All my mental energy is being spent on silently begging him to touch me again.

"It's only gonna get worse the longer I'm in here." He thumps my thigh and I jump.

He's right, I know he is. I can tell this tidal wave of need will rise so high I'll drown if he doesn't rescue me. My thoughts fuzz, my body feeling foreign.

"For both of us."

That same long finger traces my slit, teasing when he knows I need so much more.

"W-why stay?" It's a keening whisper, so shamelessly desperate.

I yelp when he grips my throat and pushes me to my back. He runs his nose down the center of my chest and along my stomach, groaning in appreciation. I can't help the moan that slips out.

"Because I can't stand being so god damn far away from you." He grinds the words out through clenched teeth against my skin, with so much venom my air leaves again, pulse skyrocketing. "I need to be in you. To fucking consume you. I need to claim you down to your soul, put my marks on you, use you so fucking hard you can't move." He paws me all over, grabs my jaw, grips my face, his fingers dig into my skin, bruising. His motions are frantic, clearly distressed as he moves to my chest, squeezing each breast, pushing his fingers into my stomach, growls and near-crazed whines filling the space. I'm too scared to make a sound other than gasping.

"It pisses me off! I never fucking asked for this." His hand finds my throat again, harder. "I didn't want anyone." He moves his face closer, so close we're touching noses.

"Was just gonna be a quick fuck like always. But you...Then I thought you were gonna die because I brought you here. Do you know what that did to me? I don't even fucking know you, and I can't live without you now!"

He cuts off my air and kisses me hard, shoving my head into the mattress by force. I've never experienced such violent affection. It's over in a second, and he lets me breathe. Tears leak from my eyes as he trails hot, wet kisses down my chin, down my chest, down my stomach, sending my body into a tailspin from the tenderness. It's all so much, so intense. I feel like I should apologize, even though none of this was my choice to begin with. I shouldn't feel anything but fear, anger, but I can't imagine not being his, not having all those things done to me and more. I'm wet, trembling, and dizzy. So dizzy.

He growls as his face moves lower, nipping at my mound. "You're so fucking lucky my beast is listening right now. Because I want to rail you into tomorrow."

He seems back in control, whatever that means for him. But he hasn't touched me where I need it, just dancing his hot breath around my hypersensitive skin, working me right back to a frenzy. I can't take it.

"Cyan, it...I need...please!"

I buck against his mouth, but he pulls back. I'm on the verge of crying out for anyone, and this utter lack of control over my own brain scares me. Did I break when we crossed the shimmering line? Maybe I'm sick.

He flicks my clit with his tongue, and I nearly choke myself on his hand with the force of my jerk.

"If I left you like this, you'd disappoint me, wouldn't you, bitch?" He flicks his tongue again and I dig my heels into the mattress. "You'd touch yourself and I'd have to deny you."

"No. Yes. Maybe. Oh my God, Cyan, it-it hurts." Tears come faster. I've never needed anything this badly. "I don't understand. Please."

"It'll only make it worse for you if you do that, anyway. If I hadn't stopped you... Hmm. Maybe that'd be warning enough." Three more rapid flicks form stars behind my eyes. "Yeah, let's find out. Rub your clit."

"W-what? But you said—"

His hand tightens, cutting off my air again. "You heard me," he growls, his eyes glowing gold, lighthouses in a pitch-black storm. "Right fucking now."

I hook my fingers under his in panic, and he loosens enough I can gasp a breath. My hand trembles as I seek to end the need myself. I slide down between his face and my skin and make contact. There's fleeting relief at first, but how much of a mistake this is becomes immediately apparent. Each rub doubles the burn, compounding the ache until I'm on fire. I try to stop, but I can't. My body knows it needs a release to fix itself, and it's franticly chasing the only way it knows how.

Sobs quickly wrack my chest, muffled now by his palm.

I only thought I was going to die before. I can feel it coming this time. A darkening in my mind, the end clawing its way through me, and Cyan could stop it, could save me. Why hasn't he? I'm as hot as the sun, crawling out of my skin. I cry out for Aeon, for Korey, for anyone, but no one can hear me under Cyan's hand, so I scream in my mind.

Large, sharp teeth grab my hand and bite down, lifting it away from myself. My other hand flies on its own to take over, but he grabs that and pins it to the mattress. If he's saying anything, I can't hear him.

I've lost all control. Nothing makes sense. Death's shadow closes in, smoking the edges of my awareness. I convulse, thrashing as shock destroys my system. My mind blanks, agony and fear and need the only things left. I barely hear the door slam open, but I do hear Aeon's voice. Distant, garbled. I'm flipped on my side and glorious skin sears against my back, his teeth bearing down on my earlobe. My hand is still clamped in someone's mouth.

"Shh, shh, hey, it's okay, stay with me, I've got you." He lines up and thrusts, arms cinched around my chest. Whatever button he hits inside unlocks the vice on my lungs, and I'm able to breathe.

"Focus on the feeling, come on." He pounds me as hard as he can given the angle, and the longer he goes, the less everything hurts. He bites down hard on the tendon between my neck and shoulder, and I shudder in anticipation. Of what, I don't know. His teeth elongate as he growls, and the skin splits under the pressure. A line of blistering fire spreads from the wound down to my heart. I can't explain what it is, but it feels right, unleashes something new as he brings my wrecked body to violent orgasm.

There's no pleasure. It's just pure, excruciatingly intense feelings. I buck out of control, only held down by Aeon and what vaguely feels like another pair of hands on my hips.

All my muscles seize, and Aeon groans, biting harder as he stills and pumps into me. The heat, the fullness is exactly what I need.

The crawling death retreats to a corner of my brain,

though it doesn't leave yet. My lungs work easier, the tears slow, and feeling comes back to my face, but I'm still hurting, on fire. Aeon unlatches from my shoulder and laps at the wound, heavy breaths bathing my skin as he resumes thrusting. "ReeRee, I'm so sorry, that was the only way."

I don't know that name, who he's talking to, or what he's apologizing for.

Another large set of hands appear in my hair. Stroking. Soothing. Who else is here? My body only knows the one claiming it. Fixing it. Helping it. Saving its life. Aeon. Aeon with the brown eyes and beautiful soul.

Shivers wrack me as fatigue sets in, and I go limp in his grip, utterly useless, gaze distant.

"Get her a blanket, you fucking asshole, or get the hell out," he snarls to the pair of hands pressing on my hip, who I finally remember is Cyan. The Alpha. My Alpha. Mine, who nearly let me die.

The door slams and part of me cries out for him to come back.

CYAN

S tupid fucking—why'd I let that go so far? I storm through the door, my beast seconds from exploding out of me on its own. I can't really explain it, and I feel bad enough, but her begging me to stay in her mind is killing me. How is she even able to do that? Maybe it's an Aruna thing. I hate not knowing shit, but I hate asking for help more.

Look at them. Neo's crouched by the fire, half-shifted, scared out of his mind, Agnar glares like he wants to murder me, and even Veikko has emerged from his little patch of ground, just to enjoy the show, I guess. They're waiting for me to explain. Too bad I've got nothing.

They all know something's seriously fucked up if I'm taking orders from the Beta. I wince, the snarling in my head growing with each heartbeat.

Take her. Take her now. We don't need them. She's mine.

I shouldn't leave but staying is too fucking dangerous. I glance at the rest of the pack one last time before I tear off into the forest, determined to put as much distance between me and her as I can before the beast gets free and does goddess knows what.

Cyan! Wait! Is she okay?

I don't answer. Truth is, I don't fucking know.

Miles of forest pass in a blur, until a thought knocks my wind out.

What if this kills her? Her reaction shouldn't have been that damn serious, not based on what we're taught. It's just supposed to hurt and hurt more. Not...whatever that was. I couldn't blame it on The Glade or magic or anything else. It'd be my fault. I'd be...just like my dad. I skid and drop to my knees clutching my stomach with a pained bellow. I really hate that I can't control myself around her.

Every time I looked at my guys I'd see it, the disappointment, the sadness. Fuck, I couldn't live with myself if that happened. It's hard enough being this far from her, losing her now would almost kill me, I'd just have to finish the job. Fling myself into the Quay.

My thoughts keep racing around her sounds, her scent, her taste, how good it felt just sitting with her like that. Natural, like that's how it should have been since the day I was fucking born.

I groan and arch back, releasing a howl to the sky before crumpling forward and punching the soft Earth. I want her so bad. My eyes widen. Damn. Not just for sex, either. I want her to like me, to look at me the way she looks at Aeon. Nah, actually, I want her to look at me in a way that's special. For her to wanna spend more time with me.

None of which will happen if she dies.

"God damn it," I grit out. If they'd just mated her like I wanted, I could have already had her. We could have figured the rest out. Now, I don't even know if she'll want me at all.

"Pack woes, little Alpha?"

Mother fucker. What is this sick weasel doing on my land? I shift and lunge, Fen's voice triggering me in the worst way. He dances just out of reach, tucking between trees.

"I don't want to fight."

"Too bad," I snarl, catching his arm with my claws. Ripping into his flesh is almost orgasmic, the beast happy and hungry for more.

"I have information!"

Squirrelly shit thinks that'll save him, but it won't. I crash into him when he faces me, pinning him to the ground by his shoulders. My teeth close around his neck just as he cries, "Mishka!"

The beast stutters to a shocked stand still, and I'm left huffing, clinging to leftover adrenaline. In a panic, I search my mind, but I can't feel any trace of Mishka. In fact, I haven't felt him in a couple of weeks. Shit. I hadn't even thought about it. I hope he's okay. No clue how I'd ever find out if he wasn't, it's not like I know the guy. But what I *do* know, is this slimy fuck shouldn't know his name. I haven't told a single person about Mishka, and he hasn't said anything either. Not big on advertising the fact we have secret brain convos.

I don't let Fen up but release his neck and shrug.

"That supposed to mean something to me?"

Fen's pulse hammers, his throat bobbing. "We know more than you think."

"Yeah? Good for you. Get the fuck off my land before I—"

"Yuli wants to make an exchange. Information...for Veikko."

I narrow my gaze at him, the beast growling back to life. "Yuli doesn't know you're here, does he, you fucking psycho?"

"He'll honor any agreement I make in his name."

That's such a greasy non-answer. I straighten and pick him up by the throat, setting him on his feet as he struggles.

"I wouldn't give you Veikko's toenail clippings, let alone the man himself. Now, I will give you to the count of three as a head start. Tell Yuli he can fuck all the way off and to keep you miserable shits away from my pack. One. Two."

He sneers at me and takes off in a blur. I take a few breaths, listening until there's only crickets. If nothing else, this has distracted the fuck out of my beast. I quickly shift to full Werewolf, my worldview changing back to monochromatic watercolor painting.

Mishka? You there?

Nothing. It's not unusual I guess, but we do end up chatting at least once a week.

First time I heard him was the day my dad died. Part of me thought he was, like, some fucked up version of a guardian spirit, but didn't take long to figure out he was real.

Neither of us can explain it, but on the off chance we're both in Werewolf form at the same time, we can talk. As clear as if he were in the same damn room. He's the Alpha for a big pack called GrimBite somewhere far away, probably on the other side of the world. Nice guy. At least, his thoughts to me are. He could be a giant bag of dicks in reality, I have no idea.

Cyan? It's been a while.

Wish I could explain the relief at "hearing" his voice, but

I can't. The guy's been a part of me for a decade. Knows more about me than anyone else.

It has, yeah. Shit's been a bit wild here. Did you tell anyone about me?

I did not. Your existence is still not something I want to share. I rather like people not assuming I'm insane. Besides, that's what you wished, to keep it secret. So, I have.

I breathe a little easier, but it still doesn't explain Fen knowing his name. Nothing I can do about that, though.

Is there something you wish to get off your chest? You know I'm here for you.

My steps drag toward the creek nearby. I guess it won't hurt anything to tell him.

We found our Aruna.

He doesn't say anything, but I can tell he's still here, so I keep going.

But she got sick crossing the barrier, and she's fucking with my wereform, and then I almost let her kill herself, and my Beta had to mate her to save her, and I'm a raging fucking asshole, which you know, but I want her to like me and somehow, my old pack knows your name. Says they have info about you, which has me worried. So, I called out to you. Didn't expect an answer, though. Has anyone freaky been hanging around your pack lately?

He's quiet for a moment before he hums.

That's quite a lot. I'll address in reverse. Not at all. Perimeter is secure as ever. It's...odd. I was in the middle of eating when I had the urge to shift, rather abruptly. Then here you are. Your old pack is full of nothing but wastrels, I'm utterly unconcerned. The rest of this I need a moment to digest.

I stare down at the gurgling water in thought. I'm glad

he's okay, but him feeling my need to talk to him is fucking weird. Nothing like that's ever happened to us before.

Cyan, are you certain she's only an Aruna?

Dead ass positive. What the hell else would she be?

He laughs in my head. *You'd think I'd be used to the way you turn phrases, but I never am. Very well, if you're dead ass positive, as you say, then her sickness is...interesting. We had an Aruna, as you know, but since she was a Nikta, and already here, there was no transition. I wonder...You say yours is affecting your beast?*

Yeah. Can't control my shift around her.

Fascinating. I'll see if I can learn anything by our next conversation. And as for the matter of her liking you—how could she possibly?

My turn to laugh as I kick a fallen tree across the creek. *Very funny.*

I kid, but in truth, you're loyal, dedicated, and capable of deep love. You may be abrasive, but I have no doubts she'll see past your gruff exterior to the heart of you. They are built to match, after all.

Yeah, to mate, but I want—

I know, friend. I know. You want what has eluded us both. A love which defies birth rights, laughs in the face of destiny, and prevails above all else.

I mean, that's a fuck load of words for 'I want her to like me for me' but...yeah.

Tell me about her. You certainly heard all about Silvin after her death.

Yeah, I really had. Their Aruna was murdered in cold blood by a rival pack, while he was out hunting. My heart broke for the guy, their whole pack, but until Reanne came along, I didn't have a connection to compare it to. Now, I know what that would do to me, and we've only been together for like a day. They'd had Silvin for years.

I take a steadying breath.

We kind of just got her, so I don't know a lot. She's smart, I can tell. She can take anything I give her and ask for more. I think she must have had a shit life before, because she seems so...I dunno. Shocked that we want her, even though she's fucking gorgeous. Inside and out, know what I mean? I can tell her heart's good.

She sounds lovely. I'd very much like to meet her. And you. Perhaps soon we shall. But I think for now, you should get back to her. Find out more about her, that's key to having her 'like you for you.' Also, apologize, Cyan. For the almost killing bit. Make it right while you can. Be good to her. I wish... Well, I wish a great many things had been different with Silvin. She might still be here had I... I don't know. Now's not the time to dwell on that.

I growl everywhere, in my head and at the water. But I know he's right. Plus, I don't want to be like my dad, so it shouldn't matter how he would have treated someone like Reanne, unless I use that as a 'how not to be a dick' guide.

Thanks, man. You keep an eye out for shady shits creepin' around, okay?

Absolutely. You do the same. Protect her, Cyan, with everything you have. If something happens to her none of you will ever be the same. Trust me on that. Until next time.

And he's gone. There's just my own thoughts, bumping around.

The guy may talk weird, but he's not wrong. I need to get back, make sure she's okay, and protect her.

Just...not yet.

REANNE

"I've got it. Stay in her, follow her over."

The hands in my hair talk. I think I recognize the voice, but I'm picked up, and terror slices through me that I'll be broken again, so with the last bit of fight left in me, I scream and claw at the attacker like a rabid animal. Undeterred, he positions me face down on his broad chest, one thick, heavy arm clamping me in place around my waist, the other holding my cheek flat against him as Aeon scrambles to his knees behind me and thrusts in.

Familiar smell. Soft hair. Warm. So warm. Safe.

I collapse, utterly pliant, hungrily giving up any semblance of control to the two bringing me back to life.

"There we go, sweetheart. Just breathe."

I know this one, too. Korey. A wiggling happiness curls around my heart. I like Korey. He smells like a salt-bleached driftwood cabin by the sea. Like home. The shivers slow and stop altogether as Aeon keeps steady movement, in and out, smoothing his palms along my lower back.

"Another load or two would help," Korey rumbles, stroking my hair.

"I know, but she drained me yesterday." He groans,

95

bottoming out in me. It almost feels good, but my body still isn't there yet. I need more. They're both only quiet breaths and grunts through the next round, and Aeon's orgasm is louder this time, the hot spurts sending thrills through me. He pitches forward, resting his forehead against my upper back, panting.

"Slacker." Korey swipes his blunt thumb along my cheek and hugs me tighter. "You better start drinking more."

"It's not just that." Aeon places several warm soft kisses along my shoulder blades as he resumes thrusting. "You didn't see her, man. It was close. Scary as hell. I had to mate her, and she won't even fucking remember it." He stills and sniffles.

Korey shushes the room when I start shaking again. "Back at it, unless you need a break."

He evidently doesn't and picks up speed as Korey cradles me. After a gloriously long stretch of soothing, rhythmic sounds and motions, he stills again, digging his fingers into my hips. With a sharp series of growls, my womb is bathed again, and this time, finally, there's a sliver of pleasure. A tiny moan slips out and they both freeze.

"You back with us yet, sweets?"

I try to answer, I do, but nothing comes out. I can't even make my limbs move yet.

"ReeRee, if you can hear me, Korey's gonna take over. You're not gonna like it, but you need food."

"That her name?"

"Nah. It's Reanne."

That's right. That's...me. I'm Reanne. A different part of my mind blinks awake.

"Aw, that's cute. You're just adorable from tip to tail,

aren't you, sweetheart?" He palms my ass in his meaty hand, and a flicker of heat forms. "We'll swap, but stay. She'll need you. Neo can bring dinner in."

Aeon sighs behind me, thrusting a final hard time. "Fine. You ready?"

I know he is, because I've been lying on his rock-hard cock the entire time.

Korey's chuckle rumbles against my face. "When am I not?"

The sound of Aeon's chuckle gives me indescribable joy, and a heaviness lifts. "Count of three."

I'm still hazy on what they're talking about until it happens. Aeon pulls out on two, and it's like I'm being ripped in half. Couple that with Korey shifting me along his body and my safe, warm cocoon shatters. I fall through darkness, clawing at the dirt walls as they close in around me. A line of fire forms on my shoulder again, anchoring me, pulling me back toward the surface.

Korey sucks in a hiss through his teeth and impales me. My mouth falls open, the darkness gone in a flash of blinding light. It's a tight fit, but he bumps his hips up, forcing more and more in. We move together, Aeon's teeth burrowed into my skin, Korey's thick cock filling me. With every thrust, we adjust until Aeon hums against my skin and releases me.

"Blood's cleaner." He places a gentle kiss on my temple and rests his cheek on Korey, placing his gorgeous face in line with mine. I can barely make it out, but I remember. My heart hiccups, and I try to touch him, but only manage to twitch my fingers. "You're in the clear, little treat. Just gotta keep you full until you sleep. Or 'til dawn if you don't."

He flops onto his back against the pillow with an exhausted sigh and drapes his arm over his eyes, but keeps his other hand on my cheek. "I'm gonna break his face when I see him again."

He must mean Cyan. I don't want that, but I know it's necessary. I don't know how, but I can feel it.

Korey grunts in answer. His movements are far more staccato, hitting different areas, just as good as the ones Aeon hits. He's much freer with his sounds, too, moaning and groaning the longer we go. I really love it. His first load is big, warming me all the way to my toes. After the second full round of thrusting and being filled, I feel almost normal, and the fluttery pleasure is back in full force.

I moan, shifting in his vice grip. He keeps thrusting, but quickly lowers his hands to my hips instead. I push up against his chest on arms that have to weigh two thousand pounds each. I slip twice, but fit into his rhythm eventually, my body equalizing.

"Holy shit, you look good riding me."

I don't know how I look, but I can imagine it's anything but good. What I do know, is it feels like I'm grinding against a chunk of stone.

Though I'm mostly whole, I'm...disconnected. Things aren't the same inside me, and I can't explain any of what happened. Regular, good old fashioned fear trickles in, and my bottom lip trembles as pressure and heat crawl through my lower stomach. I intend to ask a million questions, but I'm evidently not in control of my mouth yet.

"Aeon," I cut the word short, clearing my throat. I don't sound like myself. I don't even sound human. Nor do I know why that's the first word that comes out.

"He's here," Korey murmurs, sitting up and adjusting my legs so I'm straddling his lap. He hooks his giant hands over the backs of my shoulders and slams up into me. My head falls back, words and questions forgotten as a long moan fills the cabin.

He hums as he nips my collarbone, my chest, any skin he can reach, driving home over and over, his beard tickling. "That's right. Let it out, sweetheart. Come back to us. We've got you."

Aeon slides against my back, fondling my chest, kissing my neck until I'm panting, on the verge of coming undone. But I hover there, needing something else, something I can't name or—

Teeth slice into my shoulder again and I scream in pure bliss, releasing whatever demons still linger, trembling and moaning as euphoria takes over.

"There she is, listen to that howl. Fuck!" Korey speeds up, prolonging my orgasm, his final thrust beautifully punishing as he fills me one last time.

I collapse backward against Aeon, who quickly detaches as a trio of animalistic yowls surround the house. Aeon tips his head back and joins in while Korey buries his face in my chest, breaths heaving. I'm fully present in the now again, fully me. Whole, but...in pieces. It's almost like there's another version of Reanne who's asleep now, and I'm her dream. Or...the other way around. I'm not sure, but there's definitely something different.

I cradle Korey's head, running my fingers through his hair as his cock flexes inside me.

Chills race along my body, but it's at the beauty of the moment. Not my fear.

Still, there's a deep sadness in the air, tainting what should have, could have been a brilliant connection, a tight bond formed without my apparent near-death experience.

The details are hazy, but that part I remember. The cold grip on my lifeline.

"Mmph!"

Aeon's mouth finds mine, and he kisses me deeply, commandingly. I melt into it, until my shoulder throbs in time with my pulse. Did I get hurt? I break away and twist my neck, tugging at my skin, but I can't see anything.

He covers the spot with his hot hand, eyes seeking mine as the ache stops. "I'll explain, but you should rest."

As if his words unlock my exhaustion, my lids grow heavy. We fall to the bed together, a 'me' sandwich, and I'm asleep as soon as my head hits the pillow.

I wake up what feels like seconds later, completely disoriented. Bright light seeps through cracks everywhere, but especially the wide-open door. I'm in someone's house, a log cabin, obviously not well insulated. It's cute, though. Homey. I feel like all I've done is sleep the past few days. Has it been that long? God, I'm thirsty.

The glorious smell of warm food hits me and my stomach grumbles.

I sit up, untangling myself from my mountain and my mate, as I—

Wait. Mate?

"Hey, sleeping beauty. Got you all set up here, if you wanna come sit. If not, I can bring it to you."

I orient on the sexy, scratchy voice at the foot of the bed. It came from a shirtless, middle-aged man, with a friendly smile atop a dimpled chin. He has a hard face with thick, dark brows, simple rectangular glasses, and a head full of wild, black hair. Honestly, he's like every hot, disheveled professor fantasy ever, manifested.

God, why do they all have to be so endlessly attractive? My stomach flutters and his brows jump, that smile widening. Ugh. I've apparently got no secrets here. But he has the decency not to tease me about it. He simply crosses his arms and gestures with his chin over his shoulder. "Which do you feel up to? Or I could feed you. That's an option, too."

Time to test my voice. "What...happened?"

He shrugs. "Not exactly sure, but we all heard you screaming in our link. Like you were dying. Cy wouldn't talk and hasn't been back since he left. I've got bacon. Or ham. Hamburger. Sausage, if that's your thing. Also brought eggs, even though I don't know how anyone can eat those. Hope for your sake you're not a vegetarian. We don't have much in the way of rabbit food, here. But I'd be happy to get you something, if that's the case."

I blink several times, overwhelmed. Cyan isn't back? Where would he go? Does that mean he feels bad, or is he just avoiding drama? Is he...is he in trouble?

"Feeding you it is."

The man steps back, grabs a plate, scrapes silverware along several others, and returns. He sits near my feet, and I tuck my ankles under my legs, giving him room to scoot closer up the bed.

"What first?" He points at each food until I nod at the

bacon. "An excellent choice. The burned pig is especially crunchy today."

I can't help my laugh, butterflies forming. My reservations about meeting the whole pack are being systematically wiped away.

He picks up the piece and holds it out, flicking it away with a mischievous glint in his eye as I reach for it.

"Hey!" I giggle, grabbing and failing again.

The other two warm bodies in the bed stir, but don't sit up. I cover my mouth and shrug.

His gaze dips to my lap and sweeps back up. "You had a tiring night. Let me. As long as you can handle the chewing and swallowing. I can't do that part for you."

"I think I can manage." I grin. "What's your name?"

"Neo."

"Nice to meet you, Neo, I'm Reanne." The other version of me curls toward him, in my subconscious, but I ignore it, because it makes no sense. I thrust out my hand and he drops the bacon on the plate, licking his fingertips before wiping them on his shorts. He snags my hand and tugs it toward his face, giving my knuckles a firm kiss.

"Pleasure's all mine. And hopefully soon yours." He winks and I flush head to toe. "Now, back to the business of bacon."

I nod, matching his mock serious expression, and open my mouth.

"Mm. That really is a pretty sight. Alrighty, in she goes."

It could be because I'm starving, but it's the single best piece of bacon I've ever had. It's gone before I know it.

"O.M.G. That was amazing! Did you cook it?"

"Yes, ma'am." He mimes brushing off his sculpted

shoulders. "You're talking to the head chef of the SteelTooth pack."

"You're the only chef, Neo." Aeon sits up groggily and stretches his long arms over his head. It's the first time I'm seeing him in daylight, with eyes that aren't hazy from impending unconsciousness. He's even hotter than I thought. My shoulder throbs, and I just want to climb on top of him and never leave. It isn't until his morning wood bobs that I realize we're all still naked. Neo's the only one with half of an outfit on.

Yet, I'm so happy and comfortable, I can't find it in me to be embarrassed or care, and they clearly don't.

"Morning, Aeon! Burned pig?" I snag a piece and twist back, thrusting it at his face as I chomp down another one. "It's really good."

A sappy grin slides into place and he shoves Korey's arm out of his way, rocking forward. He pushes the bacon to the side and cups my jaw. "You had me so worried. Really, really happy to see you doing so well." He tugs me into the sweetest series of kisses, melting me to a puddle before he leans back. "That wasn't how I figured it would go, our first few times. What...do you remember?"

His eyes are weirdly hopeful, but the answer is not a lot, honestly. Bizarre bits and pieces. I open my mouth, but Neo scrambles and shoves in a bite of wonderfully salty ham. "Let the poor girl eat. Talk after she gets some strength back."

He hands me a small glass full of some sort of juice, and I down it in two chugs.

Aeon scrubs his hand down his face and scowls. "Can't

believe you're letting him feed you. If you only knew how long he's been trying to do that to one of us."

"Hey, it's not my fault none of you appreciate my attention."

I dutifully take the next proffered bite, watching them talk.

"Unless you get hurt, then it's 'Oh, Neo, can you bring me my blanket? It's so far away. Neo, this soup is too hot. Can you blow on it for me?'."

Aeon laughs, his cheeks tinting. "Soup was hot, numb-nuts, and I had a punctured lung. Couldn't breathe all that well."

"See how they use me?" He winks, encouraging me to open again by doing it himself. It's so funny, and I can't leave him hanging, so I take the next few bites the same way, bathed in his affectionate gaze. A girl could really get used to this kind of treatment. In fact, my core thinks the next bite is sexy as hell, and heat blazes to life.

Neo's nose flares, gaze narrowing on my hardening peaks. "Tell me," his voice dips low, "you're not getting turned on by being fed. Tell me I'm not that lucky."

"What have I been saying all this time?" Aeon grumbles behind me. "The Aruna is perfect for *every* pack mate."

"*I heard you,*" Neo whispers, eying me hungrily. "*Just didn't believe it.*"

He drops the bit of meat he'd been holding, and with a sexy smirk in place, touches his thumb to my bottom lip. I lick the salt off on reflex, watching as his pupils dilate.

"Open up, baby bird."

My stomach clenches with desire as I let him slip the pad of his thumb inside. He strokes it along my tongue, but jerks away with a loud throat clear. "Right. Food. Then maybe we can have fun."

Aeon chuckles, running his fingers through the length of my hair. "Those are the same thing for you, Neo."

"Yeah, yeah." Neo's cheeks flush as he grins sheepishly and pops a bite of egg in my mouth.

"I like it." I swallow. "I might not want it all the time, but it's nice. Beats starving or being ignored by miles."

Neo's smile fades and Aeon's fingers still.

"Sorry, I didn't mean to ruin—"

"You didn't ruin anything." Aeon kisses my cheek. "Trust me, we want to know every single thing about you."

"Even the stuff that makes us wanna murder your parents." Neo quirks a brow and casts a shadowed look over my shoulder to Aeon.

It's a little uncomfortable, having undivided, caring attention so focused on me.

"You'd, uh, have to find them first. I never knew them. Unless you mean my foster families, in which case, I think you'd be busy for a long, long time."

"You're an orphan," Neo mumbles with a frown. "I'm so sorry."

I shrug a shoulder and steal another bite of ham from the plate. Neo's gaze is like a laser, watching. A weird burst of bravery hits, and I lean toward him. Maybe if he likes to feed others, he'll like being fed, too. When his eyes meet mine, there's so much heat it practically hangs in the air between us. Rather than wait, he gently grabs my wrist and leans forward, taking my fingers in his mouth. The way he sucks and cleans them is so erotic and so personal, like we're the only two here. But Aeon's fingers brush my neck reminding me we absolutely aren't. And yet, even though it should probably be weird, it feels right. In fact, I feel like there should be more here. The rest of my...family.

That word scares me like always, and I pull my hand away, clasping it with my other in my lap.

Neo twists his mouth to the side, cutting his gaze over my shoulder again before settling it back on me. "Did I come on too strong? If it helps, that was really hot."

"No, no, it wasn't you." I quickly grip his knee. "This is just a lot. I'm not...no one ever..." I trail off and shrug because honestly, I'm not sure what I want to share.

His relaxed smile reappears and my anxiety fades. "Hey, there's no rush. We've got all the time in the world. Been waiting my whole life, what's a little longer?" He winks, but it hits me hard.

He's not the only one who's been waiting. I open my mouth, but Korey lets out an exaggerated sigh, bumping me with his calf.

"Why...are you all...so loud?" Korey mumbles as he rolls over, bouncing us. We share a chuckle, and as Aeon kisses the back of my head and Neo feeds me another bite of food, I forget, for a moment, why I'm here in the first place. I forget I'm an outsider, I forget the loneliness, nothing but contentment wiggling in my muscles.

That is, until a heaviness settles in the air followed by a distinct, excited tug on my insides. Cyan's back. He moves closer to the cabin and the mood shifts in less than a heartbeat.

Korey rouses like a zombie pulled from the grave, grumbling. Neo quickly sets the plate back on the table and faces the door. Aeon moves beside him, and when Korey finally hefts his mass of hard muscles and bones off the bed, he completes the wall in front of me.

Even though they're acting like I should be afraid, and a little of me is, there's a larger part bubbling with happiness, because I missed him. I really missed him.

He may have screwed up, but he's still part of me in a way I can't explain.

9

REANNE

When the door swings open, the tension in the room nearly suffocates me. I don't dare to breathe hard, let alone say anything.

The other pack members close in outside, too. I...I still don't understand how I can feel them, but their distinct connections grow stronger as they near. I may not have met everyone yet, still they definitely want to protect me. It's such a bizarre sensation. But they're worried for no reason.

"How long you assholes planning on playing house?"

Desire rockets through my body, as hot as if I haven't had an orgasm in three years.

Cyan chuckles. "Mornin', slut."

"Don't talk to her," Aeon growls, fists clenching. "You shouldn't be in here."

"Sounds like you're asking for a fight, Beta. I live here." The floor creaks as he walks closer. All three of their backs stiffen. "And that dripping little slit is mine, too, in case you forgot."

"Just," Neo mumbles, then rolls his shoulders back. "Just give her a little longer. She's eaten and her strength is coming back. She'll be able to meet the others soon."

Aeon evidently can't hold his tongue any longer and steps forward. "Cy, what the fuck were you thinking? I told you what could happen, but you let her do that anyway, I can't even wrap my brain around it."

There are mixed emotions bleeding in from outside. Fear, confusion, anger. This has the potential to turn bad, and I really don't want that. But Cyan doesn't throw him to the ground or rip out his throat or any of the other awful things I'm imagining.

"It...went farther than it should've, sure. I stopped her. Just...a little too late."

"That sucks shit as an apology. Why do it in the first place? We went along with the abduction, because you said that was the only way. Went along with the whole deal while she was still chained up, but hurting her on purpose or...or for fun...that's just fucking wrong."

It wasn't like that, it really wasn't. And it's interesting those parts were his idea. Might have been scared at the time, but that was the hottest thing in my life. I probably won't ever admit that out loud, but I can try to diffuse.

"Guys," I whisper. "It's okay."

Aeon turns heartbroken eyes my way. "But look how different you are now. How scared. It's not fair to—"

"Fair ain't got shit to do with it. I'm the Alpha. That's exactly how she *should* be with me. The rest of you could learn a thing or two. Especially you."

Korey cracks his neck, finally speaking up. "You're toeing a thin line, *Alpha*." He bites the word out with disdain. "These aren't random rules, made up to keep you from wetting your dick. It's for the good of the pack."

"The pack, huh? Which pack is that, Kor? Don't think I

didn't know about your plan to run off to the BriarMaw. Only reason you're still here is we found her. So, don't fucking talk to me about loyalty. In fact, shut the hell up."

Neo adjusts his glasses and turns a glance up at Korey, who keeps his eyes forward. "Is that true?"

"None of that matters," Aeon cuts in. "You fucked up. You almost cost us the one thing we've wanted for so long, for some screwed up reason you won't say. The fact is you can't have her yet. Period. Go, so she can rest a bit more, then we'll see about doing the claiming tonight. And one more thing."

Without warning, he lunges forward. There's a crunch of bone and a vicious growl, followed by a pained grunt. I gasp, but even though I want to run to them both and make sure they're okay, I don't move.

Aeon stumbles back, shaking out his hand.

"You," Cyan spits and chuckles, "are gonna pay for that."

There's another standoff. I have no idea how this will go. The other thing is I...I don't want him to leave. I don't know if it's this weird place screwing with my body, or if this bone-deep craving is real, but still.

My mouth opens and words tumble out before my brain catches up. "Stop. Please. I want him to stay."

The manly wall of protectors turns and stares at me with mixed expressions, but the aggression in the air is weirdly gone. It's Neo who speaks first.

"That's not a good idea, baby bird. He's not in control of himself. It's...not his fault. It's you. Well, it's his beast. The Alpha calling the Aruna, you calling him. Things you don't understand yet."

I shake my head, hugging a pillow to my chest. They

don't understand *him*. Cyan wouldn't let anything happen to me, not really. I can feel it in my heart.

"Then...you stay with us. Make sure I'm safe. But I..."

I swallow thickly, unable to voice this boiling torment inside. And I can feel the same twisted swirl of emotions pouring off Cyan from the other side of the room.

Aeon's eyes glass, and he shoots a look at Neo before giving me a terse nod. "As you wish, Aruna." He grabs Korey's arm and yanks him forward. The two stalk past Cyan and straight through the door without another glance back. My shoulder burns and I frown, clutching the wound. "Ow. Wh—"

I glance up and freeze as my eyes lock on Cyan. I slowly take in the rest of his body in the daylight, a masterpiece of hard, defined muscles with a perfect V. Every inch of me wants to be pressed against every inch of him in a more primal way than just sex. A shiver ripples through me, and when he takes a step forward, I throw the pillow behind me.

"Neo," I rasp. "Go outside for two minutes."

"But..." His eyes rake my newly exposed body, throat bobbing.

"Listen to her, god damnit, she's tryna to keep me from tearing you in half." His tone is so animalistic, so monstrous, but instead of afraid, I'm even more turned on. Neo levels an incredulous glare his way.

I pant with each step Cyan takes, like he's walking on my heart.

"It's fine. It's fine, Neo. You'll be right outside. Or go stand in the bathroom. Just...just two minutes. Don't come back in before then."

Cyan stops beside Neo at the foot of the bed, absolutely

gorgeous hard-on raging, muscles tense, fists clenched. All he does is glance at Neo and the man stalks away. Once the door closes behind him, Cyan shakes out his body, cracking his neck and rubbing his jaw. There's definite damage, but he's acting like it doesn't hurt that bad.

We stare at each other, some unspoken thing passing between us. It's almost like he's asking for permission, which I get the feeling he never does.

Honestly, it wouldn't matter if I was madder than I've ever been in my whole life. I can't go another second without touching him.

I shuffle backward toward the wall, his glowing eyes never leaving mine as he crawls up the mattress in pursuit. My lungs barely work as I flatten, and he slides his body along mine. He bites me gently the whole way, each thigh, each hip bone, each nipple, each side of my collarbone, each ear lobe, grinding that bruising erection against my hip.

My whimpers are ridiculous, and I grab every bit of him I can, molding his shoulders, his arms, his back, clawing at his neck. I need him so bad and the steady heat in his gaze tells me he feels it, too.

There's no teasing, or toying with me, or dragging it out. We're past that right now. This unreasonable need to reconnect after last night is too urgent.

He claims my lips, our harsh breaths mingling as he drives two fingers inside. I cry out into his mouth and cling to him harder as two turns to three, stretching me, stroking the perfect spot. He adds his thumb in the mix, rubbing my clit as he hammers out a punishing rhythm. I wrap both my arms around his neck, holding on for dear life as he swallows my screams.

The orgasm splinters through me like a sky full of lightning. It's absolutely perfect. Cyan moans, grinding against me faster, before he breaks the kiss with a gasp and presses his forehead to mine.

"I'm sorry." It's such a broken whisper I barely hear it over my slamming pulse. I blink my eyes open, met by his golden stare. I'm still a whimpering, writhing mess and he works his fingers apart inside me, hooking them higher as his brows pitch in regret. "I'm so fucking sorry."

I hug him tighter, moving my chin over his shoulder, bucking against his hand, my leg hooked around his hip. I know he wouldn't have said it with anyone around. And he could have said it a million different ways, none of which would have been as perfect, as raw, as vulnerable, and sincere. It means so much.

"It's okay, it's okay. I...oh, G-God, I forgive—" I lose myself in the next orgasm, digging my nails into his skin.

"Fuck," he hisses, rutting my hip harder, and claims my mouth again.

Kissing Cyan is a lesson in submission and a gift of rapture. He's vicious, angry with his tongue and teasing in the next swipe, biting and snarling or smoothing his lips across mine. No set pattern, no preferred pressure, or speed I can predict. It's so erotic. He chases what feels good and I follow his lead, utterly consumed and somehow in sync.

I don't hear the door open, but I hear it close. Cyan slowly withdraws and shoves his wet fingers in his mouth with a moan, sucking my juices. Neither of us move, save for Cyan's less urgent humping. We can't. We're locked forehead to forehead again, energy and thoughts passing to me with frightening clarity.

I should be scared. I mean, seeing someone else's fantasies isn't normal, but it feels right. Safe and logical. More than that, I deeply need the mark he's imagining, even though I don't know what it means. I need the violent claim he's picturing. The blood. If it destroys me, so be it. I want all his damage and his care and his brokenness.

Before he's halfway finished the next thought, I open my mouth and wait.

"There's my hungry little slut." He grins and slides his fingers in, followed by his tongue. It tangles with mine as we share the task. It's so hot and weirdly touching.

He seems different, more open, and way less angry. I wouldn't say I miss the aggression, but if it came back I wouldn't be mad, either. It's all part of him, and I...

I'm not sure who has the next thought first, but he breaks the connection, and slowly rolls us, so I'm on top. I grin and shimmy lower until I'm between his knees, ass in the air.

With a happy hum, I take him all the way to the hilt. His head falls back, thudding on the wall, a ripple of relaxation flowing through his muscles as I slowly make my way back to the tip.

Neo makes a strangled noise behind me. Need crawls through me again, this one more fluttery and swimmy than the consuming, choking one for my Alpha, but no less urgent. My hips roll, and I work Cyan's cock faster.

"Shit, that's good." His fingers wind through my hair, smoothing it over my shoulder in a startlingly tender move. "So fucking good." I revel in the affectionate tone, sucking, working him and grazing with my teeth. Cyan's next moan

ABDUCTED FOR THE PACK

echoes as he clutches the back of my head and bathes my throat.

It's sweet, and honestly it tastes amazing, sending even more curls of heat through me. I swallow him down and keep going. I know he's not done. Not by a long shot.

"The fuck you waiting for, Neo?"

"I...she...and you..."

I release Cyan's cock with a wet pop and glance back over my shoulder. Neo is so conflicted, I feel bad. He's hard and clearly itching to join in, but something's bothering him.

"If you make her ask, I'll break your god damn arm." There's no malice. It's barely more than a murmur as he leans up and slaps my ass, grabbing the flesh firmly and spreading me open. A blast of arousal hits me with how dirty it all is, but I love it.

Like I love this more relaxed version of Cyan, which only seems to exist when we're touching. I clutch his face and kiss him hard, moving to his ear. "Give me a second."

He growls, but with a deft maneuver, I give him a long lick as I slip off the side of the bed. I approach Neo, holding out my hand.

He gives me a timid smile, threading his fingers with mine. "So...hey."

"Hi." I grin and tug at his waistband, sending his shorts to the floor with a single tug. I don't know what's gotten into me, but this feels right, too.

"You, uh." He scratches his head. "You sure you want me right now?"

I nod and step against him, bumping into his cock as I link my fingers behind his neck. "Very sure."

He grunts and cups my hips, pulling me in tighter. Some of the tension in his shoulders bleeds away as I play with the hair at the base of his head. He melts further when I trail my nails higher and folds down for me as I pull him into a steamy, slow kiss.

Unsurprisingly, Neo's scent is comforting spices and wood smoke. I love it. His hands trail up my sides, so testing, so gentle, sending scores of goosebumps along my skin and heat through me again. He grins against my mouth and hooks his hands under my thighs, lifting me up and sliding into me in nearly the same move.

"Oh, fuck!"

Our connection twangs, strengthens. I hold onto his neck, cinching my legs around his waist and riding the wave of pleasure as he bounces me with no struggle at all. Neo mouths my skin, gentle but possessive. Cyan groans and I force my eyes in his direction, to find him slowly stroking himself, a filthy smirk in place, one arm behind his head.

That only makes this so much hotter.

After a minute of me moaning helplessly as Neo pounds me, Cy gives himself another long stroke and hops off the bed, strolling toward us. He grabs my hair, craning my head back and freeing Neo's mouth, which he covers with his own.

Shocks zip through me. Watching Cyan's particular brand of kissing is just as hot as experiencing it firsthand, and Neo's back of the throat groans are so sexy. I'm being fucked while he's making out with another guy and I never once thought I'd be part of something like this, but my GOD it's so hot I nearly come again from watching.

Cyan squeezes one of my nipples, the pain sending

another explosion of arousal through me so intense I finally come apart around Neo, who maintains a steady rhythm even as he breaks from Cyan's kiss, gasping. Cyan presses his forehead to Neo's temple for a moment, eyes closed, and my heart seizes. It's such a sweet, unexpected gesture, full of emotions I can feel in the air. It's over in a flash. Cyan straightens and claims my mouth next. I melt with the neediest sound I've ever made.

"Wow, that was...beautiful." Neo slams up into me, moaning when I gasp. "And I can't...even describe how..." He bounces me harder, faster, all while Cyan keeps tight control of my head, my lips, and my heart. "I've never felt so alive. No wonder you guys won't leave her alone."

Cyan pulls back, his mouth curling. Dirty. Dangerous. He slides his palm up to my neck, and I expect a throat grab, eagerly brace for it, but instead, he grips the side of my face and shoves his thumb in my mouth, stroking it along my tongue. Heat blooms again and I suck it, working it like it's his cock.

"She's a fucking work of art," he murmurs, and chills cover my body. "Get to it, Neo."

"Huh? Now? But—"

Cyan snaps his gaze to Neo. "Did I sound like I was asking?"

Neo doesn't say another word, and moves us toward the bed, bracing over me as my back hits the mattress. His glasses slip down his nose, and he tosses them up near the pillows, refocusing on me and thrusting slowly. I run my fingers through his soft hair.

"Reanne, I know we just met. So, this will seem fast and weird—"

"For fuck's sake, Neo." Cyan chuckles, palming his face.

"Don't rush me, this is important!" He clears his throat and smiles. "I pledge to protect and guide you, please and worship you, support and love you, until my dying breath."

My eyelids shutter, a strong tug forming in my chest while my weird shoulder ache blooms back to life. He's serious. There's a fierce determination in his eyes that takes my breath away. I don't know what to say. Do I say anything?

"Will you accept a piece of my soul, Aruna? Will you be my mate and take my mark?"

Mark. That's what Cyan wants to do, too. Pieces are starting to make sense.

"That sounds like a big deal."

"It is." He grins and rolls his hips. "We only get one."

"Ever?"

He nods and kisses my neck.

"A- and you want me?"

"Oh, without a doubt. We all do. Remember when I said I'd already waited my whole life? If you're willing, I'd like to stop waiting. You're it for me, baby bird."

I don't answer right away, because it's so much to process.

"You'll never be lonely again, Reanne. Never neglected." He presses a soft kiss to my lips. "Never unloved. Never hungry."

A tear springs up on its own and I blink it away. All my deepest fears wiped away forever? It's almost too much to hope for.

"Will it hurt?"

"Yeah. But pleasure makes it not as bad. That's why we'll do it now, during sex. I mean, if you say—"

"Yes."

He stills. "Are...you finishing my sentence or saying yes? Because I don't want to assume."

I laugh and nod, bucking against him. "I'm saying yes, Neo. I'll be your mate and take your mark."

"Yeah?" Neo grins, almost like Aeon did earlier.

I nod again, biting my lip as he rocks inside me. It feels so good, but my body has already been through a lot and it's not even midday.

Cyan lets out a hum from the other side of the room and makes his way to the bed. He steps flush with Neo's back, his hands winding around his waist and sliding up over his chest as he nips his neck.

Neo's breath leaves him, his cock pulsing inside me. I tentatively reach up and put my palm against his lower stomach, and he loses himself, eyes closing head falling back against Cyan's shoulder.

Damn, this is so hot I can't stand it. Neo's upper body suddenly rushes toward me, and I lock eyes with Cyan, as he strokes his palm along the now bent over Neo's spine. Neo claims my mouth and I melt into his sweetly dirty kisses until Cyan grabs a handful of Neo's hair and tilts his head back, shoving his middle two fingers in my open mouth.

"Get 'em good and wet, little slut."

I blink at him, confused for only a millisecond, then I work his fingers like magic while Neo thrusts, planting firm kisses along my collarbone.

"Fuck," Cyan whispers, a snarl tugging his lip as he watches. I'm enjoying myself way too much, lost in the sexiness of it all, so I actually startle when he snatches his fingers free.

My mouth isn't ignored for long. Neo takes back over, groaning as Cyan...

Oh, my God. I moan, arching into Neo as I watch Cyan finger fuck my potential mate. Cy stares at me, one brow lifted, a smirk in place.

Eyes still locked on mine, he plants his hands on Neo's hips and thrusts into him in one solid move. This pushes Neo's cock deeper into me, and I let out a high-pitched squeal.

It's like he's fucking me through Neo. I shiver with excitement, all my cells pinging to life, my nails digging into the back of Neo's neck.

Cyan leans over Neo's back and runs his tongue along his teeth, leaving a row of vicious new ones visible, like he wiped away a mask.

They grow longer as I watch, and I should be utterly terrified, not rolling toward a massive orgasm, but apparently, I have a whole new set of kinks now. The teeth return to normal in a blink, and I weirdly miss them.

Cyan thrusts into Neo again, harder, and we moan together, Neo grabbing my breast and tweaking my nipple as he sucks on my neck. No idea what's come over me, but I mouth, "faster," to Cyan, who chuckles deep in his chest, the rumble like a predator's call in the night. That does send chills of fear through me, but also makes me hornier.

They still, and Neo twists back, locking eyes with Cy, who strokes a finger down his cheek. It feels weirdly tense, but Neo nods and refocuses on me, chewing the inside of his cheek.

Cyan's eyes glow brighter, his fingers digging into Neo's hips as he thrusts harder. Neo winces, claiming my mouth, and our moans nearly match, each of us climbing the mountain toward orgasm at the same time. Cyan's head tilts back for only a second, then he locks those eyes on mine again and slams into Neo, who shouts in pleasure, and it's such an erotic moment I nearly come, too.

Neo pumps his load into me like a champion, nearly scalding as he fills me. I want to come again so bad, but it's just out of reach. I whimper, rocking my hips.

"Stand up, Neo," Cyan murmurs, palming his ass.

Neo does, his cum oozing out of me, and I whine at my sudden emptiness. He watches woozily, panting as Cyan situates himself at my head and pulls my upper half between his legs with his arm around my neck, cock between my shoulders.

"Alpha, what are—"

He gives my sensitive core several slaps, my body jerking with each one until I'm squirming and breathless.

Neo's eyes round with shock and darken with hunger.

"She needs something extra after she's had a few." He grips my jaw and turns my head to the side biting my earlobe as he tweaks my nipple. *"Isn't that right, my filthy little whore?"*

"Yes," I moan, digging my fingers into his thighs and locking eyes with my hot professor-wannabe. "Mark me, Neo."

"Fuck," he whispers. He scrambles back over me, forcing us both flat and kissing me hard as he thrusts back in.

Cyan shifts the hand on my jaw to my throat, and his other to my left nipple, while Neo ravages the right one, nibbling and licking. He thrusts faster, harder, sending me careening toward release with Cyan's rough assistance.

Right at my peak, sharp teeth slice into the side of my breast. I scream in pained pleasure, overcome with a sense of belonging. Fire sears through my flesh, crawling toward my heart as a piece of Neo's soul merges with mine. Warmth and comfort and love cover me, coaxing more tears to fall, and Neo roars around his mouthful, unloading in me again with wild force.

It's such a beautiful, raw moment, I don't want it to ever end. But it does, as my orgasm turns to aftershocks, and Neo unlatches, bathing the wound in long licks. Each one sends a zing toward my heart, followed by a matching zing from my shoulder.

"Oh my God," I pant, smoothing my hand along Cyan's thigh and playing with Neo's hair. "That was the hottest— and it felt so—"

My word catches. This sense of "home" for the first time in my life...it's too much, too intense. Tears fall over and over until sobs form, and I have to cover my face.

"Are you okay?" Neo strokes along the center of my chest. "It shouldn't have hurt that mu—"

"It ain't that, Neo," Cyan mutters and sits up. After some jostling and repositioning of legs, I'm facing Neo, still seated on his cock, and Cyan's pressed against my back, his legs over Neo's hips as they hug me close, like they can mash the sadness out of me. Maybe they can, I don't know. I don't know anything anymore. I can't shake the fear of having it all taken away, of allowing myself to settle into their rhythms, into their homes and then being ripped apart like always.

Cyan smooths my hair back and bites along the spot that keeps burning, nipping all the way up my neck until he hits my ear. "I told you, you're not going anywhere. I don't say shit I don't mean. You're ours, forever. You belong here. You feel it, right?"

I nod, crying harder, as Neo strokes my upper arms. He's not wrong and that's even scarier. I feel like such an idiot right now. All I've ever wanted was to be loved and welcomed and cherished and here it all is, literally in my lap, and for some reason I can't just be happy about it. Though...I suppose that could be entirely because they aren't human, and this isn't exactly a normal relationship, what with the kidnapping and all.

Cyan presses a hard kiss to my temple. "I don't know what you went through before, but that's all over. And...I know I fucked up. But now my head's on right, and I promise you, swear on my fucking life nothing like that will happen again. I'll protect you. We all will."

"That means your heart, too, Reanne." Neo murmurs, kissing the back of each of my hands, still plastered to my face.

"Thanks. Sorry, it's just a lot." I sniffle, resting my forehead on Neo's shoulder.

"Good thing there's lots of us to help you sort it out."

I jerk my head up at the sound of Aeon's voice from the main door. He's leaned against the frame, arms loosely crossed but with a tight smile. Korey takes up any remaining space behind him, nearly blotting out the two figures outside. Cyan's body tenses against mine, but Neo strokes his upper thigh, and he relaxes.

"Nice mark, Neo. Two down, three to go." Korey

chuckles as he crosses the room and braces on the back of a chair.

"Great, right?" He leans to the side and molds my breast to show off the angry red crescent. "I didn't know what it would look like, but I love it." He gives it another long lick, sending those matching zings through my shoulder again.

"Two?" I twist to eye Cyan. He gestures with his chin toward...Aeon.

Our eyes connect again and this time when my shoulder twinges, it all comes together. "You mated me?"

His smile falls, and he crouches on the floor beside the bed. "I did. I had to, to save you."

"I'm sorry." My eyes threaten to flood again. Knowing how precious a thing it is to them and that he had no choice breaks my heart.

"No, no, I don't regret it. As far as matings go, I doubt anyone will ever have one like ours. I'm okay with it being special, because you're special. I do wish it had been like what you did here, though." He cuts his eyes to Cyan and back to me.

I frown and cup his cheek. "I wish that too, can we do it again?"

The room erupts in soft laughter, Aeon included, as he kisses my palm. "We can only officially mate once, but we can 'do it' as many times as you want." He winks, looking sexier than any man has a right to.

Despite the fact one of these men is still inside me, manhandling my boob, and another has his still-hard dick nestled against my lower back, I manage to blush.

"I didn't mean—"

"I know, ReeRee." He stands and cradles my chin. "It

means a lot that you'd take my mark again." We kiss and it's just as breath stealing as the last time. Cyan runs his hand over my stomach, sending chills through me as Aeon pulls back. "And I'll bite you any time you want. But, there are a few more who'd love to join you, too."

I glance at Korey who juts his chin up with a grin.

Before I can do anything else, Neo nods at Cyan. "Thank you."

Cyan shrugs, tweaking my nipple again for fun. "I know I can be a prick, but I'm still your Alpha. Besides, she can't be mine if you lazy fucks don't mate her."

Neo grins, licks his mark a final time, and gives me a sweet, soft kiss. "Duty calls. Food won't cook itself. See you soon, my beautiful mate."

He lifts me and pulls out, an embarrassing amount of nut escaping along with him. No one seems to care but me, though, and he sets me on Cyan's thigh, grabs his glasses, and leaves.

Not only does Cyan not care, it riles him up even more. He leans to the side eyeing me up and down. "I can't fuckin' wait to fill you up officially."

His hand shoots out, around my jaw, and I gasp, heat daring to flare again. "Tell me, my sexy little slut, you wanna watch me put my Beta back in his place? Or do you want a bath?"

My gaze darts to Aeon, whose eyes widen for a fraction of a second before lowering.

I'm genuinely conflicted. I have a pretty good idea what putting him in his place might entail, and it could be hot as hell, but I'm also already worn thin on orgasms and starting to chafe a bit. A hot bath would be really nice.

"What if I..." I swallow and trace the outline of his shoulder muscle. He cuts his eyes down to my finger, a small smile crooking his mouth as he tugs me in close, fingers tight around my neck.

"What if you what," he mutters, brushing his lips across mine.

"If I get, you know. While I'm in there, uh, listening."

He licks the corner of my mouth before sucking my bottom lip in and biting it, hard enough to draw a gasp.

"I'll send someone with you to take care of that pretty little kitty." He gives it a playful slap, and I jump, a smile forming. I kind of love his roughness.

"Korey," he points toward the door, "go get Veikko."

"What the hell? I'm right here. I can do it."

Cyan shoots him a glare. "That's what you get for almost leaving. You'll be lucky if you're not last to mate. And you'd better not fucking complain."

Korey stomps out with a heavy sigh, not even glancing back.

"Better head in there," Cyan nibbles my chin, "it's about to get violent."

My eyes widen that time, and I nod. He lets my neck go, but I dart closer, surprising him with a kiss. When I pull back there's such a tenderness in his gaze I nearly can't move, but a rustle of fabric—Aeon's shorts hitting the floor —brings me out of the moment, and I scramble off the side of the bed on weak legs.

Aeon, for as submissive and apologetic as he looks, is also rock hard, the head of his cock glistening. I almost ask if it's too late to change my mind when a literal giant with long white hair comes ducking through the door.

126

He's absolutely gorgeous, with a huge barrel chest, thick legs, and beefy arms. Like a walking wall of breathtaking muscle. He takes in the scene, eyes finally landing on me. Or...eye, I guess. His left one is blue but the right one is milk white, a wide scar cutting from his forehead through it and nearly to his ear. The rest of his face is gentle, despite the serious expression. I can't look away as he slowly eats up the room with his strides. He's fantasy come to life, and I want to climb up one side and down the other.

"Take care of her, Vik."

At Cyan's command, I do wrench my eyes away, in time to see him grip the back of Aeon's head so hard he winces, and force him to his knees before Veikko blocks the view. He crowds me backward into the bathroom and closes the door behind himself, muffling a gagging moan from Aeon.

I blink up, up, butterflies eating me alive as I stare into his stunning face. "H-hi. I'm...Reanne. Veikko, right?"

The smallest of smiles hooks one side of his mouth as he gives me a single nod.

Ack, I can't take how cute and sexy it is. It makes me weirdly self-conscious, like I've got first date jitters, except I'm already naked, leaking another guys seed and he's only in here in case I get so horny I can't take it.

Laughter bubbles out of me, and he tilts his head, confusion bunching his brows.

"Sorry. This is just absolutely the weirdest situation. Can you show me which handles are for what?"

He gives me another nod, and I back up in time with his steps, bumping against the toilet to clear his path. But instead of telling or showing, he turns the handles himself, quickly filling the tub with water and the room with steam.

I step up beside him and test the temperature with my fingers.

"Thank you, that's perfect."

We glance at each other at the same time, and both look away quickly. I don't know how one man can be so insanely sexy and utterly adorable at the same time, but he totally is. There's a faint energy in the air around us, too, but I don't know what.

I can't wait for the tub to fill all the way and dip in a toe. Veikko quickly holds my upper arm, steadying me, and takes my other hand as he helps me in. I catch the way his gaze lingers, the flare in his nostrils, but then the water temperature zaps my brain.

"Oh my God, this feels amazing." I sink into the water all the way up to my neck with a shameless moan. "This is where I live now."

There's a single, breathy laugh from the behemoth, and I pry my eyes open. Holy wow, his smile is beautiful. Yeah, I think I could seriously get used to this.

AEON

I knew punching him was a bad idea before I did it, but how stupid it was doesn't really hit home until his cock slams the back of my throat.

It's not like this is something new, but he's extra angry, or extra Alpha, I'm not sure how to describe it. Genuinely can't be sure what he'll do.

Which...I guess I earned.

My damn dick still thinks the roughness is as hot as ever. Now, though, it's 'cause I keep picturing the softer version he does with ReeRee and the way she just melts into his touch. How sexy it would be if we were both owned by him at the same time—*fuck*.

Cyan does a particularly punishing thrust, his cock going down my throat before he snaps his hips back and crouches in front of me. I struggle for air as he cranes my head to the side and runs his nose along my neck.

"You're being quiet, little bitch. You worried she'll hear?"

"N-no. Well, maybe. Don't want to scare her or weird her out."

He chuckles, his warm breath sending a chill across my skin. I clench my fists where they rest on my thighs.

"You mean with how much you like pain?" He yanks on my hair harder, a twinge running down my neck straight to my leaking cock. "I shouldn't fucking give you any. Should fuck your face and throw you out with orders not to touch yourself."

It's the first time he's ever made that threat. And the first time I've ever felt genuine fear at his hand.

"Alpha, please. It won't happen again."

He bites my jaw so hard it breaks the skin, sending spasms through me, then licks the wound slow. "If this were another pack, your ass would already be dead."

"I know," I pant. "I'm sorr—aah!"

His hand wraps tight around my balls, tugging, squeezing just the way he knows I like, and I almost come from the shock.

"You're lucky I like you."

I nod with a light moan. I am, I really am, I know it. Neo and I are the only ones he's been with in all these years. He's different with Neo in a way I wouldn't like, but it works for them. Neo's soft, not that it's a bad thing, just a different thing. He's a great guy, funny, but soft. Can't handle a quarter of what I can take. Of what I want to take. Still, great guy. And I have no idea why the hell I'm thinking about him right now.

I force my attention back to Cyan's hand, but Reanne's muffled laugh rings out in the bathroom, and we both glance toward the door.

"How the fuck is he doing that without talking," Cyan mutters, tugging harder.

I suck in a breath rather than answer, and he lets go, running his thumb on the underside of my length and over the tip. A shiver rolls through me.

He growls and slices into my shoulder without warning, teeth elongating, burrowing deep while he makes devastatingly light strokes on my aching cock. Hot blood drips down my chest, the pain right at the edge of too much while the pleasure isn't quite enough.

It's the idea that Reanne, my mate, might appear at any moment, see this, see me, and enjoy it, maybe enough to join that has me bucking, groaning, and shooting all over the place before I can stop it.

Cyan unlatches, but doesn't give me the satisfaction of a cleaning, affectionate lick. I deserve that. He glances down with that dirty smirk and dark chuckle of his, sending even more arousal through me. "You made a mess on my floor."

I would look, but he still hasn't let my hair go. In fact, he uses it to force me to my feet and onto my stomach over the edge of the bed. He settles himself along my back, pressing me down with his weight.

"Just earning yourself more punishment by the second, aren't you," he snarls in my ear and puts his other hand in front of my mouth. "Spit."

I give him all the lube he needs, my cock throbbing as he readies me, neck still craned back. I can barely see shadows under the bathroom door as Vik moves around. There's no way I'll be able to keep quiet during this. Cyan's not gentle on a good day, and for whatever reason, he's extra wound up. But it's not like they don't know what's going on out here, I guess.

"Fuck!"

The word ends on a stunted, gasping moan as he pushes all the way in with one move. He doesn't wait for me to relax, sliding all the way out before slamming back in again. Sharp pain spreads through me, but it only makes my cock twitch more.

If I'm lucky, he'll stay man this time.

The next slap of his hips against my ass has me grinding my teeth, sweat beading on the back of my strained neck as he swells inside me. He's shifting. Damn it. Not lucky.

He finally lets my head go, in favor of digging his claws into my upper back. I manage to muffle my shout in the mattress, even as the wet spot under my stomach grows. He pounds me without mercy, dragging those claws down, slicing me open slowly. My skins ripples as the pleasure spreads.

I'm grunting when he hooks his claws under my hips and uses a powerful thrust to shove me farther across the bed. I slip off his cock with a wet slurp and scramble to my hands and knees, braced for the impact. He hefts his furry mass up behind me and shoves my upper half flat with the bed before he spears me again, over and over, railing me, each downward attack harder than the last, making the wood, and me, groan.

Faster than normal, the wounds on my back are already healing, the one on my shoulder nearly closed. I can't bring myself to ask for more, even though that's what I want.

This is supposed to be him setting the hierarchy back into place, not about—

His claws run along my bobbing cock, just hard enough to nick the skin.

"Yessss," I hiss, fireworks going off like bombs as my

body seizes. He does two more passes, the sharp burn of being cut dulled by the heavy pounding pleasure from deep inside. It's perfection.

He's usually not this controlled in Wereform, maybe it's Reanne. If so, I think I love her even more.

His thrusts pick up to supernatural speed, and instead of cutting, he fists my cock painfully hard, matching his punishing rhythm until I'm shouting through another orgasm. Ropes of my own cum hit my chest and stomach just as he fills me with a long, satisfied growl. The warmth of his load is soothing, familiar, and a sign that I've done my job again.

We both stay where we are, catching our breaths. Each time he twitches, I flinch, even though I love the ache. Finally, his beast is satisfied, and he shifts back to regular Cyan, but he doesn't pull out.

He folds his body atop mine and licks the back of my neck, forgiving me. "You gonna fuck around and mouth off in front of the pack again, Beta?"

I exhale long and loud as I shake my head.

"What about when it's just us?" He bites down hard on my shoulder again and tweaks my nipple.

His mouth stretches in a grin against my skin, the same grin eating up my face, hidden by the mattress.

"Probably not as often now that we have her, but...maybe."

He unlatches with another lick and slaps my ass, hard. "She'll like it. How many times you said she's built to match everyone? That means you, too. Now, roll over."

VEIKKO

I t's a monumental task to keep my arousal in check. Aeon is enjoying himself, loudly, and I'm beyond jealous. Not that he's with Cyan, I don't like the Alpha that way. Or males in general. Just that he's getting pleasure at someone else's hand. One more reason I stay on the outskirts. I can't take it.

Reanne hasn't moved in the last few minutes, wide eyed, shallow, rapid breaths, clutching the side of the tub as she listens. The silence in here is suffocating, in contrast to the moans and pained sounds from the bedroom.

Finally, she sits up, her soft breasts floating on top of the water. So distracting. "Is he...okay?"

I meet her gaze and hold it longer than I intend. There's still such an ingrained mental programming that buzzes to life when we do that. *Kill the Aruna Rigdis. Kill her now.* It's done nothing but stalk my thoughts like carrion around a dying mule.

I blink out of the stupor and nod.

She doesn't seem convinced. If I didn't know the two of them, I wouldn't be either. Her succulent, tiny body writhes under the water, and I hold my breath.

"I guess I...need some soap. Is there any?"

Giving her another nod, I stand and fish around under the sink. The soap I made is still here, miracle of miracles. I guess Cyan didn't have time to toss it again.

I turn around just as she's rising from the water like a nymph, rivulets running down her body, tracing her valleys. I must have made a sound, because her eyes widen and her cheeks pink.

She moves to cover herself, and I frown, lowering my brow. The last thing I want is her to feel uncomfortable around me. Besides, I like looking at her.

She studies my face, and slowly drops her arms. I relax my features, which in turn makes her smile.

"I thought you...I think I get it now. It's okay to be nervous."

I snort and cock a brow.

"Oh," she laughs. "Sorry. Not nervous, okay. So, safe to assume this is more than the silent treatment?"

I nod again.

"Is it like a monk thing? Like a vow of silence?"

I shrug and nod, even though I'm not sure what a 'monk' is.

"That's kind of cool. But now I'm super curious what your voice sounds like. Can I have that?" She points at my hand, which is choking the life out of the block of handcrafted soap.

Rather sheepishly, I hold it out and open my fist. The poor soap has indentations from my fingers. But rather than make me feel bad for my oafish strength, or for destroying something she wanted, she grins, plucks it from my palm, and gives it a testing sniff. I'm not sure what to do with the feelings swirling inside me.

"Hey...this smells familiar." We lock eyes again. *Kill her now.*

"This is what was used on me before."

I nod and smile, but it fades as she slides the soap along her torso in mesmerizing patterns. She stills and I glance up to find her staring right at me.

"Was it you?"

I don't want to lie or tell the truth. But I nod again because the Aruna asked me a direct question, and even though she's only mated with two members, her pull in this pack is infinitely stronger.

Her cheeks pink again, and she chews her lip as she resumes cleaning. "So, you've already...touched me."

Mother of the merciful moon.

I swallow thickly, compelled to nod again.

Aeon lets out a particularly loud series of moans, and Cyan has clearly shifted, his wereform's animalistic growls filling the whole cabin.

Her gaze unfocuses, aimed at the door, but her hands keep moving, lower, lower.

What is she...no she can't do—

I grip her wrist right before she makes contact, snapping her out of whatever trance that was. Or so I thought. Her glazed eyes swerve to meet mine, and I'm not sure she's fully aware. A theory proven when magic crackles in the air around us. Her subconscious has shifted to the forefront, her baser needs, her primal purpose. Shit, she's so close to becoming a deadly weapon, and I'm still such a failure all I want to do is bury myself inside her and mark her all over.

How much of that is her power and how much is my own desire I'll never know.

"I need the Alpha," she whispers hollowly, and I want to answer her, detail all the reasons that shouldn't happen, but I can't. If Cyan wasn't otherwise sexually occupied, he'd be tearing the door down.

Her skin flushes and she trembles, so I compose myself, lower her back to the water, and rinse her. As much as I both don't and desperately do want to, I take care to smooth my hands along her skin, applying deep, even pressure, soothing the fledgling power attempting to surface inside her. At first, she whimpers, flinches as though it hurts. It likely does. I'm not her Alpha, nor will I ever be. I'm also not her mate. Yet.

But she senses the pack bond, and after a few more strokes along her arms, her neck, her stomach, the whimpers turn to low moans.

"Please." She's so desperate it catches me off guard. I struggle, and fail, to recall a single time anyone has begged me for anything other than to spare their lives.

I should stop. There's no soap left. She's calmer, whereas I'm absolutely not, my cock more than at attention. She's not out of the mental flip, however, and it could be dangerous. Providing her a release would calm her completely, and it's what the Alpha commanded. That's what I tell myself when I brush my palm over her nipple. She arches into my touch, responding like the lover I've always longed for. It's difficult to believe this isn't another dream. Or nightmare.

If it's the latter...it'll end with her death as they always do. How this time?

I could bar the door and let her human remnant, the one that seeks to ease her ache, do the work for me. It's tempting. Too tempting.

Though, for something like that to work, she'd need to be far away from here. If any of us, myself included now, could hear her cries, nothing would stop us from getting to her but death. Maybe not even then. It's been theorized a fully seated Aruna Rigdis could command a legion of undead WereSpirits.

Gazing at her now, I'm fully convinced I'd rise from any grave to be at her side. And now I've returned to my even split of desire to mate and desire to murder. How can I allow this beautiful, perfect creature to fulfill her catastrophic destiny when preventing it, saving us all, is as simple as holding her under the water?

The same reason I still let Fen control me, use and abuse me. I'm weak.

She places her tiny hand on top of my massive one, slitted eyes aimed at me. I resist the siren's call, until she leans closer and cups my face. It's such a small gesture. In truth, it means nothing, but, to me, it's everything. Any hope of redeeming myself in the eyes of fate slides down my cheek in a salty cage.

What I must look like, crumpled at the feet of disaster, clinging to fractured beats in a long-dead heart. A towering redwood felled by the scrape of a dainty fingernail.

I don't resist when she tugs me closer. I don't turn away when she smears the tear across my skin with her soft thumb. Don't pull out of her embrace when she scoots to the edge of the tub and hooks her arms around my neck, bringing our faces mere inches apart.

I know what she's doing even if she isn't aware. The magic is still here, swirling, twisting, coaxing the mate urge to take over. That won't happen regardless, and I don't want any of it to happen when she's acting only on instinct. There's so much more to love than impulse, and love is the one thing worth holding on for, so when she leans close enough her hot breath mixes with mine, I tell myself that's the limit. I don't want to be seen as an aggressor when she comes out of this. I know what that does to a person.

And yet...

All I do is fail.

This hunger for her rattles my very bones. I gather her soaking wet frame in my arms, careful not to crush her as I pull her over the side of the tub and onto my lap, so close to giving in.

Water sloshes everywhere, and whether it's the change in temperature or position, her previously pliant body tenses.

I open my eyes to find hers, crystal clear, wide and searching as she pulls back. She scans our entwined bodies, stretches the fingers she's wound in my hair, and twists her mouth to the side as she plants a knee on each of my legs.

"I'm guessing something happened."

I nod, but I can't control my clenched arms any more than I can my racing lungs.

"Sorry," she mutters, "I could tell you wanted to go slow, and I was more than on board with that, but apparently my body had other ideas. Still does. This whole not being able to touch myself thing is super frustrating." She shifts on my lap, and I grunt at the jolt of pleasure. Her mind may have reverted, but she's still fragrant with need, something my system is ill-equipped to ignore. The flush on her cheeks deepens as she glances down.

"Holy…" Her throat ripples and she cuts her eyes back to mine. "So, is this…okay with you?"

Permission. If there's ever someone who deserves complete control of my soul, it's the one who asks me for the right to have it when it's already hers. Especially since none of this started with an ounce of her consent.

My nod this time is slow, accompanied by the faintest tightening of my embrace.

She grins, her shoulders relaxing. "Good. 'Cause I've got to say," she lowers her voice to a whisper and bites her lip, tugging at a lock of my hair, "you are crazy gorgeous. I could probably get off just grinding on your thigh."

My brows launch up and I can't help my shocked laugh. What an incredible visual. Maybe we'll try that some other time.

"I'm not even kidding," she chuckles. "But, it's really okay if you're not ready. I can ask someone else to, uh, help. It's—"

She cuts herself off with a small gasp as I slide my hand down her lower back, over the curve of her ass, and between her parted legs, holding her gaze. My middle finger glides between her wet lips with no resistance and when I make contact with her clit, her tiny frame shivers in relief.

I circle slow, greedily, even though I know it shouldn't be about me. But I've waited for this, and fast seems like such a blatant robbery.

She clutches my neck, her fingers still tangled in my hair, and I intend to take advantage of her chest's proximity to my mouth when she grabs the sides of my face and forces my attention up.

"What about kissing," she pants. "Is that okay, too?"

I'm focused in this moment, on her sounds, her scent, her body, so I nod. Her excited grin is infectious, and I share it right up until our mouths meet.

Her lips skate across mine, and my system registers it as an attack, adrenaline rushing through my limbs at a breakneck pace. It's been such a long time since I've been kissed in a way that meant something good, not a vicious, unwanted claim on yet another part of my body. The thunderous roar of a million hoofbeats echoes in my chest, and I'm moments from setting her down and failing yet again, when a testing, gentle swipe of her tongue scatters all remaining fear and willpower to the wind.

She's not him. Given a hundred years, she likely couldn't dream up the nightmare scenarios I was forced to endure, let alone be capable of a fraction of his immorality.

No. Reanne is good, and this is safe.

Blood on fire with unspent energy, I open to her, welcoming her warmth as I fall under the spell of her hunger-laced tenderness. I've never experienced such a sharing of passion through such a small act. If it's possible to love someone, truly love someone, in a single moment, I do. The voice in my head that cries for her death on repeat is finally silenced, and with each breathy moan against my mouth, each whine and urgent arch into my touch, I grow more comfortable, more confident.

And when she cries her release from my touch, using my air, clutching my face, pressed against my body, a new whisper forms on the fringes of my consciousness. A word I've never said.

Mine.

It scares me less than it should, excites me far more than is reasonable, and ignites a primal urge I've only heard about.

"Holy shit, that was so hot," she keens, kissing me harder, over and over, humming each time. I would have to agree.

"You are an amazing kisser, Veikko. God. It's like your entire everything was made for sex. Speaking of..."

I can barely hear Cyan and Aeon still at it over my own pulse as she trails her hand down my chest, stopping at the top of my shorts.

Finally, she pulls back and gives me the cutest apologetic look. "I'm still so...I don't know. Fluttery. I wish I understood what was going on with me. You being ridiculously sexy isn't helping." She gives me another moaning kiss, grinding on my wet hand. "I'm not complaining, but I'm worried I literally," she gulps in a heavy breath, "can't get enough. Would you... can...can we..."

I smirk and cup the back of her head, returning her mouth to mine, as I slide my other hand along her inner thigh. With a quick adjustment, I free my aching cock from the top of my shorts and guide her down. I can't help my pleasured growl. Such tight heat.

She breaks the kiss with a sharp inhalation and a deep, gravelly moan. "Oh, fuck, yes." She cuts her gaze down and whimpers, circling her hand around my base. "G-god, that won't—are you, unhh, are you half-shift—fuuuuuuck!"

Her head falls back as I thrust up, so I kiss her delicate throat and along her collarbone. I can feel the pulses of her existing marks, urging me to stake a claim, to make a home in her heart, but I can't.

I thrust again, easing more inside her, afraid it'll be over too soon. She feels better than I could have possibly dreamed. It's nearly too good.

She grabs the back of my neck, leveling her head and locking desperate eyes with me. "It's okay, you, you won't hurt me. And it doesn't have to last, I just need you, please!"

I'm not sure how she guessed that, but she takes the option away with her next breath by bouncing. She manages it once and we both groan, her muscles trembling.

"Christ, you're huge," she whispers, clinging to me harder as she descends on my mouth again. Her tongue glides along mine, and the urges take over.

I grip her hips and drive upward, slow at first, then faster. She's incoherent, the living embodiment of pleasure at my doing. This small room fills with a volley of pleas, swears, moans, searching fingers, hungry kisses, and tight embraces, each of us holding on for likely different reasons, but the result is the same. A supremely passionate encounter, the likes of which will never be replicated.

I couldn't think of a more perfect scenario for my first time with Reanne. For my first time with a future mate. For my first time with a female.

I hold out as long as I can, because watching her is fantastic, but once she starts grinding her hips, I'm done for. I hold her in place and make more sound than I think I ever have, growls and grunts and groans of my own, permeating the air.

She comes again with shock filled moans, glancing down. Once she stops convulsing, we simply hold each other like we were, breathing each other in, kissing.

After a few minutes like this, she leans back and cradles her lower stomach with a sleepy, satisfied smile. "I can actually feel it all in there. I love it."

And I love you, I nearly say.

Instead, I press my forehead to hers and close my eyes.

This is bliss. Everything I went through was worth it to get to this point, here, now, with her. I've truly found happiness.

"Aww, I feel the same way. You're so amazing. It may sound weird, but I'm glad Cyan took me, because I got to meet you."

She kisses me, but I can't feel it. I've gone numb from the top of my head down.

I grab her shoulders and push her back, eyes wide. How did she hear that? That's not possible. We aren't mated. I'm not in the pack link. She shouldn't have access to my thoughts. No one should. No one can. No one. It's the only safe place I have. The only thing totally untouchable.

"W-what? Did I say the wrong—"

I quickly lift her and set her on her feet. Confused tears fill her eyes as I stand and reclothe myself. They match mine. Even though I swore I wouldn't shed another, this is the rawest of violations.

It's too much to handle today.

"Wait! I'm sorry!"

I stall at the door, glancing back over my shoulder at her vulnerable, closed off posture, her trembling lip. My heart breaks in two, while my mind works to repair itself, to fix the damage, to rebuild the walls and protect myself above all else.

"I don't know what I did, but please don't go," she whispers. "We can be mates, if that's—no, I'd really like to be your mate. Please stay. Mate with me, Veikko."

I can feel them descend on the cabin, so I'm not shocked when I jerk the bathroom door open, and the whole pack is glaring at me. They have every right to, I've hurt their Aruna.

Her delicate hand grips my wrist, but I jerk away in blind panic, bursting through the body barricade and landing on the ground with a thud.

Agnar is the only one whose eyes I can meet. The flicker of pain there tells me he can guess what's wrong, and the clenched jaw tells me he won't reveal anything. That's all I needed to be sure of.

"The fuck, Vik, what did you do? Why is she—get back here!"

I'm through the main door, shifted, and in the woods before I can take a full breath.

Nothing but a failure, through and through.

12

ΠEO

I can't decide whose suffering is worse, hers or Vik's. I know at least a little of what they did in here, we all do, there's a sizable amount of evidence leaking down her thigh. Plus, my mate isn't quiet. I really like that about her.

But...there's not another mark, which surprises me. Veikko never struck me as the type who'd use her. Maybe that's why she's sad?

More surprising is which of us moves first.

"Reanne, what the fuck happened?" Cyan clears the few steps to her and grips her upper arms, tugging her close.

I would have led with a hug, maybe a nicer tone, but to each his own, I guess. Such is the Cyan way. And it's the absolute rudest time to be getting a hard-on, but they really do look good together.

Instead of being relieved at his touch, like she should be, he's the Alpha after all, she struggles, jerking against his hold as she sobs.

"I don't...I don't know. He..." She stills for a moment, and we all relax, until she explodes.

"Don't touch me!" Her scream is like a slap across all our

faces. The rest of us recoil on reflex, but Cyan growls low, tightening his fingers.

"I'll touch whatever I want. Just because I like you doesn't change who's in charge here. I could literally bend you over this tub and fuck you until you pass out, and you couldn't do a damn thing about it. But it's also my job to protect you, so answer my fucking question. What did he do to you?"

He should have let me stay with her, instead.

I glance at Korey's aggressive posture and frown. *You were gonna leave, why would he trust you with that?*

But I didn't leave, that's the important part!

I cluck at him in the link and refocus.

Reanne jerks her arms uselessly, tears streaming. I really just want to hold her and make it all go away. Maybe a plate of bacon would help.

"This is your fault."

"My fault? How the hell—"

"I didn't ask to be brought here," she grits out, "and I sure as hell didn't ask for my heart to be broken!"

"How did he manage that without talking? Stop... fighting me!"

He shouts the last bit, Alpha energy blasting through the room. Her exaggerated attempts to launch backward halt, only to be replaced with more tears and deep shivering.

"I asked him to be my mate, but he..." She trails off, her gaze going distant as waves of pain radiate off her.

"He rejected her," Aeon's sex-worn voice gravels, filling the space.

"Shit," Cyan mutters. One hand still around her arm in a vice hold, he snatches the drain plug out of the tub and deposits her in it, himself right behind her as he turns on the shower. He wraps his arms around her and pins her against his chest, letting the warm water run over them both.

Aeon sends his subtle Beta wave through the room, but it's not having an effect on her.

Why would Vik do something so awful? He always struck me as smart, so he had to know what that would do to her. The hell he'd rain down on himself.

I steal a peek at Agnar, who keeps glancing toward the door, but my glasses fog, so I huff and toss them onto the closest chair.

I'm glad Reanne didn't poke fun at me for them. Humans need and wear them in droves. Here? I'm the only one I know of. Werewolves are supposed to heal from almost everything, but my eyes don't. And the glasses are a big liability. Yeah, I can see okay when I'm shifted, but having to be careful with them while I'm in Wereform makes me worthless for any job outside the safety of camp.

Luckily, I'd rather cook anyway.

"Neo, get over here," Cyan murmurs, his cheek pressed to the top of her head.

I blink. "M-me?"

Would have expected him to ask Aeon, but a quick glance shows he's worse for the wear, and that broken arm'll need to heal. Which leaves me the first mate available. Got it. Makes sense.

"Okay, but I left a pot on the—"

"Neo."

"Right, yeah. Let me just..."

I step out of my shorts and slip in behind her. It's a tight fit, but the water is nice. "Not really built for three, is it?"

Cyan ignores my attempt at levity and turns her listless body around, hooking an arm over her neck, the other around her stomach. "Hit your mark."

"What? But that'll hurt her."

"She's already hurting. Sink your damn teeth in her breast, or so help me."

"Okay, okay! Sorry."

It's a terribly awkward position we're in, and without the rush of sex behind it, biting her feels wrong, but I trust Cyan. Plus, her trembling is getting worse by the second. I line up with my mark and quickly latch on, stroking her hips. That deeply connected feeling warms me to my toes again.

Her sobs grow, long, pained wails bouncing off the walls, so I send her as much love as I can, because I can't think of anything else to do. I'm too new at all this. I was always way more concerned about cooking than mating logistics. It must work at least a little, because she clutches the back of my head.

Agnar sighs. *I'll see if I can track him down. Bring him back. He'll...have to answer for it, the big idiot. Besides, I'm no good here, yet.*

I'll hunt around, too. Look after her, you guys.

The front door clatters shut behind Korey and Agnar. Aeon stumbles into the bathroom just as the bones on his arm crack back into place. Huh, that was fast. Break like that should have taken a day or two. He takes a relieved breath, shakes out his skin and finds his mark on her shoulder, slicing in with way more precision than I did.

I guess practice makes perfect.

The emotions Aeon sends above the Beta energy wash over me too, and even though I wasn't particularly upset, I'm way calmer.

The tiny room fills with steam as we hold our prize, Cyan moves his arm in favor of holding her jaw as he rests his lips against her ear.

"Better?"

"A...a little."

"So, talk. You asked him to mate, he fucked you, and left. Just like that?"

I don't have a clue how anyone could be inside her and not want to mate. I'm literally attached to her and want to do it again.

"No. The other way. You guys were, and I got, you know, and he helped, then we did it and it was," she sniffles, another tear dropping, "really great. We connected. Everything was great until I saw his thoughts, the same way I saw yours. Only his were words, yours are pictures. Anyway. He said he had found happiness and I told him I felt the same and—" she breaks into another sob.

I cut my eyes to Aeon, whose bewildered expression matches mine. Talking in pack link is one thing. I don't think I'd like anyone seeing my thoughts, either.

Cyan's growl turns deadly, his muscles rippling with an oncoming shift. "Fucker's old enough to know better. Promise you don't wanna see my thoughts now."

"No, don't hurt him or anything." Reanne tries to twist and face him, but she only succeeds in forcing our tangle of bodies to stumble, nearly hitting the floor.

I unlatch, giving the wound a long lick, before I kiss her cheek. "I hate playing mediator—"

Aeon snorts. I ignore him.

"—but what he did has consequences for our kind. It's more than hurt feelings. He upset a serious balance by rejecting you. His fate'll come down to a single choice now, baby bird."

There's a quick crackle in my head, forcing a wince. Aeon detaches as well, gripping his temple. Cyan lets our mate go, and arches back unnaturally, bellowing in pain. Reanne screams, covering her head and ducking under the shower spray.

It's all over as fast as it came on, everything quiet and normal save for one thing. I grip Aeon's forearm as we stare at Cyan, only...

"I'm afraid your mate is right, Aruna." He steps out of the shower, reaches around a confused Reanne, turns off the water and plucks a towel from the shelf, holding it out to her. "But your Sentinel isn't the only one with a choice to make."

Sentinel? I sniff the air, a low rumble in my throat, but it's more confusion than aggression. He smells like Cyan. He looks like him, but he's standing so straight, so proper. I can still feel the Alpha anchor, but it's wrong.

Aeon's growl picks up, too, but he looks just as confused as I am.

He glances at us, an apologetic tilt to his brow. "I am sorry about the intrusion, gents. I assure you, it wasn't under my control." His gaze sweeps back over to Reanne. "But I daresay the timing is impeccable. Only two marks.

Please, my dear, you'll catch your death." He wiggles the towel. "We have much to discuss, you and I."

Aeon snatches the towel away and wraps our shivering mate in it, helping her out of the tub as I step between them and this...imposter.

"I don't know what's going on, or who you are, but you're not talking to her."

Cyan cocks his eyebrow, giving me a faintly surprised once-over. "Zed's are usually seen, not heard. I won't be needing you for this conversation. Please wait outside."

The Alpha push is intense, more than Cyan ever used, and even though I try to fight it, I can't. I'm by the fire before I have control over my body again.

Aeon, tell me everything!

I will. I don't like this at all. Where's Korey? Have Aggy and Vik come back yet?

Oh, that's right. I'm alone out here. It's weird. Quiet. And my damn stew burned, great.

I don't know. And no, they aren't here either. Want me to go look for them?

No, stay put.

Rather than stare at dancing embers in panic, I grab the ruined pot, and set about making another dish. Might as well make use of the only skill I have, while I hope everyone's okay.

REANNE

I only thought I was confused before. The guy in front of me is still Cyan, with his huge neck scar and sexy, violent face, only the expression is a version of kind, patient. And he's clearly talking with Cyan's voice, but also clearly not. It's like I'm in some alternate reality where Cyan is a British nobleman from the 1900's.

Besides all that, he both feels familiar and completely bizarre.

"What did you do to Cyan?"

"ReeRee, don't talk to him." Aeon rumbles, moving me behind himself. "Who are you?"

"Peace, Beta." Aeon's body relaxes, while mine grows tenser. I can feel the energy coming off him again, just like when he sent Neo away. I don't like it.

"I bear no ill-will for you or this precious Aruna. My name is Mishka."

He bows, actually bows, and cuts Cyan's deep eyes up at me. I can't help the heart flip, even though it's all wrong. Made even more wrong when Aeon whips his head around and lowers his brow at me.

Cyan, or I guess Mishka, grins and I feel that tug in my

belly, the string connected to Cyan. It's fuzzier, different, but strong. My insides are as mixed up as my head, apparently.

Even though it's Cyan's mouth, it looks nothing like his smile. He straightens and glances toward the door.

"I'm sure what I have to say would go over better if we were both dressed." He glances at Aeon. "What do you think, hmm? Can you trust me enough to allow this darling creature to warm up?"

My cheeks flame. "I...don't think I have any clothes, actually."

Mishka's brows launch skyward, still aimed at Aeon. "Not that she isn't a glorious sight, but...was the plan to keep her naked for eternity?"

Aeon's posture shrinks a little. "Well. Maybe? We sort of hadn't gotten that far."

Mishka curls his lip, more energy leeching into the air, and Aeon shrinks further. I *really, really* don't like that. Energy of my own sparks to life, warming my chest.

"As many times as I'd spoken to Cyan, I hadn't realized his leadership was so—"

"Stop being mean to them," I snap. All the energy in the room fades, and Mishka grins again, stepping closer.

"By the moon, it's true. You felt that, didn't you, Beta? How could you not? Absolutely spectacular." He steps closer, crowding us toward the door, Aeon still my shield, though he seems confused. "Forgive the aggression, it's far from my style, but I had to be sure. My dear, do you know what you are?"

I cast a furtive glance at Aeon, who is now staring at me intently. "An Aruna. Even you said so."

"You're much more than that." Mishka is directly in front of me, palm hovering at my cheek like he's afraid to touch me.

"You are the Aruna Rigdis." Aeon inhales sharply as Mishka continues, tone reverent. "Savior of Werewolf kind."

I snort and take a half step back, hitting the door frame with a soft thud, towel slipping off my shoulder. "Right. Me, a savior. Very funny."

"This is no joke. We've been waiting for you. My people, The Vigils, have combed for generations, hoping to find you, to see you rise to your rightful place, and here this fledgling pack stumbles onto the most precious being ever created, purely by accident." He lets out a soft laugh. "Right under a Sentinel's nose. Tell me the stars haven't aligned in our favor?"

I look to Aeon again, but he's staring at the far wall, brows knitted. "It...it makes sense," he mutters.

"But of course. Facts always do. Now, please, dearest Reanne. Will you sit with me and discuss your options?"

He gestures to the bedroom, completely benign smile in place while my mind spins. Options. I haven't been given a single one since this all started, not even by my own body. And I still find him insanely attractive, because it's Cyan's drop dead gorgeous frame, but now there's the added bonus of a kinder, more respectful personality wrapped up inside.

And the pull keeps getting stronger. I nod.

"I-I guess so, sure."

That snaps Aeon to attention finally, and he grabs my hand, staring Mishka down. "I invoke Mate Guard. You cannot order me away. I'll sit in on the conversation."

If that bothers him, he doesn't show it. In fact, his smile

widens. "I expected nothing less. You're a fine Beta, Aeon. Cyan's praise has proven quite earned. After you."

Flustered, Aeon mutters something and tugs me through the doorway, the tips of his ears tinting.

We sit on the bed, and Mishka drags one of the wicker dining chairs over, setting it right in front of me, so his knees are on the outside of mine.

He gives Aeon a once-over, brow quirking. Aeon quickly grabs a pillow and plops it on his lap, which makes Mishka chuckle. "I can see the appeal of a general lack of clothing. Far fewer instances of misunderstood intent, I'd wager."

Aeon says nothing, only clearing his throat. I guess it's hard for him, too, separating the stranger inside from the body he knows intimately.

Mishka refocuses on me with a soft smile. "Would you like to ask me questions first, or should I simply surge ahead?"

I blow a slow breath through puffed out cheeks. I guess the fastest way would be direct. But what do I want to know first? Wait, that's easy.

"Where is Cyan? The real—I mean his mind, or whatever."

"Safe, I would assume. I was on routine patrol in a relatively quiet section. He's probably making snow wolves as we speak."

That makes me feel better. I love snow, we didn't get nearly enough back home.

"When will he be back?"

Mishka shrugs. "As I stated, this was entirely unexpected. I didn't know it was a possibility, so I can't predict anything."

That sucks.

"Okay, so, sentinel?"

"You know him as Veikko. Though, he's had other names through time. The Sentinels are a dwindling organization with one goal: kill any potential Rigdis. Keep them from achieving their wondrous purpose. It's no small miracle you're still here. Veikko is one of their deadliest assassins. Or...was. Clearly, something went wrong. I had my suspicions about the man as soon as Cyan mentioned him."

I rub at my chest and frown. That hurt is still so raw. But I can't believe Veikko would ever kill me.

"How do you mean you talked to him?" Aeon pipes up, composure regained apparently.

"In our wereforms. Mental communication ever since he killed his father. And no, I have no explanation beyond that. I never told anyone, and my own research into the reason was fruitless."

I blink, a cold ball forming in my stomach. "W-what? He killed..."

"ReeRee, his dad was a nightmare. Cy did the world a favor." Aeon threads his fingers through mine on the mattress. "Trust me."

Mishka's gaze drops to our joined hands. Unless I imagine it, there's a small twitch under his eye. "Quite right. Bertram's exploits reached even our ears. His was no great loss. Only in how it affected Cyan."

His eyes darken, genuine sadness etched in his features. I want to crawl onto his lap and hug him until it's gone, but he's not Cyan.

"Besides, that's how you get the Alpha power anyway.

The pup has to challenge his father, and win. Which means kill him. The problem was, Cy never wanted it. He was just avenging his mom."

I frown at Aeon's expression.

How awful. I can't imagine what Cyan went through. I had always dreamed about what it'd be like to have a dad, and if his was that bad, he probably spent his time dreaming about not having one. And then losing his mom, too. Poor Cyan.

Aeon glances at me. "I don't know how they were doing it, but there's no way he'd know that if Cy didn't tell him. We've all been under Alpha command not to talk about what happened to anyone."

Mishka nods. "As I said. We've been talking a long time."

"Why didn't he say anything to you guys about talking to..." I gesture to Mishka.

Aeon shrugs, but Mishka chuckles. "You'd have called him crazy. Grounds to break pack. Same reason I didn't tell my family."

Okay. I guess that makes sense as much as anything does.

"Why are the Sentinels dwindling?"

Mishka's smile curls higher. "Many have seen the error in their beliefs. It's easy once you have all the facts."

"And what are the facts?"

He passes a look between the two of us before leaning back in the chair. "The Sentinel's ideal that your kind are... harbingers, let's say...of destruction is based on a simple misunderstanding. They believe you destined to merge with a bloodline proven volatile time and again. The thinking is your perfection would be tainted, led down a dark path by this bad seed. However, things are different this time. There's an additional mate option with High Alpha capabilities." His eyes blaze gold for a moment as he scans my face. "Me."

That tug toward him twangs harder, but my heart also hurts. I miss Cyan—the real Cyan.

Aeon is less quiet with his emotions. "Fuck that. She belongs to SteelTooth."

Mishka's eyes never leave mine, sucking me in. "Shouldn't she have some say in the matter?"

Part of me thinks that's a damn novel idea. It'd be great to make a decision on my own. Another part was so tired of doing everything on my own, that this has been sort of nice.

"You feel the connection to me, don't you, Reanne?"

I do, but I don't want to admit it.

"I've already mated her, so has Neo."

"As I stated, perfect timing. She lacks one bite to be bound to your pack." His grin pitches higher. "If those rules still applied."

Aeon launches to his feet. "What do you mean if? That's basic pack law!"

"She's no basic Aruna, Beta. All she has to do is mate with the High Alpha to take power. The rest of you, the rest of any pack, are inconsequential. She could fulfill her destiny in a matter of moments, right here, right now, if she wished."

"That can't be right!" Aeon is fuming. "Where'd you learn all this?"

But I have a different question. A more important one. "Who is the other Alpha?"

There's finally a crack in the calm, a falter in the patient expression but it's gone in an instant.

"A pertinent question, but forgive me for not answering. I'd be a fool to use my limited time with you to talk about someone else, as I'm the soundest choice of the two. All I ask is that you give me a chance to show you how a queen should be treated. Spend time with me, come to my lands, meet the GrimBite pack. Then, you can make an informed decision."

I can't deny it does make sense that if—big if—I'm some important person here, I should learn everything I can. But Cyan is here, not at GrimBite.

This has all gotten so complicated. I'd give almost anything to be stressing an exam instead of the fate of an entire species.

"What if my decision was, I wanted to go back home?"

Mishka frowns and rests his heated hand on my knee, sending a small burst of excitement through me which I stamp out immediately. "Did they not tell you?"

"No? Tell me what?" I whip my head to face Aeon. "What didn't you tell me?"

He glares at Mishka. "We hadn't gotten to it yet."

"Gotten to what?!"

Mishka sighs. "Unfortunately, once you crossed into The Glade you were forever changed. You won't survive outside its protection."

"I...can't go home."

Tears sting my eyes. I'd held onto a tiny thread of hope that someday, maybe, if I asked nice enough, they might let me go back, at least for a little while. But now...

"I'm so sorry, my dear. If I had the power to undo it, I would."

"Aeon. You knew?"

He finally glances back and drops down beside me, regret in his eyes. "Yeah. That's what happens to all Arunas who come here from your side. I would have told you. Or Cy would have. We just..."

"You've been enjoying her at the expense of preparing her."

Aeon hangs his head. I grip my mouth while tears spill over my hand. How different might the last few days have played out if Mishka and his pack had found me instead? Would I already be mated to him?

I love the way it feels to be connected to Aeon and Neo, but would it feel like that with anyone I mate? Or does it feel like that because I liked them first? And Cyan...I thought the way I felt toward him was special. Maybe...maybe it's not. That makes me sadder than anything.

"Not to pile worse news on top of bad, but there is more. You can't ignore the decision. Each day, each moment you're here, more of you awakens. You'll soon be forced to choose one of us...or die, taking all of Werewolf kind with you."

14

CYAN

What the fucking fuck just happened? Snow beats against my face as I tug someone's jacket tighter around myself.

I'm in the middle of a forest, full of trees I've never seen, marked by a clan symbol I don't recognize. And it's snowing. I haven't seen snow in twenty years, even that was flurries. Where the shit am I?

This feels a lot like my body, but these sure as hell aren't my clothes.

I need to get back to Reanne before the pain... I rub my chest and frown. I guess this really isn't my body, I'm not hurting at all. Well, I still miss her, damn it. But I can't get a line on anyone, can't tell which direction to run.

"Fuuck."

My voice bounces off the trees and stops dead in the snow. I guess all I can do is follow the clan marks and hope they lead me somewhere safe. So, that's what I do.

It takes way too long, but eventually I'm standing at the edge of a drop-off, staring at a massive village. There must be fifty odd Werewolves down there.

Two rapid taps land on my upper back, and I whirl,

claws out, aimed for the soon-to-be-maimed asshole's shoulders. Only they stick into a tree trunk instead, above his shoulders, because he's way shorter than I expected.

"Mishka! It's me! L-Lazaros! Forgive me, Alpha. I didn't mean to startle you, I-I thought you heard me."

Why did he call me that?

I jerk free of the bark and step back, wheels turning. I wonder if I can access the...I can. This guy is a Beta, but that would mean—

That mother fucking snake. Did Mishka do this on purpose? How did he do it anyway? That means he's in my body, in my bathroom, with my mate.

I snarl and Lazaros stumbles backward, dropping to a knee with his ear pressed to his shoulder, neck exposed. "Deepest apologies! I s-should have known better than to approach you on patrol."

Wow. Talk about submissive. Or Mishka's not as nice as I thought. Maybe he is a giant bag of dicks after all. Fuck, I dunno how to play this. Do I try to talk like he does? No way I'll get that accent right, unless his mouth just...does it?

Probably end up sounding like two frogs were fucking on my tongue. Maybe I can just not talk at all.

I grunt and cross my arms, giving him a nod.

He stands, eyeing me warily.

"You... you seem...different, Alpha. Do you n-need a session with one of the Niktas?"

My stomach twists. They not only have a female Werewolf...they've got more than one. Man. I haven't seen a Nikta since my mom. I guess a bigger pack does have its perks. Wonder how long they've been using them, how they're keeping them from being bred. I'd ask, but this ain't some fucking fact finding mission.

I've been body-jacked and need to get home.

I shake my head and stare down at the village again, keeping Lazzy-boy in my peripheral. He's a good-looking little dude, with a hairless face, short, tousled hair, bright blue eyes, high-arched brows, and a straight nose with a flat ridge. Cute as hell. I didn't know they made grown Werewolves this small. Could put him in my damn pocket. Hard to guess what he looks like under the coat and pants, but there's a 100% chance he's got a nice, compact body. I don't think I've met a fat Werewolf. I almost laugh out loud but bite the inside of my cheek instead.

"Ah, alright. Alpha. M-may I, and you can certainly tell me no, say something?"

I nod, the back of my neck pricking as he sends heady Beta vibes my way. That's a sobering punch to the gut. I miss Aeon. I miss all of them.

But Lazaros pumps another wave out and my mind gets a little hazy. Horny. Unh…that's way too dangerous right now, no matter how much the idea makes my dick jump. And anyway, maybe he's doing it on accident.

"I've heard, which it could be incorrect I suppose, but that you're holding secret meetings with a questionable pack…well, to be direct, Alpha…"

Secret meetings, huh? It hits me he talks a lot like Mishka. I guess they all would.

I sway, practically drunk as he mutters, "I'm…w-worried about you."

Another soothing wave of energy hits, and my knees

almost fold. This dude didn't come to play today. Fuck. He could teach classes.

Why is he still standing here, staring at me? Leave, damn you.

I cut my eyes back to him and he smiles. Fuck, he's got a nice one of those, too.

"Do I...need to be worried?"

I shake my head again. We stand in a thick silence as more snow falls.

Lazaros inches closer and my throat tightens. I recognize the submission, now, and so does my beast. Or... Mishka's beast, I guess. Weird, actually. It still feels crazy familiar, like I could call the shift the same way.

"I...have a confession. My finding you here was no accident. I wanted, well, needed a moment alone. Just us. Ever since Silvin's death," he takes a deep breath, and his pain hits me square in the heart, like I lost her myself. "You've been different. Please," he holds up his hand, "Don't deny it. Let me say what I need to say, I-I beg you."

I'm way too caught up now, his energy stroking down my spine like a hand, so I nod again. He's a damn good Beta.

He stares at me in shock and blinks, getting his composure back. "Uh, right. I didn't expect—thank you." He clears his throat. "I know I'm your last choice, everyone's last choice for...everything, really, that's no great secret, and I'm endlessly grateful you gave me these last two days of freedom. N-not to say I'm not grateful for my, uh, my home, as it is, but I believe, and please correct me if I'm wrong, that I've proven I, well, that I could be..."

I wanna eat him up. He trails off, unease filtering into

the air, so I send him a quick Alpha burst, and the reflected relief digs right into my heart.

"Thank you," he breathes, staring up at me like it's the first time he's seen me. Shit, maybe that was the wrong thing to do. What the hell kind of Alpha is Mishka?

Neo would fall all over himself to love on this guy. Hell, Reanne, too, probably. I could see them in a sexy little cuddle pile, just waiting for me to dive in. I wince and adjust myself in these tight ass pants. This is why I wear shorts or nothing, can't stand being all cooped up.

Lazaros tracks the motion, and cuts wide, hopeful eyes back up. I can't look away. It couldn't be clearer how he feels about Mishka, but I have no fucking clue what I'm supposed to do here.

And I'm hard as a damn rock.

Not that I'll die if I don't screw something, but he couldn't be asking for it more if he was naked, on his knees, waving that ass like a 'fuck me' flag.

Ugggh. Wrong time for that visual.

I know what I'd do if he was my Beta. If I could have two, I'd steal this glorious bastard.

"Uh, as I was trying, failing really, to say, I think that I, in the absence of, well, anyone better, could...would like to be..." He closes his eyes, gulps, and says, "yours."

I laugh, not because it's a bad idea, but because he's so god damn adorable I can't stand it. Swear to the moon, I think I'm blushing. The fuck kind of shit is this. Get it together. He's not even saying it to me. He thinks I'm his body-snatching Alpha. I wish like hell I was.

His eyes pop open, and before the hurt on his face rips

me to shreds, I grab him by the back of the neck and duck down, searing my mouth to his.

He lets out a shocked little whimper that sets my blood on fire. His tongue invades, and I moan, even though I don't mean to, but holy Moon Mother, he can kiss.

I grab his entire ass in both hands and lift him, grinding his cock along mine. We groan together, and he clutches my head as I spin and press him to a tree, where he gasps at the impact. I break the kiss as I rock my hips, nipping a harsh trail along his jaw and down his neck. I nick the skin several times, just so I can taste him. He's like a damn drug, fogging my brain.

I'm a second from ripping these clothes off and saying to hell with everything when he mutters, "Mishka," with such shocked reverence, it kills me.

I pull back and stare at him. Hard. He's beautiful, panting, flushed. I can't stand him thinking that sorry sap is the one making him feel like this, when it's me, damn it.

I have to tell him. I send out a wave of Alpha command, and his pupils dilate as he stills, listening. I'm literally holding him, suspended against this tree with my hips, and if I forced the issue, I could pin him to the ground no problems. But maybe it won't come to that.

Even though I know this is probably a shit idea, I cover his mouth and put a finger to my lips. "Not Mishka, Lazzy-boy."

I rock against him again, because I can't fucking stop.

He blinks over and over, hot little breaths fanning over my hand. But he doesn't look scared. More excited than anything.

"He and I swapped brains or some shit. He's off in my

body, and I'm in his." I keep my eyes on Lazaros's as I work my other hand between us and palm his hard-on. "But I really fucking wanna be in yours."

A fast, harsh breath hits my skin next as his eyes roll closed. It's worth the risk, mostly because I need to kiss him again, so I slide my hand away from his mouth and into his hair instead, gripping it tight as I rock again. He groans and I tangle my tongue with his, sucking his bottom lip before diving back in again.

These pants are murdering my blood flow, but there's something to this whole anticipation thing, I guess.

I break away again, and we both suck in breaths. I fumble with the clasps on his jacket, growling when it doesn't give way.

He chuckles and rests his hands on top of mine. "I... knew something was wrong. Or-or not wrong. Never wrong. You could never be. But different. Mishka would have...well, and *never* would have, he doesn't...it-it was foolish of me, anyway, I thought it might s-save me some abuse later, so stupid, but then your Alpha power felt, *whew,* so good. And the way you, you're..." a deep red flush hits his cheeks.

I bite my lip before I bite his, tugging it hard and releasing it with a pop.

"Bloody hell," he whines, leaning up and gripping the back of my head as he kisses me even deeper. My dick nearly shatters the zipper.

Yeah. He's mine.

When we separate the next time, I rush to get all the thoughts out, 'cause there's no telling how long I'll have.

"Cyan, Alpha of the SteelTooth. Lazaros, I can't promise you a Beta seat, even though you're the best god damn Beta

168

I've ever felt, but I can promise you a pack who will fucking love you, and a spot in my bed any time you want it, right beside my Aruna. And that you'd probably get tired of being fucked long before I got tired of fucking you." I kiss him again, hard and fast, stopping just as quick. "Leave. Come find us. Come find me."

Part of me is in full on what-the-fuck mode, because this isn't like me, but the rest of me knows this is right as hell, and he can't stay here because he belongs to me.

I do my Alpha best to keep his sudden sadness at bay, but even I can't fix a broken heart. He gives me a faint smile.

"I would love that."

"...But?" I growl it. I don't mean to, I just really fucking can't stand people telling me no, especially people I want. He winces, a tremble wracking his muscles, so I Alpha wave him again, anchoring him. Mm, fuck, those eyes.

"The rest of the pack, this pack, I mean, they-they might need me. E-even if they don't, well, like me."

How the hell could anyone not like him?

"Are you mated?"

That sadness hits his eyes again as he shakes his head. "H-hardly. I haven't even, uh, well I've, you see, this is—you are—the first, no one..."

"Fuck 'em. They'll choose a new Beta, but there's only one you. And I want you."

"Mercy," he whispers, swallowing. "I-is this how you get a-all your pack mates? You must have hundreds."

I grin. "Including you and my new Aruna, just eight."

He tilts a brow at me, adorably incredulous and I can't even help myself as I nuzzle his ear. His Beta energy is so damn good and the breathy groan he lets out as he digs his fingers into my shoulders is fan-fucking-tastic.

"Trust me, I can be a bit of a dick. It ain't easy to admit I'm not emotionless, but I've been all up in my fucking feelings these past few days. I'm glad, otherwise I might have let you slip away." I bite his lobe and grip his cock at the same time. "Say yes."

He thrusts against my hand, so needy. I cannot fucking wait to tear into him.

"B-but...how would I...where...I'm shite at directions."

He's so genuinely put out about that. I laugh and bite his smooth neck, harder and harder until he gasps, arching away from the trunk and into me.

"That doesn't sound like 'no'. We'll go together, then. Right now."

I can tell he's considering it, but he frowns. "That will only work until M-Mishka swaps back. Then I'd be..."

I rock against him again. "So hurry the fuck up and say yes. We'll figure the rest out. I'll build you a cabin with my bare hands and fuck you on every surface. Say yes."

I have no idea why I need him so bad, but my beast isn't taking no for an answer, not now. Laz feels like a missing piece. Like there's some bizarre, desperate puzzle Reanne and I are stumbling around, trying to put together in the dark, and now we can.

In fact...

I hoist him over my shoulder and start walking. He lets out a series of strained laughs in his soothing tenor voice. "Okay, okay. But I can walk. P-put me down. Uh, please. Alpha?"

"What if I don't wanna?" I slap his ass, giving it a firm squeeze.

"W-well, I, then I guess, oh...fine." He gives up and goes limp, but I'm laughing too hard to hold him, so I set him down, and gather him in my arms for another kiss.

"Let's hurry."

15

REANNE

What am I supposed to do with all this information? I've stopped crying, but that sure as hell doesn't mean I've stopped being sad. I'm never going back home. I'm not even human like I was before, apparently. And if I don't pick either this guy, the real him, or some other guy, I die and murder them all.

Mishka's smile is soft and understanding, his index finger tracing small circles on my knee. "Do you have any more questions?"

As a matter of fact, I do.

"You said take power, but what power?"

The circles stop, but he doesn't retreat. "The power to command all Werewolves as their rightful queen. Surely, you've felt that already. You did so just in there, when you wiped away all my energy. And I'm no mere Alpha, my dear. You're strong, but once you reach your full potential, you'll be unstoppable."

Is...that what happened? I did feel something, but it's so weird to think of myself as anything other than completely pointless and taking up space.

"I'm not sure I'd want to be unstoppable; I just want to have a little say in my new life."

"And so, you shall, because you'll have the power to do so."

"Okay. But why? Like, for what? What's the point of any of it?"

His eyes glow a little as he continues. "You and your chosen will rule in supreme. Packs become superfluous. No more frivolous wars, or animosity, or territory disputes. Just a unified population of shifters who can finally be happy, and who will serve at your feet."

I blink at him. It sure sounds like a good idea, but if human history has proven anything, it's that nothing is that easy.

Aeon clears his throat and I jump. He'd been so quiet and still, I forgot about him.

"Even if she does that, sets all that into place, that's not going to change decades, generations of hate. What if some of us don't want to give up packs? Or if you force two rival packs together with no protections, what's to say they don't kill each other?"

Mishka's smile hasn't faltered yet, but he leans back again. "You'll want to do whatever she commands, as if it were your lifelong desire. With the proper Werewolves around her, a powerful Beta, for example, she can, quite literally, rewrite souls, Aeon. She could take the most depraved, violent individual and fix them."

"Or make them worse."

Aeon voices the one thought that popped into my head, too. I feel sick. This is way, way too much power. I don't want it. I don't think anyone should have it.

Mishka shrugs a shoulder. "She could, but I believe Reanne to be good. She'd never do something like that. Not without reason."

My stomach turns, and I launch to my feet. "I-I need some air."

I tuck the towel under my arms as I stumble through the door.

It's my first look at anything other than the inside of Cyan's cabin, but I can't even appreciate it. I grip my waist and press my back to the wood.

Neo glances up and tosses some utensil on the table before racing to my side. "What's wrong?" When I don't answer he curls his arm around my shoulders. "Come on, you need to eat."

I almost laugh. If nothing else, I can count on Neo's belief that food is some magical cure all.

But what do I know? Maybe here it is. Maybe Neo has his own powers and there's literally love in everything he cooks.

I have no idea why that thought makes tears spring back up in my eyes, but I scrub them away as he sits me on a large, smooth stump near the roaring fire.

He takes a step toward his long prep station, but I grab his hand and hold it.

I can't voice what I want, because my emotions are essentially soup, but he crouches in front of me and cups my face before giving me a sweet, lingering kiss.

"What do you think about it all?" He smiles at my confused expression, and taps his temple. "Pack link. Aeon's been filling me in. With colorful commentary. Newsflash, he doesn't like Mishka."

A chuckle finds its way out, and I feel a little lighter for a second. Only a second, though. "Are they talking now?"

Neo nods. "Aeon's getting as much info as he can. But Mishka's less talkative without you in there. I can't believe we didn't know any of this. Then again, I was never one to worry about weird history or fables. Still. I have to think if someone knew, it would have come up at some point."

It helps to know Neo wasn't hiding things from me. I lean into another kiss, because it feels good, the warmth from his mark helping to wash away the sad.

He pulls back and grins, adjusting his glasses. "Can't get over how good you taste. So, talk to me. What does the powerful Reanne, with her love of burned pig have to say?"

I chuckle again, lighter still. There's no way I'd feel like this with just any mates...right?

My smile falls, because Veikko's face forms in my mind, the rejection. He's the only one I asked, and besides Cyan, the only one I want desperately. I'm sure I'd have connected with the other two, sooner rather than later if Cyan had his way, but I feel real feelings for Vik, just like with Cyan. At least...I thought I did.

"It's scary. Weird. I don't want to be a queen or change souls or crap like that. I was just getting used to the idea of belonging to you guys, being your, you know. And now I can't go home. I can't even step across that line thing to see how life got on without me. That's awful." I snort, letting my head fall back so the tears run into my hairline. "Not that anyone's noticed I'm gone. The school will, eventually, when I don't pay my fees. But they'll just drop me at the administrative level. Send a bunch of sternly worded letters to the dorm." I groan and rub my forehead. "Neo, I know I don't have anything there to miss, but it's the principle of the thing."

"I get it, baby bird, even if I don't know all those words. Here." He tugs me to my feet and deposits me in front of a cutting board littered with vegetables. "Can you cut those?"

I nod and shrug, wiping a rogue tear with my wrist before I pick up a carrot and tap his shoulder with it. "I thought you guys didn't eat rabbit food."

His grin is so pure, my breath catches. "We don't. I'm trying an old stew recipe. Without veggies, it would just be soggy meat. Which, before you, we probably would have eaten anyway."

I snort. "That sounds so gross."

"What, never soaked a hunk of raw rabbit in a bath of water and salt for a few...you know, it does sound gross, actually."

I laugh and pelt him with a carrot piece. "See? That's what I'm saying. At least give it a name. What about The Neo Special?"

"I like that. For something else, though. Not soggy meat water. Hey, I could come up with a unique dish, just for you, how's that sound?"

"Really?"

"Yeah! That'll give me a chance to stretch the brain. See what I can make, worthy of your name."

My heart lights up, Neo's mark tingling as he leans in and steals a quick kiss before returning to his task.

We fall into a rhythm, chopping and sorting, but it's short lived, because he makes short work of it. Perk of doing it for so long, I guess. Whereas my skills are a bit rustier, consisting mostly of scalding pre-packaged noodles in my rusted saucepan.

I'm left with nothing to do again. This lack of electronics or books is going to murder me slowly by boredom.

I amble back to my stump and watch Neo assemble everything.

A burst of adrenaline shoots through me, stealing my breath as I spin toward the cabin. Excitement warms my stomach as the tug I recognize forms again, stronger than before.

Cyan's back.

16

VEIKKO

The sheer gravity of what I've done doesn't hit me until I'm over five hundred miles away. I rejected the Aruna Rigdis. I rejected the pack's chosen mate. For all my thoughts of killing her, I never once wanted her to suffer like that. It would have been mercifully quick, had I the guts. And because of what she is, I can never go back. They'll give me the ultimatum, mate or be cast out fully. I can't mate her. Can't give Cyan the permission he thinks he needs to seal everyone's fates. And I shouldn't be pack-less. I'll have no protection from BriarMaw and...Fen...if that happens. A sick shudder winds through my bones.

I should have handled the situation better, I know. But my thoughts are so dark, so private, no one else but me has the right to see them. She didn't know it was wrong, I understand that. Everything is new to her, who's to say that's not how it works for everyone? Except—it isn't. It never has been. It's something special to her. Because she's special. And I'm just a broken failure who doesn't deserve to feel the way I do about her.

There's eerily familiar laughter on the frigid wind,

dancing along the snowflakes in the distance. I stop running and duck behind a copse of trees.

I don't understand what I'm seeing, not fully. I'm far beyond our lands and any lands he could know about, and yet, here's Cyan, in clothing, stomping through the woods with a terribly short Werewolf from another pack… laughing. Touching him, quite possessively, but with care, too.

That sharp pain hits my chest again. I could have had that, with Reanne. She asked for as much. Maybe dying with her would be better than living forever alone in the wilds. I've already failed to kill her. What's one more abysmal tally mark in my celestial chronicle?

"I think you're gonna love it," Cyan croons. "Be able to get out of these damn clothes, for starters. I'll introduce to you everyone. Neo will cook something ridiculously complex, but so fucking good, just to impress you. I know it."

"T-that sounds lovely." His voice is so quiet, I can barely hear it over the wind. "I don't want to be any trouble, though."

Cyan leans down to his ear, smirking. "I hope you are trouble." He gives him a quick kiss and straightens, resting his forearm on the man's head like he's a fence post. "But nah, he has a food thing. Trust me, he likes it. Then there's Aeon, my Beta, Korey, Agnar, and Veikko. But most importantly is Reanne. Our Aruna."

Cyan's gaze hits the horizon, wistful and clearly infatuated.

"I love her. I think we all do, though. Bet you will, too. And after we all get more comfortable with each other, we can..." Cyan leans down to his ear again, muttering things that have the poor guy's face turning increasingly bright shades of red. He gets so flustered he trips over a root and stumbles right into Cyan, who snickers and kisses him again.

I blink and rub my eyes. I've known Cyan his entire life. He's never been this open and playful and honest with anyone, not even himself. He's practically a different person. I dig a claw into my thigh just to make sure I'm not dreaming.

As they near, the wave coming off the short werewolf nearly knocks me over, even this far away. Mother of the merciful moon...that's terribly intense Beta energy.

Cyan steals another kiss and volleys several nips on the man's skin until he gasps, flushing yet again with a shocked grin. My mouth curves on its own, my unease lessening. He could be the thing Cyan needs to tide him over until he can mate Reanne. Wait, no. That can't happen.

It's so bizarre to see Cy act this way, but I can't deny I feel a pull toward a version of him that isn't an insufferable prick. I have to look anywhere else. I glance up at one of the trees and spy the GrimBite Pack's marking. Cold dread slithers down my spine. Oh no. I hadn't realized where I was running. Or maybe I subconsciously had. The quickest way to certain death is to run headlong into the lair of your enemy, and GrimBite houses all the remaining Vigil members.

What is Cyan doing with one of them? I squint at the man, struggling to place his face, but he wasn't in The Obscurance with the other Vigils, so we never met in battle.

A skill like his, though, it could have turned the tide in

their favor. He must be a secret weapon, something they're holding on to if it comes to a stand-off again.

Which leads me back to the question, why is he with Cyan, acting like a lover?

I'm left no more time to ponder, as Cyan's gaze lands on my hiding spot. He stops short, tucking the GrimBite behind himself.

"Vik? Is that you? What the shit are you doing here? How did you find me? Get out from behind the damn bushes."

There's nothing but Alpha waves blasting toward me. I stand slowly, and the GrimBite's eyes widen little by little until they're bugged. He mouths something that looks like a prayer.

Cyan grins, but now that we're closer, I can tell there's something off about him. He's *almost* Cyan. Like someone made a copy but didn't quite get all the parts right. Most obvious thing being his missing scar.

Dread covers me in an instant. If it isn't Cyan, there's only one werewolf it could be. Mishka.

Blood of a dead moon...the Harbinger is still alive.

"This is lucky as hell. Listen, this," he tugs the short man out, "is Lazaros. He's joining our pack. I might not have a lot of time to explain, but the nuts are I need you to take him home. I'm trusting you, he's really fucking important. Protect him. Don't let anyone but our pack touch him. Got it?"

Lazaros has the most awe-struck expression as he gazes up at Cyan.

I'm not sure what to do. This isn't Cyan, not by a long shot, but...he's clearly here. Somehow. Whatever is happening, it's like he's completely forgotten what I did to

Reanne. But that doesn't mean the rest will. And she surely won't. He's also right about Lazaros. In the wrong hands, under the wrong Alpha, he could be as dangerous as Reanne. But what about in conjunction with her? There isn't a single expletive that conveys the depth of my despair as the bottom drops out of my stomach. It feels like my failures compound by the second.

All I had to do was kill her. Now, the weapon will have a weapon of her own. Is it too late to run? Beg the GrimBite to tear me limb from limb before I witness the end of everything?

"Vik, this is a command. I ain't fucking asking." His eyes flash, the push nearly crushing, and that's that. My fate is decided. He placed no time limit on his order. And the command energy was the same as all his others, so...this must be Cyan after all...somehow. He's still my Alpha, and I have to obey. I'm the short werewolf's protector until I'm released.

Damn the moon.

I nod.

He glances around, stares at his hands, cracks his neck, and continues. "Good. Okay, a bit more time, I guess. Me and his Alpha swapped brains or something, and I dunno when it'll go back."

My heart stops. Mishka is with Reanne in Cyan's body? I shouldn't have left. Failure after failure.

"But when it does, I'll be waiting for you guys, so don't take your sweet ass time bringing me his sweet ass." He grabs the ass in question and Lazaros blushes furiously again, a quieter beta wave forming.

Nothing to do now but follow the command. All I can

hope for is that I prevent a greater catastrophe than the ones I've allowed to happen.

I firm my expression again and gesture back the way I came. We walk together, Lazaros between us, but I'm lost in my own mind. My own guilt. I should have realized when Reanne appeared that Mishka would make a move. So much has happened to me since we met last, that I allowed the memories to fade. I grew complacent in my torment, and then in my solitude with SteelTooth.

"Vik may not talk, but I know he's got my back, which means he'll have yours."

His words are a knife in an already flayed heart. Up until they found Reanne, that might have been true. But maybe I can do something to redeem myself. Or condemn myself further, depending on how the bones fall.

I hold up a finger and scan the underbrush until I spot the herbs I need.

It only takes a minute, but I fashion two wards for his wrists. Since I know I'm intimidating to people twice his size, I approach slowly and crouch in front of him, gesturing to his arms.

He glances at Cyan, who shrugs, before allowing me to apply them. Lazaros trembles, but still meets the gaze I dare to cut his way as the last coil winds into place.

There's an immediate dampening of his energy. Such a drop-off in fact, Cyan and I both stagger. There's a faint ache in the back of my skull, but Cyan winces, holding his temples.

I hope he doesn't scare this poor man to death with an outburst or something equally damaging. I can tell Lazaros has been through something dark, and while it likely isn't the same as my situation, it still left a permanent mark.

It's a rare thing indeed to find a soul so kindred in its devastation.

"What...the fuck..." Cy shakes his head and blinks like he's waking up from a dream. He glances at Lazaros then at me. There's the recognition I expected. The rage. It's almost comforting to be proven right.

"You hurt—"

His shift comes on suddenly in sporadic waves, one body part after the other, from Wereform back again to man.

"T-that's what he did. Um, my Alpha. I saw him. Before he-he, uh, well, became him?"

That means the other one is on the way back. I can't begin to understand that magic, but I understand the danger.

If my life is forfeit either way, if I've done everything in my power to fail like that was my goal all along, then there really is no reason to keep up my silence. I have a command now, to protect Lazaros, return him home, and I can't do that with wild gestures alone.

I face him and point to the woods, nearly afraid to test my voice, but the time has come. "Hide. Now. Keep the wards in place. Stay quiet. Wait for me to collect you."

To his credit, he doesn't delay at all, dashing off into the tree-line faster than I expected he could move. Soon, I can't hear his footfalls over Cyan's mixed growls and groans.

Then the forest drips with silence. The body in front of me straightens, adjusts his coat, and spins a slow circle until he faces me.

Shock twists his features, followed by an unsettling smile. "Sentinel. How delightfully unexpected. What brings you to me, after all these centuries? Have you finally come to die like your brothers?"

His posture and speech are darkly familiar now, fueling my dread. My mind wants nothing more than to assume this is another waking dream.

"Tell me, Spectre, do their ghosts haunt you yet? All the innocents murdered at your hand?"

My focus narrows to a pinpoint. I haven't worn that name in so long, I'd forgotten it. It cannot be denied now. I'm not asleep, no, but this is truly a nightmare.

17

REANNE

I race to the cabin and throw open the door, expecting him to still be sitting in that chair, where I'd last seen his body. Only he's standing right here, glowing hooded eyes cutting into me like erotic knives.

I'm on fire again, just this fast. The marrow-deep need I'd been feeling since I got here bursts back to life, and that's when I realize, it isn't the weird air, or magic, it isn't that this new, changed version of me has to have orgasms or I'll die—it's him.

It hadn't felt anything close to this level when Mishka was in his body. I'd been so caught up in the strangeness of the whole thing I didn't notice how calm my insides were.

But now they're a hurricane.

"Cyan," I whimper, throwing my arms around his neck, my towel now a long-forgotten puddle at my feet.

"Fuck, I missed you." He kisses me with as much passion as I feel, clutching the back of my head with one hand, the other gripping my hip. He breaks the kiss with a vicious growl and turns, pushing me against the door with his body as he runs his nose down my neck. "Wasn't even gone that long, but I forgot how this feels. You're so god damn—I

186

need—" He cuts himself off by melding his mouth to mine again, robbing me of my oxygen and my last thread of sanity.

We grab for each other at the same time, his fingers diving deep, thumb on my clit, my hand curling around his length. It's fast and frantic and violent for both of us. My moans and whines fill his lungs, his shouts and groans fill mine, until there's nothing left but heated panting, several wet spots from both of us, and an only slightly dulled ache.

He presses his mouth to my cheek, still just as hard in my hand. "I can't fucking wait to pound you until we pass out. These shits need to mate you tonight, 'cause I'm tired of being patient. You're mine."

I nod in a daze and tug his mouth down again for more. I'll never get tired of the way he kisses, not in a billion years.

My eyes flutter open to see Aeon standing in the bathroom doorway, holding some sort of flowering plant, gaze vacantly focused on the empty chair. Weird, maybe he's still feeling confused about the mind-swap. Or he's talking in the pack link. That's probably it.

Cyan pulls back and catches my face in his palms. "Found us another pack member while I was out there. Someone for me. For you. He's on his way here with—"

The word cuts off in a gargle. His eyes widen and he grips his throat, staggering back a few paces.

"Cy?!"

I watch in horror as his skin pales, all the veins in his body making themselves known in a terrifying roadmap of pain while blood trickles out of his eyes.

"Oh my God, Cyan!" I barely manage to catch him, and we crumple to the floor together. "Aeon, somebody, help!"

He doesn't move. Neo explodes through the open door and pulls Cyan from my grasp, quickly laying him on the bed.

"What happened?!"

"I don't know, I don't know, we kissed, and he was talking and then he..." I cover my sob as Cyan convulses, blood at the corners of his mouth now.

"Aeon." Neo wipes at Cyan's face, and pins him in place by his shoulders, the bed quaking. "Aeon, you can Beta wave him any second here. I can't check him out until he's calmer."

But Aeon still hasn't moved. Still clutching whatever plant that is.

Neo finally glances at him, and there's a snap in the air, the dark unknown above us finally coalescing.

"No," he whispers, before he launches across the room and slams Aeon into the wall. "No! What the hell did you do?"

I stumble over to Cyan, and stroke his face. "You'll be fine. You have to be fine."

Korey appears, haggard and worse for wear, but quickly surveys the scene and stomps over. "Go." He grabs Neo's shoulder and pushes him back toward us and grips Aeon by the top of the head.

I catch his eyes as they tilt toward Korey. Blank, distant. Tears streaking so fast they drip to the ground. "I...I couldn't stop him."

"Couldn't stop who?" Korey growls, but Aeon keeps whispering the same four words, until he lets the plant fall and drops to his knees.

Korey lets him and twists a panicked look at Neo. "Holy shit...all that while I was gone?"

Neo grunts, straddling Cyan's chest and twisting a strip of fabric between his hands. He gestures at Aeon with his chin. "Get him to do his job or I can't do mine. Quick, please." His voice trembles.

Without hesitation, Korey rears back and clocks Aeon so hard his head leaves a dent in the wood, a dull crunch hitting my ears.

I scream and run over, but Korey catches me in a bear hug, ignoring my flailed attempts to escape.

"Shh, sweetheart. It's okay. Just wait a second."

Aeon shouts in pain and clutches his broken nose, walking himself up the wall with one hand.

The next second, we all relax as Aeon sends soothing energy. Cyan's tremors stop, but that's the only change. Neo lets out a rushed breath and wedges the cloth between Cyan's teeth, slipping off his chest and wiping his forehead on his arm.

"Okay. That was intense. But, hey, good news is he's not dead. And I don't think he'll get worse. I hope. Aeon, how much did he—"

"Enough to kill three of us." His voice is nasal, clipped, heartbroken. "He could feel Cyan swapping back."

Oh my God, why would he do that? He seemed so calm and collected, so rational. And how can I trust anything he said?

"He...he saw the dose in Vik's bucket there, and grabbed it before I..."

"Veikko's? Why did he have..." I stare at Aeon's tear-raw eyes. Mishka said Veikko was something. Some sort of killer whose mission was to wipe out, "Me." He really was going to kill me. If that's true, maybe the rest is, too. Or at least enough of it I can't just discount everything.

My knees give and Korey lifts me into a fireman's hold, cuddling me close. "Somebody needs to fill me in, now."

I can only assume a conversation is happening in their link because the only noises are Neo's as he examines Cyan's face and arms for damage with gentle fingers stroking along his cheek bone, smoothing along his forehead, Aeon's sniffling, and Korey's increasingly erratic breaths.

"Damn. I don't know the guy that well, but even if he planned to, he didn't kill you. He's had a ton of chances, yeah?"

I wipe a tear off of my chin and nod. That's true.

"Maybe he was waiting for a better time," Neo rumbles, covering Cyan with a blanket.

"Nah. I think," Korey adjusts his hold on me, lifting me a little higher and tilting his chin, "he fell for you, just like I did, sweetheart. And he couldn't do it."

I've felt so many emotions in such a short time, I'm having trouble sorting them, but Korey's sparkling gaze and grin warm me to my toes. I rake my fingers through his beard in thought. "Maybe."

That version of events hurts less, for damn sure.

Korey continues after kissing the finger I poke at his lip. "But I still don't get why that Mishka guy would go after Cy. He said they were friends?"

Aeon grunts and pinches his nose. "Well, he said they'd talked for a while."

"This Alpha we don't know and have never heard of,

chatting up ours. Okay, but why? Was he keeping tabs on him or something?"

My eyes widen as pieces slide into place. The tug I felt for Mishka was close to Cyan's, familiar. What if...

"He said he was just in time, right? That I only had two mates. But he also said mating you guys, or any pack members, was pointless because I only had to mate him or the other Alpha. What if that's because he knew Cyan would wait to mate me until after you guys. And if that's the case, that would only matter if—"

"Cyan is the other High Alpha," Neo breathes, staring at me.

Korey's jaw jumps, and Aeon grunts.

I nod with a shrug, even though my heart is racing. "It makes sense, I guess. Take out the competition."

"Okay," Korey sighs. "Okay, if all that's true, the answer's clear, isn't it?"

I glance up at his downturned face. "No, not even a little."

"It is, though. All you gotta do is mate with one more of us to give you a pack claim. If Vik comes back, we'll give him his ultimatum, which if he's smart, he'll choose you. I don't think we can afford to be down a member, now, anyway. But, pick another guy to mate with, then, when you're ready to choose Cyan, you do the thing and you're Queen Reanne and that murderous fuck loses. You can command him to fall off a cliff."

He smiles, but I can't feel anything except dread. This decision is bigger than that. Bigger than me. This power—if that's even true—could be really dangerous. Mating Cy might be a terrible idea.

Ugh, the thought of not being Cyan's mate hurts. My body wants that more than almost anything else. But if we mate, what'll happen?

"I have so many questions, still. I'm pretty sure Mishka didn't give us all the info, and clearly Veikko knows a lot, too. I don't want to make a decision right away."

"There's a problem with that." Aeon checks his fingertips again for blood, makes his way to us, brushes the hair off my shoulder, and kisses his mark, sending a soft wave of warmth through me. "Cy doesn't know any of this. The second he finds out he can mate her without us, that's that. He's been trying to do it since he laid eyes on her."

I can't control the lurch in my heart. That makes what we have even more intoxicating and wonderful. He doesn't want to mate me because he thinks he gets to be king or because I'll have some mystical powers, he just wants *me*. But I still don't want to get this wrong and end up destroying everything these monsters love about their lives.

"Can we...keep it from him? For just a little while?" Guilt at even the idea of hiding anything from him gnaws at me. No one else seems comfortable with that idea, either. "I guess not. Maybe..."

"If you think asking him to wait is gonna work, you don't know him at all."

The truth is I don't want to wait either. I want Cyan, mind, body and soul, but it's not about what I want anymore. All I have now is an illusion of choice. One Alpha or the other still gives me powers and control I don't want. Another tear slides down my cheek as I tuck my head under Korey's chin.

LAZAROS

Magical bracelets. Mind-jumping Alphas. A daring escape. Potential capture. Bleeding hells, this is dangerous. Thankfully, that gargantuan male is courteous enough to be loud, otherwise I'd wither from terrified boredom whilst I wait to be reunited with Cyan.

My heart rams against my ribs, cock uncontrolled again. He likes me. More than likes. It feels better than I dreamt it might, to be desired like that. Desired at all. And I don't know what the real him looks like, but it matters not. I think I'm bloody well in love.

I never, in all my wildest imaginings, thought anyone would find me even a minuscule level of attractive. I'd certainly not heard as much, so utterly stepped on and bruised, brushed aside, used for my power. I still expect the punchline any moment. For Mishka to have the pack pounce again, mock me, beat me to within an inch of death and put me back to work.

But Cyan...the way he looked at me, it has to be real. That passion, how he ravaged and teased and claimed— hell, I'm panting here in the snow again.

Composure, Laz.

I don't know why I thought it was a good idea at the start. Confess my undying devotion to a blithering psychotic? What then? Did I hope he'd give me flowers? Outstanding line of planning, top notch. Too long without food this last time, I wager. Looped in the brain.

I would laugh but dying of embarrassment is easier.

And now I don't regret it. If Cyan's telling the truth, if this isn't some other cruel trick, a carrot of hope he'll just thrash me with, I might be on my way to an actual pack family, where I could well be valued, not live in sub-par quarters as a servant, for all purposes.

I can't be his Beta, sadly, but pet has a nice ring to it. Especially with the scenarios he promised. To go from friendless slave to cherished prize in mere minutes is hard to believe. My lip still throbs, much like another part.

For blight's sake, I need to stop immediately.

I adjust myself and inch closer to the towering white-haired giant as he's stalked by the one-time recipient of my unrequited infatuation.

Knowing another Alpha wants me so completely casts Mishka in a new light, a rather unflattering one, at that.

"I'm not here to die, Harbinger."

The brute has a deep, broken, rumbling, husky tone. Terrifying, really. Fits him to a T. He seems a mite haunted by his own thoughts.

"So, you do remember. I wondered if time had burned it all away."

Snow crunches as Mishka circles Vik like the predator he is. It brings too many nightmares to surface.

"You know, I used to be wary of you," he continues,

taunting. "The fearless assassin. I would check around corners, light all the dark places. But you're just a husk now, aren't you? What happened?"

A thread of jealousy wiggles through me at his tone. He's genuinely curious, almost marveled. But Vik only stares at him.

"No? Still not big on talking, I see. Very well. There's still the matter of why you're here."

"Took a wrong turn."

Mishka actually snorts. "No. No, this is not coincidence. No error in directional judgement. You, here, just as I return from time with your precious abductee? I have a spy, don't I? How long have you had eyes in my pack, Sentinel?"

"Delusions have always been your only friends. You are not important enough to spy on."

"Not import—are you attempting a joke? Oh, well done. Well done."

Mishka applauds, each slow, aggressive clap echoing off the trees, but Vik isn't the least bit intimidated. I'm bloody shaking, wishing Cyan were here to burn my ear with his dirty words.

"If you met Reanne, you know I failed."

"Yes, that was most interesting. She's prettier than the last one. Being a human makes a marvelous difference. You should know, I won't lose again. I'm prepared this time. And, I have no doubt she'll—" Mishka opens his mouth, but cocks his head, listening. I hold my breath and clutch my knocking knees together.

"It seems you're in luck. We'll finish this chat another time. I have work to do. Something tells me, I'll be hosting a terribly important guest soon. Then, perhaps, you and your zealous brethren will finally see how wrong you've been. Reanne is a shining beacon, a paragon of goodness. It'll be utterly marvelous having her as my Queen."

"Your queen?"

It's the first chink I've seen in the big beast's armor, and I'm covered in a head-to-toe blanket of chills. If he's afraid, I've got no shot. I might as well roll over now. Bury myself, save everyone the trouble. It's all I can do not to cry out in terror.

"That's right, you weren't there. Ever on the outskirts, the lone Sentinel. Well, I wouldn't want to ruin the surprise. I have it on good authority there are a few waiting for you. By the way, brush up on your kneeling."

Mishka chuckles and...leaves.

I nearly jump for joy. He doesn't know I'm here. I could kiss these grassy manacles. We have, or had, I suppose, a healer of sorts, but it's mostly just wound cleaning, and setting breaks and such. Nothing like this.

Vik stands alone for too many minutes, puffing small clouds, clenching and unclenching his fists.

Oh, the poor mammoth. I'd go see if he's okay, but I'm under strict orders to wait. The good news is Cyan will make it better for him. That surge earlier was the most wonderful gift. I haven't felt so protected and important in my whole life. Direct attention and care from an Alpha? Stuff of dreams, that.

Finally, Vik blows out a large cloud and turns, clomping through the underbrush toward me like a tree come to life, just learning to use its roots as feet.

Blimey, how does a man get that big? Downright monstrous. I know he's not here to hurt me, but he's still so scary, I can't make myself move. Oh, no. If he doesn't spot me, he'll walk right on top of me.

I'm so sure of it, I cover my head and tuck it against my knees, shaking.

His steps grow louder, closer until they stop. It isn't until it's quiet I realize I'm whimpering.

There's an exhale in front of me, and I lift my head to see Vik crouched with a frown in place.

"He is gone."

I nod and scramble to my feet, brushing imaginary attackers off my clothes. "T-thank you."

His soft grunt is the only reply as he stands, too, and continues his path through the woods. It's work to match his pace, but I manage it.

"Are you alright?" I ask because I'm concerned, but I whisper it because I also wish I were invisible. Drawing attention to myself is as uncomfortable as stabbing a branch in my eye.

He doesn't look at me, but shakes his head slowly, trudging ever forward.

"I can't believe you stood up to-to him like that," I maintain my hushed volume. "Or, I suppose if anyone could, it-it would be you. Or Cyan. Blimey, what that might look like."

"Cyan fights with his whole soul. Catches opponents off guard. He does not lose."

I nod, even though I can't picture it at all, that sexy, fabulous beast tearing into something or someone. Heat floods my face and I fight to keep myself in check.

Vik's somber expression cracks, a small smile forming

with such hesitation you'd think it was painful. "You really like him."

"Bloody right!" Well, that was far too loud. I clear my throat, hoping for a stray lightning bolt to strike me dead, as Vik cuts me a side-eyed glance with a raised brow.

"I...it's hard not to love the first person who actually sees you. Makes you feel special. I-I mean like. Hard not to like."

"Mmhmm." Vik chuckles.

"W-what, eh, what about you? You like him?"

Vik shakes his head slowly again. Oh good, I couldn't imagine competing with Vik for anything, let alone Cyan's attention.

"So, that wee bit about a queen—"

There's a faint blush on his cheeks and I grin. "Ah, you like her!"

He hefts a breath and pins me straight on with a glare. It's so heavy, even if only one of his eyes is whole. "The way you 'like' Cyan."

My brows lift, my lips pursing. I had an inkling he felt big emotions in that big body.

"But it is beyond complicated," he growls, swinging his gaze back forward.

"Skinning a mouse is complicated. Love, that's easy, innit? Just a feeling, and-and you either run at it or, well, from it. At least, that's what I tell myself. This is, quite literally, the first time I've felt anything like it. I'm as far from an expert as the moon is from the sun."

He tilts his face slightly back in my direction, less glare, more curious glance, though he doesn't say anything. I guess he really isn't a fan of talking. Which reminds me...

"I-I couldn't help but overhear, you know, primarily because I was trying, that you and M-Mishka know each other. Or did."

Vik makes a non-committal sound.

"Is that a yes?"

"You didn't ask a question."

"Oh."

I cross my arms tight, feeling suddenly vulnerable, weak, and stupid. An unfortunately familiar cocktail.

"The less you know, the safer you will be." He eyes me over his shoulder, like he's not sure what to make of me. "I also...endured abuse. If you wish to...talk."

I stare up at him, this massive male who could wear two of me for boots. It's hard to imagine him being anyone's victim.

"R-really? That's terrible. I'm sorry to hear that. Do you, well, rude of me to assume you'd share with the likes of me, but I would very meekly point out that you broached the subject first, and—"

"Ask."

"Right. How? Not-not the specifics, no one needs to talk about that. But you're, well, you. Me, that makes sense. I'm nothing. A speck."

He stops and takes a deep breath, keeping his eyes on the horizon. "An Alpha. Commanded me to be Fen's..."

The fist sized lump in his enormous throat bobs.

Poor thing. Good to hear it wasn't Cyan, though. Not that I ever suspected him.

"Why didn't you leave? Surely, a command like that is, well, more than enough grounds to break pack."

He cuts his gaze to me again. "Why haven't you?"

Ah, another battle of wits in which the winner isn't me.

He refocuses on the trees ahead. "I had to stay. To watch over Cyan. I promised his...mother." The word cuts off, his heartbreak murdering me from the inside.

A whip of wind grabs a few strands of his hair as I stare. I owe this giant everything. He endured who knows how many nightmares just to guard the sleep of a boy, who grew to a man, who became an Alpha, and eventually saved me in every way possible. By direct causality, Veikko is the architect of my salvation by his own destruction. But his pain is almost suffocating.

"I-I can help, more if I touch your arm. Please don't obliterate me."

He gives a single nod, eyes wide like a spooked deer. I place my hand on his bare skin and send him as much energy as the bracelet allows.

A tremor travels across his bulk, and he exhales shakily, giving me a small smile. "Thank you."

"N-no, thank you. You couldn't have known how important Cyan would be."

Something about the look he gives me tells me he knew way more than I realize.

We continue to my new home, the off-rhythm crunching of snow under our feet the only sound for a hundred feet or so before I work up the nerve to talk.

"I...couldn't leave. Had nowhere else to go. When Mishka took me from my pack as a pup, he...he killed them all. I didn't know that at the time, you see. Too young. Only found out eight or so years on. By then I'd been pretty well cemented as an easy target, and a slave. Mostly the target bit. What's more, as I am clearly determined to make myself seem as pitiful as possible, this is the most I've talked to someone in years. I've still no idea why he wanted me, not really, other than he needed my power."

Oy, that feels much better. I take an easy breath and glance up, not sure what to expect, but it certainly isn't such compassion.

"You are far from pitiful. In fact, you are terribly important."

I can't help the derisive snort, my built-in defense for uncomfortable things. Suppose it's good to know even giants can be wrong.

He continues with a sigh.

"Those words I spoke earlier, before Mishka arrived, were the first I have said to anyone in well over one hundred years." He looks fully at me. "A vow of silence, at least one year for each of my brethren who died."

How noble and sad.

"Deepest sympathies for your losses. Mine was-was no vow. More of, you don't talk to the pile of dirt under your foot. I'm the dirt. Simply put, no one liked me."

"You are not dirt. You are powerful. Power can be hard to understand. Others often dislike things they misunderstand. They seek to destroy...it..."

He pales, cutting wide eyes to the sky like he's heard the answer to eternity's riddle, and the solution is so intense he has to stop walking just to process it.

In fact, what little color he has left drains away. I'm so afraid he'll pass out and leave a crater when he hits, I grab his arm again. Not that a twig can support a boulder, but I do send some energy his way. It's not enough, though, thanks to the bracelets.

"What is it? Wh-what's wrong?"

"I...I've been...we've all been...what if she's not..."

"Who's not what? The Queenly person?"

He whips his face around, and I shrink under his stare, withdrawing my hand as tremors rack me.

"What do you know about her? What did Mishka say?"

"N-nothing! Well, nothing to-to me directly. I-I overheard he was searching for someone, an Aruna, and he talked about her with that other pack. They wanted to make sure M-Mishka would favor them after she took-took power. But I don't really understand what that all means, remember, conversations with Laz were not on anyone's priority do list."

"What other pack?"

"I don't know, um, the guy had black hair, glowing blue eyes, big, though, nearly everyone is compared to me."

Vik narrows his eyes. "Yuli."

"Y-yes, that sounds familiar. Is that, is that bad?"

"He is the Alpha who..." Familiar pain and fear reappears in his eyes. Like I'm looking in a mirror. If that mirror was stretched and wider and far more handsome and generally not a mirror at all but instead a portrait of someone I wish I was.

"Oh. Yes, I would say that counts as bad. Like with like, I suppose." I dare to touch his arm again, going so far as to give it a pat. "Chin up my enormous, uh, well, friend. This Yuli chap can't order you to do anything. You're with Cyan." I swoon internally, but quickly clear my throat. "And-and once you get back, you can tell her how you feel and set about protecting her, right?"

"Protecting?"

I blink and shrug. "Do you want Mishka to have her?"

"No," he barks, anger sweeping his features. "Absolutely not. That cannot come to pass."

"Then the great protector should protect!" I grin, but he stares at me until it falls away, replaced with a swallow. "You know. If that's, well, something you feel you should— given the way things..."

He cuts his razor glare to the left and I exhale, gripping my chest. Too much stress for one day on my poor heart.

"Once we reach home, they will issue me a choice. I will choose exile. I cannot protect her."

"Why would you choose that?"

As soon as I ask, I wish I hadn't, because all I expect is rage at being questioned, as is my history, but his face is still stony.

"Because I cannot mate her."

"You already have a mate?"

He shakes his head.

"Oh. I see. Bit awkward, this, innit? W-well, I haven't done it myself, but I've seen it plenty of times. I can, you know, explain it to-to you. Ins and outs, as they say. And Ins. And outs."

His expression cracks, eyes crinkling at the corners. "I know how, Lazaros."

"Thank heavens, because I was not looking forward to that conversation. I-I would have, of course, but, this, whew. This is much better."

He chuckles and resumes walking finally, with me two steps behind from the start.

"I should let you just to watch you sweat about it."

"S'that right?" I laugh, and it feels good. It feels bloody

good to have a real friend and a real conversation. Albeit he's a scary giant, but still. "So, since you know how, why can't you?"

Aw, there's the sad face again.

"If I mate her, it...even if she is not as bad as I, we, thought, I still...what if my doing so changes the course of events...or somehow alters her? What if my interference ushers doom? I may be too close to it all. That had never been factored in. What if my avoidance is all there is between..."

He's rubbing his temples, muttering to himself, really, which is fine. Less intensity aimed at me.

"Ah. I understand. No, it makes sense, really it does. It's a scary thing. No better way to protect her, though. Than being mated. If Mishka wants her, she will no doubt find herself in trouble.

"I am not scared."

I'm well and goodly prepared to give him what-for with my cocked brow and squinted eye, but he doesn't look down.

"Perhaps I am a little scared. But...you might be right. It will not matter, though. I hurt her, she will not want me."

I can tell that's the end of any conversation, as he gives his skin a shake and transforms into a stunning silvery-white Werewolf. My jaw won't close. I've never seen one this color. Never even read about them. Perhaps that's why he's called Spectre. On top of that, I know we're all bipedal, but he's just so enormously tall in this form. Even more terrifying than his man form.

He rolls his shoulders, cracking his neck and swivels his head to face me.

"Channnnge."

Change, but why would—oh, I suppose we're running now. Why he's so eager to race toward such an awful, assumed fate, I'll never know. But I hurriedly shrug out of my clothes and ball them up, snagging them in my claws as I speed to catch up to my new, and only, friend.

19

KOREY

I rest my chin on the top of her head with a sigh. It's really hard not to think about how good it felt to be inside her when she's on my lap.

What more is it gonna take to show her I'm serious about mating? She's affectionate with me, she's letting me hold her, so it's not a dislike situation. Picking me makes sense, I'm right here, plus I want her. I know I'd thought about leaving, but other than that, I'm loyal.

If I was the High Alpha, she'd absolutely choose me. But, not a damn drop of alpha blood in me. No blood of any importance, actually. Part of why it's so hard to feel like I belong anywhere.

But I'm still a solid mate choice. I'd never hurt her. Eh. Again. Getting her riled up that first night as a 'fuck you' to Cyan was pretty stupid, even for me. But, I never claimed to be the smart one. I do have my moments, though.

Like this mate idea. It's brilliant, if I say so myself. She doesn't have to pick Cy or that Mishka-prick yet, just mate with me and be a bit safer. I can't figure out why they don't see it that way.

"What I don't know is why he's not dead, if he had as

much as you say." We all glance at Neo, wiping his hands on a towel. "But...I did notice your broken arm healed pretty fast earlier."

"You're right." Aeon cocks his head, eyes darting as he sniffles. "My nose is already better. Some, uh, other bits, too. You know, Cyan also healed from that attack really fast."

"Could it be her?"

Aeon shrugs. "I think so. It makes sense to me."

Reanne sits up a little. "Is that a normal thing for an Aruna to do?"

"Well. No. But, you're—"

"Not normal, so I've heard."

Aw, she sounds so sad. I hate that. Kissing her forehead, I cuddle her close again, and she melts into it. Damn I really, really want her.

"I like you just as you are, sweetheart. Mystical weirdness and all."

She laughs, but it catches at the end as she draws in on herself. After swallowing a few times, she clears her throat. "How long until Cyan gets better?"

Neo catches my gaze and crosses his arms. *I don't want to scare her, but I have no idea, guys. He really should be dead. She's the only reason he's not. I'm not above saying I'm this close to panicking.*

Well, if she's keeping him alive, maybe she'll heal him up, too. I smile, but he doesn't share my optimism.

Aeon sends another subtle wave through the room, before answering. "Hopefully not too long."

She nods and rests her head on me again. We're quiet for a few moments, watching Cyan's chest rise and fall in stutters when Agnar's energy registers on the outskirts of our land.

We glance at each other, searching the link...but no Veikko.

I frown. *Can't believe he's just gone. Who's gonna make me another rabbit skull mug for my collection?*

Aeon barks a laugh and Neo bites at his smile as he shakes his head.

What? I'm serious. Now, I'll have an uneven number.

"Please, share what's funny. I need something else to think about."

I could give her something else to think about, something to scream about, but nooo.

"Your mates are silently making fun of me."

"No," Aeon leans back with a small grin. "Not you. Just your need to have things in order."

Reanne cranes her head and glances up at me. "Order like how?"

The back of my neck burns from embarrassment, but Neo and Aeon couldn't look more pleased with themselves. Asses.

"Things...unfinished annoy me," I mumble. "I don't like odd numbers."

"You eat all of one food before moving to the next," Neo pipes in.

"Your pillows have to be facing the same way. Can't stand an open cabinet. Less than precisely eight full hours of sleep and you're a grump all day, even if you're not tired." Aeon is enjoying himself way too much.

"Okay, okay. Enough."

Reanne is grinning, though, and it almost makes it worth it.

"That's cute."

Neo chuckles. "Cute unless you untuck his blankets."

"Guys, seriously." I rub my hand down my face and Reanne giggles.

I peek at her over my fingers and wink, cupping her chin. "You can mess up my bed anytime you want, sweetheart."

Her cheeks flush as she blinks those long lashes at me.

"Just as long as you fix it after. Sharp corners." Neo ducks behind his arms, Aeon laughing. I jam my tongue in my cheek. I can play at this, too.

"We sharing secrets now?"

"No."

"Nope."

They are both quick to straighten, regaining their composure, but Reanne is fully into the game now. She sits up and twists to eye me excitedly.

"I want to know! Tell me something about them."

I was half-way kidding, but that sentence had a distinct command thread behind it, way softer than Cy's, but just as unavoidable. I guess if there was any question about her having extra power, that answers it. I cut a glance at the guys, but they don't seem to notice. Maybe because she said it directly to me? Whatever the reason, I have to answer.

"Well, Neo won't drink water from the river unless he boils it twice, even though we don't really get sick that way. And Aeon is a total slob. Has no idea where anything is in his house, ever."

"Bruh!" Aeon scoffs, even though he's smiling. "Rude."

"Do you have any idea what lives in the water?" Neo shudders.

Reanne glances around the room appraisingly. "It's pretty neat in here, basically like it's not lived in at all."

"That's 'cause Cy bed hops," Neo blurts out before shooting a quick look to Aeon, whose jaw clenches.

"Oho, really?" She's fully engaged in the convo, eyes sparkling with curiosity instead of sadness. "Whose beds?"

"Uh," Neo scratches the back of his head and leans against the foot of the bed. "Mine. Aeon's. Korey's. Agnar's."

"Cy can't stand sleeping alone, so mine and Aggy's are just for body heat." I throw up a hand. "These two are his pound pals."

Neo laughs while Aeon groans and buries his face in his palms. "That's the grossest way you could have possibly described it."

I can't help chuckling. "Really? 'Cause I feel like that's pretty tame. Unlike what you're into, Mr. Beta."

"I, uh, heard, and saw a little of that." Reanne tucks a bit of hair behind her pink tinted ear. Neo tosses her a grinning wink, but Aeon is still mortified. "Don't worry," she says. "I think it's nice. Hot, honestly, that you guys are so open with your sexuality."

Aeon's face appears little by little before he leans back. "That's one thing we've got up on humans. We like what we like, and usually no one's forced into a role they don't want. Plus, our females are scarce and die quickly, so if you aren't open to guys, you're basically alone. Not many choose that." He cuts a glance my way and I can practically feel him thinking 'Veikko.'

"Also, an Alpha won't attract pack members who won't

or can't help the pack be strong, whatever that takes. Usually. I was pretty sure Cyan wanted me as a partner before I joined. If I wasn't, uh, open to it, I could have stayed with BriarMaw. I sort of knew what I was getting into, we learn all about Alpha urges from the start, but it's still intense. I don't think I could have ever prepared." A faint smile hits his mouth.

"Me either. I fell into the 'was going to stay alone' category, until I found BriarMaw on my Pack Hunt. And met Cy. He's just...he had this energy about him even before he took the Alpha power from his dad. I knew I wasn't staying behind when he broke off to form his own. He wooed Aeon first, and me the next day. I think I was sore for the first two weeks after I accepted. Even though we heal." Neo chuckles, swallowing as he stares at Cyan. "Whatever he needs, however many times, it's worth it. There's nothing like feeling his gratitude, that peace he gets because the pain stops for just the smallest bit of time."

Aeon nods, passing odd glances between Neo and Cyan.

"Are you saying...having sex with the Alpha is...part of that?"

"Oh, yeah, sweetheart." I kiss her shoulder as she stares at Cyan. "Big time. Being Alpha comes with perks, but way more negatives than you'd think."

"Really?"

"Yeah. Sex isn't an optional thing for them. I couldn't imagine having to do it multiple times a day, no matter what. And we're a small pack, he doesn't like wearing these two out so much, so he does the bare minimum, just dealing with the pain. The longer an Alpha goes, the uglier it gets. It's why we search for Arunas. You're able to slow the beast's drive, leave them satisfied longer, which makes things better for everyone. Plus, if we're lucky enough to find one who can carry the Alpha's seed, it's like a vacation."

"I heard one Alpha slept for, what was it, a week straight? After his got pregnant."

I nod. "Something like that. Of course, you have to live past the final mating, that...oh."

Aeon is drawing his thumb across his neck and Neo's eyes bug before closing.

Reanne twists to face me, fear in her eyes. "Do what?"

"I wouldn't worry about that," Aeon urges. "You're not a standard Aruna, you're apparently the Queen. I have a feeling you won't have any issues. But...there's a reason there aren't any rogue, pack-less Alphas out there claiming mates. They'd just die. It's all of our jobs to make sure you stay, uh, alive. Both of you."

Reanne blinks, eyebrows up. "I need way more explanation."

Neo blows out a slow breath through pursed lips, adjusts his glasses, and crosses his arms. "When Cyan, or whichever Alpha you pick, I guess, finally claims you, he'll fuck you for days straight. Maybe longer. He won't be able to stop. So, in addition to," he clears his throat, "participating, the pack also has to make sure you don't die of dehydration or starvation while you're in the thick of it and after you're," he clears it again, cheeks flushing, "knotted."

"That's why the pack mates first, so we can use our links to urge you to drink and eat even if you don't want to, and so that the Alpha recognizes us as not a threat during."

"Good grief," Reanne whispers, gripping her throat. "He,

uh, knotted me in the woods. The...bigger part? That's what you're talking about, right?"

"Heh, what he did out there was the mild version." I adjust in the chair, willing my dick to calm down. All this talk of knotting and sex and she's right here, thigh pushing on the damn thing...

"It'll be bigger." Neo's tone is thoughtful.

My teeth grind. I can smell her excitement but can also feel her unease and general sadness. I know it's not the time. I know it's not. Maybe I should go take a walk.

I'm about to suggest that when Agnar bursts through the door, holding a disgustingly familiar man by the scruff of his neck. He's wearing a pair of black sweats and that's it.

"Look who I found playing grasshopper with our perimeter."

Neo stands at the foot of the bed, quickly joined by Aeon, protecting Cy. I would but holding her is way more important.

"You must be Reanne," Fen smirks, shouldering out of Agnar's grip and giving her a head-bow. "Pleased to meet you. I'm Fen."

"How do you know her name?" Aggy growls.

"Same way I ever know anything, brother." He taps his ear and shrugs.

"You're brothers?" Reanne shouldn't be gracing this bastard with her voice, but I'm not her mate so I can't say anything about it. I can understand the confusion. They don't look anything alike. Fen is like a dark smear of negative energy, and Agnar is a bright eyed, fair haired, pleasant guy. Literally night and day.

"Guilty as charged." Fen smiles as he scans the room. "Someone important is missing. And...why the long faces?"

"Cyan was poisoned," Reanne answers so un-helpfully. Before we can stop her, she adds, "Do you know anyone who can help?"

"*Shit,*" I mutter under my breath. Neo and Aeon cut their concern at me before glaring at Fen again.

She glances at me, brows drawn tight, but Fen's excited titter draws her attention.

"Your power is so interesting," he whispers, hands clasped at his chin, nearly crazed. "I'm not remotely connected to you, but even I feel it. Just there. Fringe feathers on a newly hatched bird."

I hate this guy. Pretty sure the feeling is the same for all of us, including Aggy.

"Yes, future Queen, I happen to know two people who can heal your Alpha."

"Really? That's great!" I clutch Reanne's arm, but she's ignoring me. "Who are they? Do we know them?"

Aggy sighs, crossing his arms. "I'd ask how you found out about her, but there's no point, is there?"

Fen shakes his head and approaches Reanne with a deference-heavy sidestep. "I'm only too happy to answer your questions, but I'm afraid they come with a price."

I wish she could talk in link, that would make this way easier. As it is, the only thing I can do is cover her mouth.

"Sweetheart, whatever help this guy would give isn't worth owing him anything. We'll figure it out without him."

She yanks my hand down. "But what if we can't? And if it takes too long to get him back later, after we've given up? I'm not ready to choose, but I also don't want the choice taken from me. Cyan's life is worth everything." Tears flood her eyes but she grunts them away.

Fen is unfazed, as usual, still smirking. "I will make it easier, future Queen. One small price for any and all information I have about who and how. Sound fair?"

"Yes." She blurts it out before I can cover her mouth again.

His smile widens and a chill hits my spine. "Decisive. I like her. I will even give you the answers first, to prove my good will."

Reanne gives me a smile that says, look I made the right choice, but I have a bad, bad feeling.

"Veikko can easily heal whatever ails your Alpha."

Chalk that up to yet another thing I didn't know about the guy. Too bad he's not here.

Her smile falls, but she keeps a brave face. "Who...is the other one?"

Fen is calculating something. I can practically see wheels spinning in his brain as he steps closer. "Me."

20

Reanne

I'm not sure why the guys are being so weird about getting help from Agnar's brother. Yes, Fen is...creepy. That's the nicest way to put it. Like an emo kid from school, but one you're sure has a few bodies hidden under his parent's basement.

But what choice do we have? Now that we know he can heal Cyan, I don't know why they aren't all jumping for joy.

I smile. "That's great. What do you need to get started?"

His expression doesn't change, yet somehow, he seems a little scarier. "As agreed, in exchange for a price, I gave you all the information I had. If you would like me to heal him, that, I'm afraid will carry another price."

Ugh, why is everything so convoluted?

"Fine! Just please fix him."

"Are you serious?" Korey stands, expelling me from his lap so quick I hit the floor on my hip. "Shit. Sorry." He grabs my elbow and lifts me, continuing. "Sweetheart, I get you want him healed, but now you're in for two with this guy and we don't know what he wants. What if he asks for our land? Cy will lose his mind."

"But he'll be alive to do it!" I fume, snatching myself free and crossing my arms. "Your plan to wait and see is too dangerous."

"Owing him is dangerous!" Korey barks. "Guys. Back me up here!"

Agnar is silent, but Aeon frowns. "Sorry, ReeRee. I'm with Korey."

"Thank you!" He throws up a hand.

Fen side steps closer to the bed. "The future queen has already agreed. Don't worry, I don't want your land."

He takes one more step, closer to me this time, and that's when I feel it. Maybe it's the same energy the guys are picking up on, or maybe it's something different, something only I can sense. But Fen didn't come here to play savior.

"Wait. When I say heal, I mean get the poison or whatever out of his body so that he makes a full and complete recovery as soon as possible."

He meets my gaze, but not like a normal person, there's no motion, just a point-blank, unblinking stare, dead into my eyes. "Of course. What else would I do?"

There it is again. This weird cold spot in the center of my chest.

Neo finally speaks out loud. "What were you doing near our land to begin with?"

"Excellent question," Korey spins to face Fen, bulky arms braced across his chest.

Fen breaks the stare down and straightens. "I was coming for a visit. Diplomatic, I assure you." He glances back at me, friendlier now. "Time wears on, future queen. If you'll ask your mates to allow it, I'll get started."

The pit of unease grows, almost exponentially. So much

so, I look down, half expecting something to be crawling around under my skin.

Did I mess up? No, it'll be worth it. I need Cyan to be better, we all do, and this will guarantee it.

"It's...okay, guys. Please let him fix Cy, so we can figure everything else out."

Neo and Aeon step apart, clearing the line of sight.

"Oh, dear. That looks painful." Fen stares a moment longer before slipping to the side of the bed and looming over Cy's face with a small smile.

The pit grows again, wriggling, and I slap at my chest, whimpering as I look. But there's nothing. All eyes turn to me. I don't want them assuming I've lost my mind, so I say the first thing I think of.

"S-sorry. I thought there was a bug on me."

Fen grins. "Small and shy, a weaver, I, build my house with silken thread, and drain my visitors until they're dead."

"What in the hell," Korey mutters under his breath.

Spider. The answer is spider. It's a twisted version of a riddle I've heard before, and it doesn't make this feeling go away at all. Fen refocuses, picking up one of Cyan's arms and watching as it falls, limp.

Instinctively, I step against Korey, needing his warmth, his protective arms, and he doesn't disappoint, wrapping me up tight, no questions asked. But the pit wriggles on.

Fen takes that same arm and tugs it over the side of the bed. He transforms his thumbnail into a claw and rakes it along Cy's vein, opening it up.

"No! What are you doing? I said heal him, not hurt...him...oh."

As I watch, a dark vapor curls up from the wound, and he takes a deep breath.

"A little bloodletting can do wonders. This will keep him from getting worse while I collect the herbs and plants I need."

"I'll take you to Vik's garden." Agnar has decided to be helpful again, I guess.

At the mention of his name, Fen's eyes light up. "I'd dearly love to see him. Do you know when he'll be back?"

The pit turns into a gaping hole, taking with it my ability to breathe. I clutch my throat and gasp, nearly doubling over. Korey grips my shoulders. "Woah, what's wrong?"

Neo and Aeon both approach, each placing a hand on me.

"Breathe, baby bird. Is it the blood?"

Their marks throb, and it's like there's a battle inside me, their light fighting whatever this darkness is. How can I explain it?

"Does the future queen need my help as well?"

Korey practically vibrates with rage as he shouts, "No! No more help."

"I'm fine. Go. Herbs," I manage in barely a whisper, even though it feels like the light is losing.

Agnar takes Fen without another word, and once the door is closed behind them, I straighten with a gasp, smoothing my hands over my torso. It's gone.

Aeon cups my cheeks, chasing my gaze. "You're starting to scare me again. What was that?"

"I don't know. I don't know," I gulp air. "Check Cyan. Please. Is he better at all?"

Neo speeds to his side, while Korey makes soothing circles on my upper back, and Aeon kisses one cheek then the other.

"Huh. His color is coming back a bit. Maybe he really will heal him. I have to say, though. It was a bit reckless to agree to whatever price he set. Still, I get it. It's Cyan. Plus, I can't help thinking if it was you lying here, I'd give Fen the rest of my soul to make sure you were okay, too. So, I get it."

"Damn," Aeon whispers, glancing back at Neo. "You're right. I would, too."

"Mates," Korey grumps. "Oh. Oh, hell. Blech."

"What? What's wrong?" I lean back, eyeing his contorted expression.

"What if he asks you to be his mate? You know, as payment."

My eyes widen, slowly, and don't stop until it's physically impossible to get any wider. Nausea takes hold of my stomach. There's no way I could ever have sex with him or accept a piece of his pitch black soul. There is absolutely nothing "right" about him.

"No...he wouldn't, right? Why would he want that?"

Aeon and Neo shudder with their whole bodies.

"Who wouldn't want that? Ah, hell, don't cry." Korey tugs me back into his thick arms as I sniffle. "He probably wants something stupid. Don't worry about it. I shouldn't have even said it."

"It's okay, I'm glad you did. I need to be prepared." I sniffle again. "I mean, I said Cyan's life was worth anything, and I meant it. But, can he even mate with me, since he's not in this pack?"

"I think you can have as many as you want from

wherever you want, if what Mishka says is true." Neo gives me a very small, very fake smile. "Besides, pack claim isn't set until you've mated with three. Again, though, I don't think most rules apply anymore when it comes to you."

I step out of Korey's embrace and cross to Neo, who straightens with a sniff, adjusting his glasses. "What's wrong," I say, rubbing his arm.

"Tired. Hungry. Fairly certain I burned another dish, and I should care, but I don't. I'm worried. About Cy, about you, about us, the pack, werewolf kind in general." He takes a deep breath and pulls me into a hug, his mark twanging on my heart. "And I have no right to feel overwhelmed because just look at all you're having to deal with. You didn't ask for any of this, but you're taking it way better than I would. Than I am. Plus, I'm perfectly healthy, while Cy is lying here, nearly..." He cuts himself off, tucking my head under his chin.

"Neo, you have a right to your feelings. They're yours. You've known Cyan way longer than I have, and he's your Alpha. More than that. I can't even imagine how scared you all are right now. You having emotions doesn't cancel out my emotions or anyone else's. You're right. I didn't ask for this. And frankly, I don't want it. The power, I mean. But I'm glad you guys took me, because I finally started to feel like I had a home, like I belonged."

"And now what's going to happen?" Aeon's somber tone cuts through the room.

"Right," Neo sighs. "If you don't...choose Cyan, will you leave? Will we have to come with you since we're mates? I can't imagine being apart from you for a long time, so that's a yes."

"Agreed," Aeon says.

"Which means leaving the best home I've ever had. Leaving my best friends, if you don't mate us all. And let's say you did, mated all of us, but still didn't choose him. He'd be alone." Neo's silent tears drip onto me, while mine stream down, soaking his bare chest. "Who'd keep him warm at night?" He whispers, ragged and heart broken.

His pain radiates through my mark, through my heart. He loves Cyan, but he loves me, too. I can feel it. I wish it were as easy as mating Cy and hoping for the best, but I can't help thinking there's so much more to this, so much I need to learn, because it's too important to get wrong. And there's apparently a whole collection of people dedicated to killing me and others like me because they're so afraid I'll do just that. I have to get it right.

After another few seconds, he clears his throat. "I'm not trying to sway you one way or the other. I know you're not ready. Just answering your question."

"Thank you for being honest with me." I kiss his chest before pressing my cheek back against it. "And for being understanding."

He presses his mouth to the crown of my head, murmuring, "I'll always be those two things with you, baby bird, at the bare minimum."

Aeon's breath hitches, and Neo's chest stills.

"Wow. Guy's got balls the size of boulders, I'll give him that." Korey shakes his head, smile forming.

"Huh?" I twist to eye him.

"Veikko's back."

My stomach flips over my heart, as nervous energy zips through me. Neo pushes me out of his arms, scanning me with amusement. "You really do like him. Even though he was probably going to kill you?"

"But he didn't," Korey chirps. "That's really important, guys. I'm telling you. He may be a loner, but he's been loyal for a long time, and that has to count."

"I guess." Aeon scrubs his face.

"I think Korey's right. Plans change, right Aeon?" I give him a wink and he smiles back, softly.

"Sure do, ReeRee."

"Will you guys stay here and watch Cyan? I want...I want to go talk to Veikko alone."

They all exchange glances, probably internal conversation, too. That's super frustrating, like a boys only club.

Finally, Neo nods. "But if you're gone too long, Korey'll come looking. Just to be safe."

"Okay, that's fair. Thanks."

I pull Neo into a kiss which turns more heated than I expect. I'm a little glaze-eyed when I pull back, and he's entirely too smug as he wipes his thumb across my lip. But I'm happy to see something other than heartache on his face.

"See you soon, baby bird."

I nod dumbly and stagger back, only to be spun around and dipped, by an equally hungry Aeon.

My shocked gasp is muffled by his searing mouth as I cling to his neck. I know my body wants to respond, but I'm still too worried about Cy and conflicted about Veikko to be fully in any moment.

Doesn't change that I love how they both kiss or how their marks hum to life when we touch.

223

He rights me and, after a quick series of pecks, steps back, leaving me swaying.

"You guys just can't stop showing off," Korey grumbles, crossing his arms.

I spin like I'm tipsy, because that's sort of how it feels, and step up to him.

Instead of saying anything, I grab his beard and tug gently.

With a soft grunt, he lets me pull his head down toward mine, and I hesitate, our breaths mingling before I kiss him.

I know we've been intimate, but this feels weirdly more vulnerable.

He grips my waist tightly, deepening the kiss with a consuming urgency. I can't help grinning, because I've never kissed anyone with a beard before. It tickles here, too. Apparently three hot men kissing me in a row is enough excitement to drown out any trepidation I had, because I'm throwing my arms around his neck, grinding against his thick cock before I realize it.

The only reason it doesn't go further is Korey himself. He breaks the kiss with a low rumble and pushes me back.

"I want to. Fuck, I want to. But this isn't the best time or place. Go talk to Vik, sweetheart. I'm not going anywhere."

Now I'm horny, damn it. My skin tingles, need rising. But he's right. I know he is. I force myself to think of the way Cy looked as the poison took hold, of how scared Veikko was when he ran, and once I'm back under control, I nod and head out.

I'm not sure what I'll say to him, what he'll say to me, but I know I absolutely need to see him again, at the very least.

21

VEIKKO

L azaros is...interesting. Pleasant enough. I don't know what the future holds, but he seems convinced we're friends, and perhaps we are.

His wereform is faster than I expected, which is good. We made it here in only slightly longer than it took me to retreat in the first place.

Stepping across our territory line lifts a weight off my shoulders I can't deny. It's home. My safety, for the most part.

Though, I am not the same anymore.

I'm no longer a Sentinel, not since betraying the code. And given that the code could have been wrong since its inception, I don't feel quite as bad about that. I am, however, on my own.

Or perhaps...perhaps, since I'm a member of the SteelTooth pack, Cyan's pack, I should finally join them, in all things, and together we can find a solution. It's been a long time since I've been fully invested in a pack, it's a nerve-wracking thought.

The Vigils will back Mishka, which is an atrocious idea.

The Harbinger has always been power hungry, since the beginning, and he will not change now.

Laz is correct. I must keep her from him.

Cyan is the only choice. The rightful High Alpha. And perhaps with the right werewolves around her, the right mate, she won't spell doom for us all.

We shift back to our man forms, and Laz quickly redresses, mumbling about impropriety.

I can't help but smirk. If general nudity bothers him, he will be supremely uncomfortable here.

I tug my shorts back on for his sake and lead the way through familiar trees until we reach the clearing.

My feet stop working. I stare at the approaching figure, not sure what do to. I'm not quite ready.

"Bleeding hells, why is she naked?"

Laz jerks his coat off, leaving him in his jeans and plain white t-shirt, and trots to meet her. I'm still too worried to move. Worried she's angry. Worried she hates me. Worried this violent spark inside means I love her far more than I should, and knowing what she is, I worry how wrong that is.

"Hello madam, I don't know what happened to your clothes, but here, take this. Not-not that you're not attractive, don't read me wrong, you just can't be comfortable, right? I suppose, if you don't wan—"

"Thank you, that's sweet." She smiles and tugs it on, zipping it halfway. It hits just at her hips. "They aren't into clothes here for some reason."

I clench my jaw, forcing my mind to blank. Somehow, that vertical strip of visible skin on her chest is more erotic than when she stood here in nothing.

"Happy to help. If I might ask...oh, yes, of course. I'll just, I'll wait right here."

"Sorry, I...need a minute."

She leaves him scratching the back of his head and glancing around as she steps up to me. Her deep eyes seek mine, and I can't look away. We stare at each other, until tears stream down her cheeks, surprising me.

But the real shock is when she launches up and throws her arms around my neck. I don't want to, I don't deserve it, but I greedily crush her in an embrace, burying my face in her curtain of hair.

"You came back," she whispers, clutching me tight.

I nod, breathing in her scent like it'll be another figment of fantasy gone in a blink. It would mean more if I'd returned on my own, but I've never been more grateful for an Alpha command in my life.

"I'm so sorry, Veikko. Whatever I did, I—"

"No," I rumble. "I am...sorry."

She jerks her head back, wide eyed as she clutches my face. "You-you broke your vow?"

I shrug a shoulder. "I had no choice."

"Christ, even your voice is dripping with sex," she all but gasps. "Can we please kiss and make up?"

I chuckle despite myself, but shake my head.

"Oh. I understand, it's okay. I can wait." She forces a smile, but I set her down and drop to a knee, taking her hand.

"I am so sorry I rejected you." Not really sure what else to say, I rub my thumbs across her skin, staring at her until her eyes brim.

"Please don't leave me again." Her lip trembles. "I know

227

you thought about killing me, and I was upset, because who wouldn't be, but then I realized there's so much I don't know, and Korey pointed out that, clearly, you didn't kill me, which has to count for something big, if your whole goal was that. Sorry, rambling. My point is, I'm not mad at you. I missed you. It didn't feel right without you. I won't ask you to mate me, or force you to be my friend, or anything like that, just, please, please stay."

Her sadness is my fault. I hurt her, and instead of hurting me back with knives or claws as is her right, she's maiming me with love and forgiveness.

I don't deserve her. None of us do. She's simply too wonderful. Maybe she is strong enough to fight the darkness. But even so, even if she could do it all on her own, she doesn't have to. I don't want her to.

"I promise I will never leave you, Reanne. I do want to be your friend." I wipe her tears away and cup her cheek. "Your protector. Your champion. And perhaps someday...your mate."

"Really?" She grins under her tears, and I feel it in my soul.

I nod, finally pulling her into a deep kiss. She tastes as perfect as before, her searching tongue setting me on fire. The fear I'd felt before is just a blip in my pulse, because I know now what must be done. I can only hope the choice is the right one.

LAZAROS

I've got nothing to do but stand here and wait, while Vik makes out with his pretty brunette.

This is such a small village. No—quaint, yes, very quaint. I could guess which house is Cyan's, but I don't want to be rude. It hurts a little that he hasn't come to greet me. Maybe he's...forgotten about me already.

No, stupid Laz. He hasn't. Stop wallowing.

I sniff and cross my arms. It's not cold here, like on our land. Well, ah, my old land, I suppose. This is my new home. I glance around again. It's very cozy, with its log cabins and big cooking fire and stumps for chairs. Homey and rustic. Very different. I think I'll be happy here. Who am I kidding? I could live in the bottom of a slimy barrel if Cyan's there with me.

A door opens on the nearest cabin and my breath catches. A huge, bearded man with a dark smattering of chest and stomach hair trudges out, head down, hands jammed in his loose shorts pockets. He's not as big as the white-haired mammoth, but wider than Mishka by half a person, and at least a foot taller. Is this...Cyan?

I send out a small testing beta wave, but there's no answering Alpha energy. The man doesn't even seem to notice it. No, then. Not Cyan.

Mercy, whoever this is, he's...so...gorgeous. My heart trips, and I can't stop my addled brain from picturing myself playing with all of his hair or having those thick arms around me.

I—I'm going to die here. Death by excitement, by pleasure, by pining alone, likely. Oy, I'm ready. Take me now.

He looks up as he nears and stops cold, gaze traveling my body. I've bloody well forgotten how to draw a breath.

"Helllllooo. Who are you?"

Chills cover me from head to toe. I expected a deeply male voice, but it's more than that. It's rich and warm, like a hug from someone who loves you. What I imagine that would feel like, at any rate.

He glances at Vik and Reanne, watches them for a second, and slides his gaze back my way as he steps closer, sniffing the air.

"Well, whoever you are," his smile widens, "you smell fantastic. And you're clearly not a threat, or they wouldn't be sucking face."

I chuckle, nerves eating me alive. "H-hardly. I'm essentially the-the least threatening—I'm the danger equivalent of light snowfall."

He laughs, a sumptuous sound that washes right over me, and that's it. This is my final resting place. A patch of dead grass housing one stick of questionable origin and eleven leaves. Here lies Lazaros, he died a virgin, and he's eternally sorry for ruining the aesthetic with his grave.

The likely sex-god stops right in front of me, sizing me up with his heated gaze and telling grin. I want to mash my face right against his skin and breathe him in.

"Damn, you're adorable. I've never really had a thing for other guys, but I am seriously rethinking my entire life right now."

To go from not feeling anything like this ever, to twice for two different men in the same pack in a single day seems like another trick. Maybe none of this is real and I'm unconscious at home. Oh. Oh, why did I have to think that?

All the delicious feelings fade, and I draw in on myself in preservation mode.

His brows pitch up, concern forming in an instant as he crouches in front of me. It's a heady, heady sensation.

"Aw, hey, what's wrong? I didn't mean to upset you, if I did." He strokes the backs of his thick fingers down my cheek, over and over, like he's soothing a skittish creature.

I suppose he is, isn't he?

"It-it's not you," I manage on a whisper. "I'm just, in general, a coward."

He clucks his tongue and lets those fingers continue down my neck on the next stroke, his index finger dipping just under the collar of my shirt, sending bolts of lightning through me. He withdraws and lightly taps my nose a few times before returning to my cheek.

The sweet gesture freezes me in place again. Well, most of me, but I don't dare adjust myself. I don't dare move. Yet all his attention works. My fear mostly vanishes, replaced by heat, heat, and more heat.

His smile comes back, and I could live there, look at it all day. "There we go, that's better." His voice is softer now, teasingly erotic. "Now, if you don't tell me your name, I'll have to come up with something to call you."

I don't know what I'm responding to most. His absolutely mouth-watering look? The bone-melting timbre of his voice? The strong, mind-hazing scent of a salty sea scape? His gentle touch, both calming and setting my blood on fire? Who knows. I'm useless right now. I can't make my brain work. I don't want to.

"Alright," he chuckles, stroking the other cheek now. "How about...pup?"

It hits me in a weirdly vulnerable spot. I scowl, which I'm sure looks nowhere near as intimidating as I hope.

"I-I'm an adult, I'll have you know. Just, eh, well. Small." I manage to sound both indignant and microscopic. Quite a skill I'll have to be proud of later.

"Oh, I know, little pup. Trust me, I can tell." He gestures down with a head tilt and winks, killing me a third time. "And you're not small, you're perfect."

Ah, I can't breathe again. This can't be real. My mind rudely supplies a fantasy scenario wherein Cyan is his gloriously intense self and this man coddles me until I explode with happiness.

"But you also like that nickname, don't you?"

Criminy on a cracker, I do. I still can't make myself answer, but obviously something screams it from the rooftops.

"Yeah, you do." He grins wider and stands. "I'm not sure why you're here, but I'm sure glad we met. My name is Korey."

"Lazaros." It stumbles out of my mouth like I've just learnt it.

His brows lift as he mouths it silently, flicking his tongue. I'm fairly certain that squeaking sound is me, but it stops before I can be sure.

"That's a sexy name, little pup. So, now that we're not strangers, you can tell me what you're doing here."

"Uh, w-well, I was invited, by-by Cyan. While he was, you know, the-the thing, with the mind swap. He had Vik bring me here to, erm, join your pack."

Korey's eyes light up and he strokes the top of my head with a grin. I lean into it like the touch-starved mongrel I am.

"You mean I get to see you every day, from now on?"

"If-if that's what you, er, want. Then, I guess so, yes."

"Oh, that's definitely what I want. But what do you want?" His gaze is so earnest.

Is it too soon to say 'you and I in many compromising positions, spanning several days'? It's too soon. Yeah.

"Nothing." I clear my throat. "Well, to see Cyan, actually. Would be nice. And to get the joining, you know, started."

Korey frowns, and I fight a flinch with all my might.

"I can take you to him, but he's not awake. The Mishka guy poisoned his body, while he was off inviting adorable men to join us."

He winks at me again, but I feel sick and wracked with guilt. Did he find out about me after all? Er...no that timeline doesn't add up. So, not my fault, potentially. Still, I thought I knew Mishka. Poison seems so...Well, I should say, I thought I knew his methods, more than the man, and I suppose were he desperate enough, anything is possible. If it's true, he's worse than I ever realized.

233

"Don't worry, little pup." He strokes my cheek again and dash it all, my lids grow heavy. I swear I'm being brainwashed this very moment and I couldn't care less because I might well do anything to keep this level of care and attention, keep his kind eyes on me.

"Someone's here fixing him up, even though Vik could take over now, probably. We didn't know when, or if, he was coming back."

That does make me feel better, so I smile, and it's apparently everything Korey's been waiting for. He grins from ear to ear, which embarrasses me, ergo I smile harder against my will, and glance away.

His chuckle draws my gaze, but instead of his eyes, all I can focus on in the sizable, growing bulge in his shorts. It does absolutely nothing for the state of my own arousal. Bother.

He shrugs a shoulder. "What can I say, I like you."

You can say that. Say that over and over. I'm perfectly fine with that.

"Come on, I'll take you to see Cy."

"We'll come with you."

Reanne has Vik by the hand, passing very sweet coy glances at him as they approach. I quirk a brow at my smiling gigantic friend who rolls his eyes, but twines their fingers together.

It's not nearly as big a difference as everyone else, but unsurprisingly, she's taller than me, too.

"Thanks again for the coat. Sorry for before, we had stuff to work out. Do you want it back?"

"N-no, that's quite okay. Keep it as-as long as you need.

I'm Lazaros." I thrust out my hand. Doing so jostles the grassy bracelet. Now that we're here, I can't see a reason I need them, so off they go before I hold my hand out again.

"Veikko told me. Cyan mentioned you were coming, too. Welcome to the pack, I guess!"

She grins and grabs my hand. There's an immediate, sharp energy transference, like a severe static shock, traveling from her, to me, and back to her again.

Both our smiles drop, replaced with confusion as the shock grows, warmer and warmer, spreading farther up each arm. I know this, because what she feels, I'm feeling, too. I can only assume it's the same for her, with the glances she keeps flicking to my arm.

It's...not unpleasant. Just unexpected. She nods, like she heard, or thought that, too.

Korey takes a deep breath and stares at me. "Wow. Are you a Born Beta?"

I blink several times and break my connection with Reanne as I focus on Korey. "A-a what? I mean, yes, I am a Beta, but as-as to my origin, you see I was—"

"You are." His reverence only grows as he faces me dead on. "You are, you're a Born Beta. Holy shit. You're so rare!"

Fabulous. Another reason to be singled out.

"What's that? How can you tell?"

I nod at Reanne, grateful she voices the questions for me.

"Well, it's obvious, but only if you know, I guess. So, Betas are Betas because there's an Alpha. It's a, well it's hard to explain. The ice to the fire, moon to the sun, sort of balance you have to have to run a pack. Any non-Alpha werewolf can become a Beta, if there isn't one in the pack already, but it takes Alpha energy to make Beta energy. If they break pack, they lose the ability to do it at all, since their next pack, they might not even be in the hierarchy. He's nowhere near his Alpha. And he's not bonded with Cy yet, which means—"

"He should not be able to form Beta energy at all. Let alone so much. I should have realized that," Vik rumbles.

I pat his arm. "To be fair, even I didn't know and-and it's me we're talking about. You were, ah, a bit preoccupied."

Korey's jaw drops.

"What the absolute—you can talk? Are you serious? I thought your throat was damaged or something!" Korey slaps Vik on the shoulder with a wide grin. "Wait until the others hear this!"

"Hear what?" A smooth voice calls from the shadows. "I do so love a secret."

Confusion mixed with dread dumps over me like a bucket as the man steps into the light carrying an armload of plants. What is he doing here? He was with that other Alpha, oh what did Vik say...Yulish? Yulon? Regardless, he doesn't belong here.

Reanne's confusion is coupled with a wince as she rubs the center of her chest.

But Vik is barely breathing, eyes wide with genuine terror.

"It doesn't concern you, Fen." Korey growls.

Fen. Fen! Oh no.

I curl up my fists and step in front of Vik without another thought.

"Y-you, you stay back! Get away from him!"

Fen smiles, utterly unfazed.

"Ah, that won't be possible." He eyes Reanne. "You see, there's still the small matter of my price. And that price, is Veikko."

REANNE

This is all my fault. Everything is in slow motion. The cute, short guy is trying to protect an utterly checked out Veikko, Korey is gesturing wildly, shouting something I can't hear over my own heartbeat, and that blackness, the dark, cold spot in my chest is back. If Lazaros and Vik's reactions weren't clue enough that something bad went down, the way Fen is so certain I'll give him an actual person is disturbing. How can anyone want another person as payment?

Neo and Aeon race toward us, already shouting, anger pouring off of them as they loom around the monster we invited into our homes. I...invited. And Fen is simply smiling, gazing at Veikko like he's already won, like he knows he'll always win. A spider with prey trapped in his web.

Sound filters in slowly, then all at once.

"—have him. Cy would tell you to go fuck yourself, and you know it!" Aeon is in Fen's face, each word punctuated with a hard point.

"My deal was not with Cyan." Fen finally cuts his eyes to me, unnervingly calm.

Neo clutches the back of his neck, knuckles white, pacing. "She doesn't speak for the Alpha," he grits out.

"But she does have ultimate say over all our fates."

"That doesn't matter," Korey seethes. "She's not queen of anything yet, and Veikko is a member of this pack. If you want him, you'll have to fight us for him."

Fen chuckles. "No, I won't. You all fail to realize," he steps closer, and Vik closes his eyes, defeated, trembling. "That he wants to come with me. To come home. Isn't that right?"

My heart stops before it races so fast, I get dizzy. The blackness grows, spreading through my chest, down my arms until my hands burn, like I've held ice cubes for too long.

"That is-is a known tactic! He's attempting—Veikko, do not answer—"

He nods, and I break inside.

There's shouting again, and not all of it aimed at Fen. The guys are scared, confused, mad. They're a family at risk of being torn apart. I get it, completely.

But Lazaros is suddenly silent as death, staring me straight in the eyes. I...can hear him again, even though we aren't touching. I won't even begin to guess what this weird connection thing is, but right now I don't care. I sat through enough group therapy and 'motivational talks' with social workers back home to know what he's thinking is right. Fen is an abuser, the worst kind, and Veikko has serious PTSD and some sort of twisted sense of belonging. I can feel Lazaros has been through something like this, too, which makes me sad, but it's rage I feel most of all. Violent rage.

"No." I say it calmer than I expected, but I think I've crossed that line from shouting angry to scary, quiet angry.

I step between Fen and Veikko, my arm brushing against Lazaros. There's another spark, but it's not warm this time. All it does is make the darkness in me even darker.

"A deal was struck, service provided. Payment is due, future queen. You need not worry, I'll take good care of him." There's a sick glint in Fen's eyes. "Just like I always have."

More muffled shouting, more crystal-clear feelings from Lazaros. Or maybe they're my own feelings, being reflected back at me. I had always thought I was levelheaded. That what I went through made me...not stronger, but resilient. Even so, I'd assumed I would live out the rest of my life with no family, no real friends. Maybe I'd find a steady boyfriend someday, maybe a husband, but I wasn't holding my breath.

Then these guys showed me what it would feel like to belong and be loved and feel cherished, and this monster is threatening to take someone important to me. A member of the first family I've ever had. All I can think is how I want Fen dead, how he doesn't deserve to live in this world, a constant dark cloud, threatening a storm that could destroy Veikko at any moment. But it isn't until he reaches out a hand toward Veikko, around me, almost making contact that I lose all control.

"NO!"

It explodes out of me, a blindingly bright concussive wave of fear-fueled anguish.

All shouting and arguing stops. I stumble backward into Veikko with a sharp gasp, hands locked over my mouth to muffle the scream that follows.

Fen, or what's left of him, is crumpled in a charred heap on the ground, surrounded by untouched plants. Even the grass under him is fine, it's only his body that burned. I can't look away. I killed someone.

No one speaks, the shock too intense, the weight of what happened smothering me.

I killed someone. With...my mind.

Lazaros clutches my forearm, telling me with his emotions that I did the right thing, sending massive waves of calming energy but they don't touch me. Instead, they skirt me, this dark ball in my chest acting like a stick in a stream.

I'm a murderer. I don't deserve to be soothed.

Night insect songs fill the sound void as Veikko pushes between me and Laz like he doesn't know we're there, severing our connection. He stares down at Fen, fists clenched, breathing. With a single, slow, measured step, he crushes Fen's charred skull under his bare foot. The brittle bones crunch, crackle under the pressure. Without warning, he releases a massive roar, his body contorting with frightening speed until he becomes an absolutely massive, scarily beautiful nightmare creature. Even his scar is still there, somehow more noticeable, harsher. I had no idea what they looked like in their fully monster forms, and I'm almost too numb to be afraid, though I do stumble back another step.

He roars again, grabs Fen's body, and flings it into the woods. It crumbles against a tree with a dull thud, and Veikko races to meet it, grabbing it in both massive, clawed hands and ripping it straight in two.

Tears hover in my eyes from his unbridled emotion as

he takes one half and bashes it against the tree, until there's nothing left, then repeats it with the other half. With another terrifying roar, he punches a gouge out of the trunk, like he can't even stand for specs of Fen to be left.

He turns then, blood dripping from his knuckles, giant teeth on display from a snarling maw, pointed ears flicking, eyes locked on me.

It only takes three of his long running strides to put him directly in front of me. My neck pinches as I crane to keep his face in sight. He grabs my arms far too tightly, his elongated fingers letting his razor claws cut into the coat as he yanks me against his furry body. I can barely feel the pain. Whether that's Laz's doing, or I'm dead inside, I don't know. I wonder briefly if he plans to destroy me, too, until he slowly shifts back to himself around me. His face is the last thing, milliseconds before he crushes his mouth against mine.

He's untethered, no trepidation in the way he hungrily kisses, like he's a different person.

When he pulls back, there's fierce determination in his gaze. His grip tightens, and he slowly presses his forehead to mine.

Jumbled words explode in my mind as he openly gives me access to his thoughts. Grateful, love, forever, mine, gone, free, thank you, mate, forever, free, beautiful, mine. They repeat without order until he plainly asks me to be his mate. I nod, tears forming as he pulls back and kisses me again. Slowly the dark pit inside me shrinks, smaller and smaller, then the weight is gone, and all I feel is his warmth and love.

I sob, shattered, limp in his hands, before I'm crushed in a mass of hot skin and soothing words.

Neo and Aeon stroke my back, rub my neck, and kiss the parts of me they can reach, each of their marks flooding me with heat.

Everything stills, both of them staring at Veikko with shock on their faces. Slowly they smile and nod, adjusting behind me. I nearly ask what's going on, when Veikko rips the jacket open and descends on my chest, licking, biting. I gasp as Neo tugs it off my arms and tosses it somewhere behind him, kissing and tonguing my neck, the outside of my arm, and eventually the other side of the same breast Veikko is mauling, while Aeon nips at his mark on my shoulder.

"Oh, ffffuck!" I suck at the words as Veikko latches onto the side of my neck and pushes into me. Even in the throes of passion, he's careful, easing his enormous cock in little by little. It's maddening and wonderful.

Neo and Aeon share my weight, holding me, caressing me while he moves faster, faster. Someone's hand slips down my stomach, dancing on my clit, coaxing me toward my release, while Neo takes over tonguing my nipple with his sexy throaty groan. Aeon's teeth cut into his mark, and a vibrant burst of pleasure darts through me. I tangle my fingers in his hair.

I moan louder, utterly out of control, and as my orgasm crests, Veikko slices into the side of my neck. My eyes fly open, and I scream, colors shifting around us like we're inside a rainbow. He's not giving me a small part of his soul, like Neo and Aeon did. He's giving me as much as I can possibly hold. Everything that makes him who he is, everything he holds dear, every dream, every fear. I clutch at him, digging my nails into his shoulders as his teeth burrow deeper.

It's intense. There's an undercurrent of some sort of power I can't explain. I want him to stop as much as I want to completely consume him, absorb him into myself until we're one being. It's scary and amazing and like nothing I could ever imagine.

He lets out a deep, guttural moan against my skin, ramming up into me with speed before filling me with his hot seed, pump after pump, warming me from the inside out. I truly don't think I will ever get enough of how it feels when they come inside me.

I finally come down, whimpering, trembling, the colors fading as Veikko unlatches and laps the wound softly, shyly. There's so much of him inside me, physically and emotionally, it feels crowded. My heart overflows, and I grab at all three of my mates, tears streaming as I kiss them all in turn, Veikko last.

We finally break and I catch his watery gaze. "I love you."

"I love you, Reanne," he rumbles. "My mate for eternity."

There's a small sniffle behind us, and I twist a look over my shoulder. Korey is grinning behind Laz, hugging him around the neck. Laz wipes his eyes. "That was quite beautiful. And-and hot, in case you were, you know, worried. About that. Also, I forgive you, that was my favorite jacket, but under the circumstances it-it was unavoidable."

I laugh, shocked that I do, and then we all chuckle as Veikko pulls out of me. A thick stream leaks out, but I don't even care as he gathers me against his chest for another soul-searing kiss.

One of my other mates teases my opening from behind, running his fingers through Veikko's nut. Unnh, why do they have to keep being so hot all the time? I moan a little, pushing back, but he withdraws, giving my ass a quick squeeze as Vik gives me a small parting kiss.

"I'd love to watch that over and over," Korey says, "but Cy still needs your help, Vik."

He cuts a sharp look at Korey. "What's wrong?"

AEON

Vik really shocked us. Not only can he talk normally, he jumped in the link like it was nothing, asked us for help, which he's never done a single time as long as we've known him. It's nice. Feels more complete with him in there. And now we're connected by Reanne, which is even better.

I can't stop watching Korey fawn all over that short guy. I only thought Neo was soft. Lazaros is a cloud nestled on a feather pillow.

It bugs me a little that Cy invited another Beta here. But...maybe he had a reason. It probably has to do with Reanne, since they seem to have some sort of connection, too. At least, I hope that's why he's here.

His energy is insanely powerful. Makes me a little jealous. Maybe I'm just grumpy because I'm still worried about Cyan.

Or still swimming in guilt since I'm the reason he's lying there in the first place. I'm also peeved that Neo seems to be taking this way harder than I am, emotionally. I shouldn't care, it's not like I'm in love with Cyan.

Veikko growls, throwing the last of Fen's previously gathered plants away. "He was going to finish the job."

ReeRee gasps, clutching Vik's bicep. "But if Cy had died, I wouldn't have given him anything."

"It would have been slow. He would be long gone."

"What a shitty guy," I grumble.

I knew letting him help was a bad idea.

I narrow my eyes at Korey. *You better hope she didn't hear that. She feels bad enough as it is. For all of it.*

Veikko clears his throat. *I can hear you, even if she can not. And Aeon is correct. Do not hurt my mate with your words.*

I'd never say that to her, give me some credit. But seriously... you guys saw that, right? Her eyes went full black. Is that normal?

Nothing about her is normal, but she's still our Aruna. We brought her here, became her family, and she's bound to the SteelTooth now, for what that's worth. Pack over All. Neo makes weighted eye-contact with each of us.

Pack over All, we echo, silencing the other lines of thought.

I should have been the one giving that command, reminding us. Damn it, I'm slipping. Maybe he is going to replace me with Laz.

"I need to see Cyan to know the proper herbs."

"Good idea." ReeRee takes Vik's hand, giving it a squeeze. "I'd...like to see him again too. And Lazaros has been waiting very patiently."

She smiles at Laz who returns it with a shrug. "N-not patient, entirely, just quiet. And, well, ahem, distracted."

His cheeks tint and I almost roll my eyes when Korey puffs up with pride. I guess I should be happy for the guy.

Anything that gets him to lay off Reanne for five seconds, give her space to make the choice to come to him is a good thing.

I get it, she's magnetic, smells amazing, feels really damn good, is super responsive, and if I hadn't been her first mate I'd probably be all over her, too.

Her smile isn't as radiant now, though. There still seems to be some unease around her, but it's hard to get a full read on her energy with Laz's Beta waves blasting all over the place.

We're headed toward Cyan's cabin when Agnar stumbles out of the tree line, a bloody gash on his forehead already healing.

"Oh my gosh, are you okay?" ReeRee runs over to him, stopping short as he keeps trudging forward. "What happened?"

"Fen knocked me out when I noticed he was grabbing the wrong plants," he grunts. "Where is he?"

I cut a quick glance to Neo, keeping my mouth shut. However, my gaze follows the subtle lines of his muscles like I haven't seen him shirtless and/or naked a billion times before. I blink rapidly, setting my brain back on course to something less utterly baffling.

Reanne's face falls, and Veikko stalks over, pulling her into his protective cocoon. "He is dead."

There's a tense standoff as they stare at each other, but it's silent in the link. After another few seconds, Agnar speaks, but it's low and measured. "I'm surprised you finally did it."

"He...he didn't. I did."

Aggy's brows lower. "You killed my brother? How?"

"I didn't mean to. It-it just happened."

Didn't mean to? That's even more worrisome. Korey locks wide eyes with me. I'd hate to see what happens if she really wants to hurt someone. I keep that thought to myself, though.

"She was protecting me."

"Protecting. You."

"That payment he wanted? Was Veikko," her voice breaks.

"I wasn't going to let that happen." Aggy's voice is nothing like his normal, light tone.

"Wait," I step closer. "You knew he'd ask for Vik? And you didn't say anything?"

"Fen is...was...obsessed with two things in life. Me and Vik. I was going to go with him, instead. He would have been satisfied with that."

"You know I could not have allowed you to take my place."

Agnar nods, jaw tight. "It wasn't a fight I was looking forward to. But one I would have won."

What the hell is going on around here? Cyan needs to be here to slap some sense into these two. I'd talk in link, but Aggy is connected, so I can't. There's also no point in trying to Beta wave anyone, Laz has that covered. Hmph.

"That's stupid," Korey growls. "Just proves that the world is better off not having that psycho in it."

"He was my brother," Aggy seethes, advancing on Reanne. "You had no right to interfere."

Veikko's palm slaps against the center of Agnar's chest, stopping his movement. "No matter our past, I will kill you if you hurt my mate."

"Your m…" Agnar's eyes widen, and he takes a deep, loud breath, stepping back. They stare at each other again, before he stalks past the two of them, then all of us, headed for his own cabin.

I get it, he and Fen grew up together, and blood brothers are exceedingly rare, since the Niktas almost never survive giving birth the first time, but there has to be a reason Agnar didn't stay behind, and Fen didn't come with. I just hope once the shock wears off, Aggy will remember why he picked us.

"Guys, we really need to take care of Cyan." I'm probably being a dick, but my guilt won't stop eating away at me. "I get that other people have things that need to be dealt with, but our Alpha still isn't well."

Veikko thumbs ReeRee's tears away, and nods at me. He grabs her hand, and we finally all reach Cyan's cabin. Neo and I go through first, followed by ReeRee and Vik, and lastly Korey and Laz. It's a tight fit with all of us in here, but I free up some room by sitting on the top of the bed, near Cy's head.

Laz gasps and freezes once he sees the bed. "Is-is…why does…that's Cyan? Do you know that he, I suppose you wouldn't know, and I suppose that leaves me to be the one to tell you all that he—oh, dear. I feel ill." He paces a small circle, one hand on the top of his head, the other on his hip, before Korey stalls him with a shoulder grip.

"What is it?" He leans close and whispers something into Laz's ear that has him stutter a breath. He pulls back and grins, giving his cheek a single pat.

Laz stares up into Korey's face like he sets the moon in the damn sky, and gives him a nod. I have no idea why that makes me jealous, but it does. I also don't know why my gaze snaps to Neo, or why he's already looking at me, or why my dick twitches when he cuts his gaze away, flustered.

What the hell is up with me today? He and I are a big no. I'm not into soft guys. I must be taking this thing with Cy harder than I realized.

And if not...I seriously need to figure some of my own things out, apparently.

"Right. Apologies. Ah, so. If the man there, in that bed, is your Alpha, is Cyan, you-you should know, that, uh, well." He closes his eyes and takes a steadying breath. "He looks exactly like the Alpha, my-my old...Mishka. He looks like Mishka."

25

REANNE

Veikko rumbles a hum as he shoulders his way through the tightly packed room to Cyan's side. "I noticed. Surely some trick."

Laz shakes his head emphatically. "I assure you, sleeping, awake, uh...engaged in activities, he has always looked that way.

"Mishka is more powerful than you know," Vik mutters.

I don't really know how to feel about it, honestly. I love the way Cyan looks, his rough angular features, his hard body, I even love his scar. And part of me had wondered what Mishka looked like, which is stupid, I know.

"Fen was correct about the bloodletting. He is stable." Veikko moves to the bathroom, rummages around, but comes back empty handed, frowning. "Where did the poison come from?"

I swallow. "Your bucket."

Veikko cocks his head, brows low. "I left no bucket here."

I glance around the room until I spot it, but Neo beats me to it, and holds it up. "This isn't yours?"

"No."

"Then whose is it?" I'm not sure I want to know at this point, but we need to.

Veikko shrugs a shoulder, and opens Cyan's mouth, pulling out his tongue, which is an awful, sickly yellow color. He places two small flowers under it, one blue, one white, and sets everything back into place, silently mouthing something.

Neo turns the bucket over and over, his expression growing more confused. "Guys. I think this...I think it's Agnar's."

Aeon shakes his head. "It can't be. When would he have even been here?"

"I'm telling you, it is. Do you remember when we wanted to see how far we could throw them, and his hit that big rock?" He points to the bottom ridge, to a sizable dent. "This is his."

"So...why would he bring poisonous plants into Cy's cabin?"

Veikko frowns and catches my gaze. "There is only one reason."

I nod, even though the facts don't make sense.

"I will return with a poultice for additional help." My giant mate ducks through the door, leaving a heavy atmosphere behind.

I sniffle and crawl up onto the bed beside Cyan, draping an arm over him. His heart beats a steady, slow, strong rhythm under my ear, but there's none of that intoxicating energy he normally exudes. I miss it. Aeon takes up the space behind me, curling around my body as he covers my arm with his.

"He'll be alright, ReeRee." He kisses my shoulder.

Laz approaches the other side of the bed, filling the space left by Veikko and leans his head sideways, scanning Cy's face. "I do see the subtle differences now. And-and the more obvious ones. You'll be happy to know, ah, he's slightly more attractive."

I smile despite myself, and bury my face on Cy's chest. "That does make me feel better," I mumble.

Neo sets the offensive bucket down and sits by my feet.

I glance at him. "What do you guys use buckets for anyway?"

"Carrying things." He quirks a brow. "What do you use?"

Aeon snorts. "She has a built-in pocket."

"Gross!" I reach back and swat his hip while he laughs into my hair and Neo chuckles. I tuck my arm back over Cyan. "Forgot you guys are naked most of the time."

"The lack of clothing in your pack is-is most interesting. We have many options where I'm from, more with each supply run, and mostly no one is without. These pants actually have the least quantity of pockets you could have." I eyeball Laz as he pats the front of his jeans. "Still, very handy for, ah, well, hands, and various things."

I laugh and bury my face again. "Yes, pockets are awesome. Though, hard to find on dresses for some reason."

Aeon hums. "I forgot about those. They're my favorite. Maybe I'll swipe you a short one to wear."

"I'd love that! But, seriously make sure it has pockets."

"Done deal, mate." He plants a kiss on my head and snuggles closer.

Laz tentatively steps back over in front of Korey and turns to face us again as Korey squeezes his shoulders.

I can't help my smile. It's such a pronounced size

difference. And Korey is covered in hair essentially, while Laz is all young looking and smooth, at least from what I can see, not even any scruff to speak of. They're cute together. He's a nice-looking guy. But, even though we do seem to be connected somehow, which still doesn't make sense, there's no sexual vibe between us. Honestly, it's refreshing. It would be really nice to just have a friend. I was beginning to think my new magic-infused body would legitimately want to bang practically every werewolf I met.

Neo sighs. "What do you think Cyan would say if he woke up right now?"

"Either, 'get the fuck off me' or 'get the fuck on me,' depending on his mood," Korey chuckles.

"Or 'why the hell are you all in my house'," Aeon says, grinning against me.

"He'd wanna know why in the god damn fuck you were talking about pockets," a familiar voice whispers. It's scratchy, raw and painful sounding, but it's the most wonderful thing I've ever heard.

Ice and fire zip through me as I sit up, met with the slightest sliver of gold peaking out of Cy's cracked eyelid.

It's all I can do not to pounce on him and smother him with kisses, but the slight pained grunt he makes when I move is all it takes to calm me back down.

"You're okay," I laugh-sob, stroking his cheek. He leans into the touch as his eye closes.

"That...what we're calling this?" He chuckles once and grimaces.

"Welcome back, Alpha." Aeon props up on his elbow and gently rubs Cy's arm. "Vik's on his way back with something else to help."

Neo squeezes Cy's knee over the blanket, scraping a thumb discreetly under his eye as he clears his throat.

Cy's eye cracks back open, aimed at me. *"Whose mark is that?"*

I rub my neck, delicious zings traveling to my heart, and smile. "Veikko's."

"Good." He closes his eye again, working his mouth. *"Why am I eating flowers?"*

"Do not swallow, Alpha. You may remove them, now."

Cy's head jerks up as Veikko comes back through the door. They stare at each other, the room falling quiet as he spits the flowers over the side of the bed with a puff of air. I bet they're doing the brain talking again. I pout.

"So jealous you guys can talk to each other like that."

Aeon rubs my neck. "Just filling him in on everything."

I hope...I hope he doesn't mean *everything*. I'm not ready for that conversation, for hurting him by not choosing him immediately.

There's still no talking, but Veikko crosses the room and folds Cy's blanket down, revealing his chest. It does look better, but it's still a spiderweb of visible veins. Cyan lets his head fall back, brows pitched, staring at the ceiling. As Veikko applies his fragrant medicine, Cy's eyes dart to me and widen, before they cut away again, back to the ceiling.

"Shit. I had no damn clue, Vik."

There's a deep wave of sadness mixed with anger, confusion, and I can guess which part of the story they've reached. I stare down at my fingernails, but he grabs my hand and squeezes, drawing my gaze again. He gives me a wink.

"You did good. I'll show you how good later."

I didn't do good. Why doesn't anyone understand that? I'm being strong, I'm pushing it down, but I killed someone.

My focus fuzzes as his particular energy fills the room, little by little, until the pressure and heat steal my breath again.

Thrills dart along my skin and I bite my lip, nodding. He's almost back.

"What? Are you fucking—" I jump when he pushes up to his elbows in a single quick motion, taking his hand back, a dark scrunch of his brow. "Bring him here since he's not fucking answering." Veikko keeps applying the substance, making interesting white patterns on Cy's skin.

Korey nods, and bolts through the door, leaving Lazaros alone at the far wall.

Cy locks his attention on him. I glance between the two of them, as a smile slowly plays on Cy's mouth. "Hey there, Lazzy boy."

"H-hi, hello." He waves awkwardly, cheeks tinting. "Thank you, uh, again, for inviting me here. It's, well it's lovely."

Cy chuckles and lets his head fall back against the pillow again. "Work faster, Vik. I've got lots of fucking to do."

Laz rubs his face, blushing, and crosses his arms.

"Your blood must be clean to form a new bond." Veikko smiles and shakes his head. "It won't be long."

"You almost died, Cyan," I murmur, trailing circles on his hand. "It's okay to rest a bit."

He snorts. "You know how hard I'm tryna to keep myself under control right now? If Lazzy wasn't blasting his Beta juice at me, I'd already be in one of you."

I shoot Laz a shocked look. I didn't realize he could send it direct to a single person, instead of just a wave.

Aeon's face falls, but he clears his throat, and Cy eyes him with a smirk. He tries to sit all the way up, but Veikko shakes his head. "Too soon."

Korey comes back through the door, expression dour, followed by Agnar.

"I'm breaking pack." He announces, without so much as a hello. "Returning to BriarMaw. Release the bond."

Cy pushes Vik's hand away and sits up slowly, hooking his arms loosely around his knees. "You think I'm gonna let you live after you tried to poison me? That's your bucket, isn't it?"

Agnar stares at it for a moment, and I can't read his expression until he glares at Cyan again.

"You owe Yuli for the...life she took. This will put the count even. No need for him to retaliate."

"I give exactly zero fucks about Yuli retaliating," Cyan seethes, hurt lacing his words, "you traitorous piece of shit. After everything we've been through."

Agnar chews the inside of his cheek. "I did what I had to do."

"Yeah? That'll make two of us. Get out of the way Vik, I'm ripping him apart."

But Veikko doesn't move.

"If," Neo speaks softly, "he wants to leave, and this will placate Yuli so we can have peace, maybe it's the best idea."

I stare at Agnar, who refuses to meet my gaze. "Did Mishka put you up to it? Say you had to or something? I just don't understand why you'd want to hurt Cyan."

His eyes radiate sorrow.

"There's too much you don't understand. But you'll know soon. Release the bond, Alpha."

They stare at each other, and I can't tell if they're talking in link or not, but Cy is so tense. Eventually, he holds out his arm, turns his thumb into a claw, and carves a crescent into his flesh, followed by a wide, violent slash through it.

Agnar winces, clutching his chest as a shudder of power sweeps the room, full of emptiness and loss. It's gone in a flash, and without another word he leaves. Forever.

26

CYAN

Almost dying does wonders for a guy's perspective. That, and losing someone you thought you could depend on no matter what.

If I'd known how much cutting a pack member loose would hurt, I'd have damn sure waited until I was a bit farther from death's doorknob. That settles it, though, no one else is leaving this family. Fucking ever. Feels like my heart had a chunk taken out of it.

I'm hit with another warm, heady wave of Beta energy, and my shoulders relax. I flop back to the bed with a heavy sigh.

Lazzy boy is earning his damn keep already. He seems to have cozied up with Korey, which I'm not mad at. Mostly, because I know I can still have him any time I want, but also, I can already tell Korey is about a hundred times happier.

Before all this happened, that didn't matter so much to me, but it sure as hell does now. I love them, all of them, I really do. Even Veikko, now that he's joined up officially and I've seen some of the shit he had to deal with. If I'd known all this before, I'd have ripped Fen in half and ate his heart long before we left BriarMaw. So, I don't blame Vik a damn bit for how he needed to protect himself. Anyway, if me letting them know they're important, instead of only being an emotionless ass hat is what it takes to keep them with me, then that's what I'll do.

'Cause the truth is, there isn't a luckier Alpha and you can't tell me otherwise. This is the best pack out here, claws down. Aeon had never been a Beta before me, but his instincts are killer. Knows just when to send and only sends what I need to get sorted. And Neo's so fucking nice, a great cook, and really good kisser. Korey may be an idiot sometimes, but he's the best hunter I've ever seen, and a damn fine listener. Then there's Vik with his magical medicine mumbo jumbo and his trapping and carving skills. And Reanne. Fuck. I almost feel too many things for her to name. I may love my guys, love this pack, but I'm legitimately *in* love with her. She fits us all so perfect, and I can't imagine a single day without her in it.

Evidently, I'm a grumpy ball of fuck you with a warm, gooey center.

Hmm. I wonder if Laz is messing with my head again, like in the woods, or if I'm really feeling all these things. I guess it doesn't matter. It's not like he's putting the ideas in there, he's just making them too loud to ignore. Or making all the other noise quieter. I don't know, but I'm glad as hell he's here, too.

Aeon runs his tongue along my wound, warming my skin with his softer Beta vibes. I can't help the twitch on my mouth or in my dick. Does sappy me equal hornier me? No idea, but the urge wells in my chest, letting me know it's been too long. I need to get ahead of it.

I grip the back of Aeon's neck and jerk his mouth up to meet mine, his surprised muffled grunt setting sparks in my blood.

"You should wait a little longer, Alpha." Veikko, aka buzz-kill-gigantus rumbles above the two of us in a disapproving tone, smearing yet another pass of the cold white, goop on my chest.

I break from Aeon's kiss with a growl and flop my head to the other side of the pillow. "Hate waiting."

Reanne giggles and I shoot her a playful glare, sitting up. "Vik, what happens if this stuff gets on someone else?"

Her eyes widen as Vik sighs.

"Nothing, it is simply—"

She yelps a laugh as I grab her and drag her onto my lap, this damn blanket keeping us from truly connecting. She hooks her heels behind my back and holds my face just like I hold hers.

"Hi," she whispers, scanning my features like she's studying a map.

"Hey, my little slut," I whisper back, grinning as I claim her sexy mouth. The way she lets me lead and curls into me is the best fucking thing. Just as I hoped, it turns heated in a heartbeat, her scent, her energy wrapping around me, trickling through me, meshing with all my parts like nothing else I've ever felt before.

I seriously fucking love it now. Can't believe I fought my body so hard at first.

She hugs my neck and I hug her lower back, mashing her to my chest, until she sucks in a breath and pushes back.

"Ah—holy—that's so cold!" She laughs and wipes at her skin, smearing the bits on my arms instead.

262

"Hell nah, I've had enough of that shit," I laugh and twist away, snagging her wrists.

Something heavy and real hits me in the heart as I stare at her twinkling eyes and happy smile. My gaze dips to her stomach, and I can almost see it. Her, swollen, carrying my pup. It's scary at first, but then it's the most beautiful fucking thought I've ever had. It's so real, I fling her hands away and press my palm to her belly, like I could feel a kick from the future.

All I lack now, to be able to claim this woman as officially mine, is for Korey to mate her.

"Not much longer, now that we're down a member," I murmur, spreading my fingers. The thought of her body swollen and even needier has my dick jumping. She's got no idea what's coming.

Her breath hangs, no one says a word. Finally, she rests her hands on top of mine. I expect her to be smiling when I glance up, but she's crying, and they don't look like happy tears.

"S-sorry. Ha." She wipes her wrist under her eyes. "It's been an emotional day."

I glance around at everyone else's weird expressions. Am I missing something?

Veikko comes at me with another smear of the stuff, but I hold out my hand. "I'm good. Thanks, Vik. Can I wash this off now?"

He eyes me a moment, then his mate before nodding. "A shower could be useful. The steam might—"

"That's all the okay I need." I hoist her onto Aeon's lap instead, and fling the blanket off. Vik only just clears the way as my legs swing over.

Woah. Damn. I wrinkle my nose as the room sways a little. Maybe slow would be better.

Neo appears from nowhere and takes my hand, steadying me the whole trip to the bathroom. He closes the door behind himself with his heel and grabs my face, pressing his mouth to mine.

Fuck yes, I could do this all day.

He's hungry, kissing me deep and harder than normal. The leftover fear thrumming around him is thick, so I send him a heavy dose of my energy. He groans, muscles rippling in relief, and I grip his shoulders, pushing his back gently to the door as I trail kisses down his neck.

"Help me clean all this shit off, first," I mumble into his skin, shoving his shorts to the floor.

He nods with a gulp and holds my hand as I walk backward to the shower. He turns on the water and climbs in with me. I expected his touch, but I didn't expect him to actually clean me. It's fairly fucking erotic. He slides the rag along my skin, lip locked under his teeth, gaze flicking between the task and my eyes, and even though I was hard before, by the time he's done I'm throbbing, waiting to see what he'll do.

This is nothing like our normal dynamic, but I can tell he needs this. Needs to show himself I'm still here, and everything's still good. I'd joke that he's trying to kill me, but it's probably too soon.

"I really thought you might die," he whispers.

Yep, definitely too soon.

A tear hits his cheek, but he wipes it on his arm with a smile. "Guess you can tell I'm glad you didn't."

Instead of waiting for him to move, I curl my arm

around his waist and tug him against me, kissing him again. I let my other hand glide down his wet stomach, loving the way he twitches. Lining my cock up along his, I wrap my hand around both our cocks and gently stroke them together. His sharp exhale is so hot, like he's always surprised at how good it feels when I touch him.

He scratches at my hips as I move faster, but breaks the kiss and grips my wrist. "W-wait. Please. I have another idea."

I grin and grip his chin between my thumb and index finger. "What's with the blushing?"

"You'll find out in a second. Just...trust me?"

He's so unsure and it's tearing me apart. It won't destroy me to let him control things a little, especially if it helps him out.

"I trust you with my life, Neo. Lead on."

KOREY

I know what the rest of them have planned for when Neo and Cy come out of the bathroom, just like I know Lazaros and I don't really belong in the middle of it. I'm not mated and he's not in the pack yet. Sure, they wouldn't exclude us, and I damn sure wouldn't turn down a chance to be with Reanne again, but there's only one of her, and I know which of them will be in her. I'm not interested in being with any of the others.

Not like I am this adorable, squirming man in front of me. Still trying to wrap my head around that. It's hard to think I just hadn't met the right "guy" this whole time, but I have not, one single time, felt anything like this for any other male.

This man is mine as sure as the sun's gonna rise way too damn early tomorrow. Cyan feels just as strongly for him, so I'm not sure how that's going to play out, but for now, for at least a short while, I can have my little pup all to myself.

Reanne pats the bed beside her, coaxing Veikko to be present. She's good for him, even with her slightly scary mental murder thing.

266

Aeon rubs her inner thigh, while she threads her fingers with Vik's, and holds it on her other leg.

Annnd that's our cue.

"I'm going to show Laz the rest of the village," I announce, gaze locked on his suddenly upturned face.

"Uh, a-alright. Yes, that would be, I mean, it didn't look all that large, but I could do with a, a proper tour." He gulps audibly. "As it were."

Damn, I can't get enough of how he reacts to me.

She looks up and smiles at Laz, then me. "That sounds fun. I haven't even had a tour yet."

"I will, uh, give you the highlights. Probably. At-at least most of them."

Reanne laughs and nods. "I'd like that."

Are you sure? Aeon's brows mash together. *They'll be out in a second probably.*

Even Veikko eyes me. *He would likely appreciate your presence.*

I grin back, squeezing Laz's shoulders again. *I'm absolutely certain. Give it to her good, Vik.*

His eyes nearly bug, and he manages to look embarrassed even as his lips curl into a smile.

I maneuver Laz through the doorway, him passing backward glances the whole way, and once we're outside I step to his left, but he stalls, glancing up at me with wide eyes.

"Korey."

Heat hits my spine at the way he says it.

"Little pup."

His lids flutter before he pops them back open with a throat clear.

"Blast, I really do like that nickname. A-anyway. They're all going to have...sex...at the same time, together, with each other, aren't they...with-with Cyan, as well?"

I can't help my chuckle. "Yep. Neo's idea, actually."

He taps his mouth with the side of his index finger before pointing it at me.

"Have they done that before?"

"Nope. Vik's never been involved in anything pack related, and Reanne really just got here. Aeon and I have been with her together, but that wasn't just for pleasure, we were saving her. Neo and Cy have been with her together, while Neo mated her. And you saw the three of them with her out here, even though that was mostly the Vik show. But Neo and Aeon have never been with Cy at the same time. Not even in the same room while he's with the other. Huh. In fact, that thing with Vik was the first time they've even been near each other during anything sexual."

"I see." He taps his mouth again, and points again. "And-and you didn't want to? With them? If it's a first, perhaps it's a pack bonding moment."

"There'll be others, I'm sure. Besides, I have another bonding moment in mind."

He blinks his wide eyes at me twice and ducks his chin to his chest.

I chuckle and snag his hand. Mine is so much larger, it's crazy. He stares at it and smiles.

"That is, ah, rather nice. Isn't it? Not an unpleasant feeling."

"What? This?" I twist our hands.

He nods and rubs the back of his neck. "I haven't, been, with anyone in-in any capacity. Never held hands. Hadn't even kissed anyone be-before Cyan, using M-Mishka's...body."

My brows lift. "Wow, seriously? Have to say I'm a little jealous he was your first kiss."

"You're my first this." He twists our hands the opposite way, smiling up at me.

I grin back. "I'll take it. Hopefully I'll be a bunch more of your firsts."

"Ah..." He blushes furiously, and I shake my head at how full my heart feels.

"How can you have never had anything at all?"

He takes a deep breath, eyes on the ground as we approach my cabin. "I was kept in a rather small, well, you know, I told myself my whole life if I called it a-a house it would make it so, but the harsh truth is it was a prison."

"Aw, that's awful, I'm so sorry." I squeeze his hand tugging him closer.

He shrugs. "It is. Was. They, he, brought me out if they needed me, sometimes not even then. Now-now mind you, I had all they felt I required. When...they remembered me. I wasn't the only Beta, you see, so I wasn't needed all the time."

I nod. "Another sign you're a Born Beta. Can't have more than one if they're just made from the Alpha bond."

"Mmm. Still such a odd thing to hear a fact about myself from a virtual stranger." He cuts his apologetic gaze up. "I'm grateful, truly, please don't misread. I just...I find myself wishing you knew more. That I knew more. I was taken as a-a pup, you see. GrimBite is all I've ever known. Hearing I'm something of a rarity...how bizarre is it that it makes me miss people and a place I've never known?"

"Not bizarre at all, little pup." I duck and kiss the back of his hand. "And I wish I knew more, too. I'd spend all night telling you, and tell you again any time you asked."

"You absolutely cannot be real," he whispers.

"I keep thinking the same thing about you."

He grins at me and jostles our hands again. "That, ah, was another first."

"The hand kiss?"

I repeat it, lingering longer, holding his gaze.

"Yesss," the word leaves his mouth like he's deflating. "That. With the beard and the mouth. Whew."

I laugh. "You're so adorable."

We finally reach my cabin, and Laz chuckles. "I see. Not much of a tour to report to Reanne, is it?"

"Well," I say, nudging the door open with my foot. "She hasn't been in here, either."

His eyes light up. "So, you're having a first of your own, eh?"

"Everything about you is a first for me, little pup."

"Really?" The teasing tone is gone, just awe and maybe something else as I lead him inside.

"Mmhmm. Like I said, I wasn't into guys before you."

"I thought that was a line," he chuckles, scratching his thumb on his forehead. "A good one."

"Oh," I laugh. "Then let's pretend it was. Anything that gives me a better chance of racking up firsts tonight, I'm down for."

He gives me the most winning grin. "I'd say your chances are, as chances go, fairly magnificent."

28

ΠΕΟ

I'm more nervous about how he'll take this idea than I was the first time he and I had sex alone. It could go horribly wrong if Cyan resists too much, gets too stressed, or any number of other things. In the beginning, after we first broke pack from BriarMaw, this would have gone over like a hunk of moldy meat. He's different nowadays, so...

I gulp and crack open the door, Cy gripping my hip. Aeon has a hand on one of Reanne's thighs, and Veikko has his on her other, each of them kissing her neck. She's in bliss, her need thick in the air.

Heat crawls along my spine. They all look so good together, it's crazy. Especially Aeon. I blink, shaking that thought away. Cy can smell her now, too. I know, because his energy twangs behind me, and Reanne's eyes pop open, aimed at the door.

Okay, can't delay anymore.

"Cyan," I say, pushing the door open, met with three sets of eyes. "We want to show you how much you mean to us."

"That right?" Cy's breath is hot on my neck, body flush

with mine as his hand slides around my hip and grips my cock. Reanne's gaze flicks down, mouth parting.

Veikko's jaw clenches, but he glances back at Reanne, reading her face instead.

And Aeon. For some reason, his eyes are locked on mine. I can't read his expression at all, and it's unnerving. I furrow my brow, glancing away and back twice before I clear my throat and spin around, adjusting my glasses.

"Yes, so, kneel on the bed."

Cyan's brows launch sky high, a wide grin splitting his face. He mashes his body against mine, grabbing a double handful of my ass.

"You're giving the orders?" He runs his nose along my neck, a low growl in his chest. "You?"

I almost instinctively melt away, but barely hold my ground, muttering, "It'll be worth it."

He chuckles and steps back, thumb swiping across his bottom lip as he scans us all. It's a tense moment, because he has the final call on everything, so he could decide none of this is happening and handle things however he wants.

But he finally says, "A'ight," and rounds the bed. He knee walks to the center of the mattress, that delicious cock of his hard and ready as always.

Thankfully, the only one I really have to give any instructions to is Reanne. The other two and I worked everything else out after Vik mated her, you know, provided Cy had survived. Which he did. Really glad for that. Super glad. And I'm stalling.

"Okay," another throat clear. "Reanne."

Her attention snaps from Cy's brilliant, hungry eyes to me. "Hm?"

The mate bond sizzles, overwhelming me for a second, and I hold my hand out. "Come here, baby bird."

She grins at me and hops up. I cradle her face and kiss her deeply for as long as I think I can get away with before breaking. "Mm mm. Okay. You wait right here for a bit."

"Alrighty," she whispers, uncertainty in her gaze, right up until Veikko stands and crosses in front of me to loom behind her.

He rests his hands on her shoulders, sliding them down her arms, and she's back to sending out warm, desperate vibes again. Much better.

Aeon moves finally, twisting from his position on the edge, staring at me of all people, to sitting at Cy's right leg.

"Lookin' good down there, bitch," Cyan murmurs, raking his fingers through Aeon's hair, the same time Aeon strokes his hands up Cy's thigh. Once my knees hit the mattress, Cy's attention splits, his energy scattering in all directions. He doesn't look comfortable anymore, which is what I was worried about. I had a feeling he wouldn't like what this would do to his system. At least, not at first.

He growls, deep enough our instincts kick in and we both recoil, but he's wide eyed, which means he's still present, at least.

Aeon sends a wave of Beta energy, just as I make contact with Cy's hip.

I lean over and run my tongue along the side of his cock, to the tip and back again. His other hand lands heavy on my head as I cup his balls. When he groans, Aeon takes that as his cue to move closer, his tongue making the same path on the other side of Cy's cock.

"Fuck," Cy whispers, but he's still completely

disconnected, energy bouncing around the room like a swarm of lightning bugs trapped in a jar.

Aeon and I are supposed to alternate, but on the next pass our tongues somehow cross. Electricity arcs through my mouth, but I pretend nothing happened. That works, with me *not* avoiding his touch like I thought I would, until we end up at Cy's tip at the same time. Totally not part of the plan, at least not mine. Aeon's? I don't know, but we stare each other down, our tongues tangling around his head.

Reanne's breaths are short and sweet, eating up too much oxygen, but I know Vik will keep her satisfied. I would look, but that would mean not passive-aggressively licking Aeon's pre-cum coated tongue, and that's apparently what I'd rather do right now. We somehow come to a mutual, silent decision that we'll move in the same direction, at the same time, sucking, licking, tangling tongues around Cy's cock. It's one of the hottest things I've done, since kissing Cyan while being inside Reanne. And my own pre-cum has dripped onto my leg. Is Aeon stroking himself? I want to see and I don't. What a weird day.

Cy still isn't able to manage his Alpha waves, what he uses for Aeon being too much for me, and what he uses for me not nearly enough for Aeon. But it's also hard to ignore having your dick worshipped, so he's a grunting disaster, bucking and gripping each of our heads. His chin lifts, a long, loud groan filling the space as his first orgasm hits. Aeon takes the first few spurts, I get the rest and we keep going, only neither of us has swallowed. To my utter shock, we're licking each other's tongues around Cy, while trading his cum. I have no idea what's happening, to be honest, but it's all sexy, and it's all working.

Reanne lets out a few stuttered moans, and I need to see why. On the next trip down Cyan's cock, I tilt my head a little and glance back. My eyes widen and I swallow on reflex.

Veikko has her back pressed against him, his mouth planted on her neck, licking and nipping his mark, one arm around her shoulders, that hand playing with her breast, the other hand between her legs, fingers dipping in, swirling. Her eyes are glazed, and she keeps fighting to open them, watching the three of us. He's basically a Vik blanket, his massive body wrapped around her.

It's hot as all hell.

I can't take it any longer, but I only manage one stroke on my cock before I bump into another hand.

Shocked, I pull back and jerk my chin to my chest, following the arm even though I know whose it is, but I need to convince myself it's real. Aeon is absorbed in sucking Cy's cock alone, but cracks open an eye and aims it at me, pushing my hand out of the way as he takes over.

My teeth grind, the pleasure intense. His grip is almost too firm, but he uses his long fingers better than I do. I gasp a moan and he grins around Cy. I have no idea why that bugs me, but it does.

Not to be outdone, because this is apparently a contest now, I scoot closer, and grab his cock, too. He does a sharp inhale, and okay, yes, that's a solid victory feeling if I've ever had one.

I meet his mouth at Cy's head again, and since I accidentally swallowed my share of the cum, I suck on

Aeon's tongue, hoping to steal some. It's a good plan, until I realize it means we aren't actually sucking Cy's cock anymore, we're solidly making out, stroking each other's cocks.

This is not a road I want to travel tonight, or any night, really. We're not compatible that way, but holy hell, it's so hot. Okay, no this is about Cyan. I pull away, and open my eyes, met with the same hooded, confused look I know I'm giving off.

"Shit, do that again." Cy's voice tumbles down from above us, his hand taking over where our mouths should be.

I want to play dumb and stick to what's left of the plan, but Aeon grips the back of my head and delves in deep, tasting my mouth, lips bruising like he's angry, even though his cock is practically drooling in my hand.

It's too rough for my liking, but in the mix of everything, it's still kind of hot.

Vik gives Reanne what sounds like a massive orgasm, which sends Cy over the edge again, since he's no doubt watching, and he shoots his load on the sides of our faces. The shock of it all, coupled with Aeon breaking the kiss and lapping Cy's nut off my cheek, while he strokes me even faster, has me exploding in his hand with a shout, panting as I watch Reanne cling to Vik.

He smooths his fingers along my tip, playing with my cum, still licking my face even though I know it's clean, and I seriously can't make sense of what's happening, but it feels so good I could probably come again just from this.

I don't know why I bothered to plan anything out at all. Now I'm irritated again. When Aeon finally returns to Cy's cock, leaving my face and insides tingling, I dive onto his, determined to force one out of him, too.

The loud, muffled moan he lets out is too much of a reward, though, and I'm back to hot and throbbing and confused. I suck his cock for all I'm worth, and it's not long before he bucks, hand tangled in my hair as he shoots into the back of my throat with several long, chesty moans. He tastes so different, and I don't want to like it, because I have no idea what that means. But I do like it, damn it.

Okay, something has to get back on track here. I release Aeon, who tackles Cy's cock again, and motion to Vik. He whispers in Reanne's ear, and her breathing stops, but she nods, whimpering as Vik removes his hand.

They move toward the bed as a unit, but when her hands hit the mattress, Cy's energy flatlines before spiking uncomfortably in every direction. Aeon quickly fills the space with more Beta waves than I think he's ever produced, and there's a different energy swimming just underneath. Is that...

I cut wide eyes to Aeon, who, of course, is already staring at me. He nods with a small one-shoulder shrug.

We both stare at Reanne, practically radiating lust as she crawls toward Cyan. Our hands go to her automatically, playing with her nipples, and smoothing over her back once she reaches Cy. She pushes to her knees, aided by his grip on her face. His hands slide to her neck as he holds her in place and ravishes her mouth.

The new energy is stronger, brushing along my skin, mixing with the mate bond. It has to be her, I can't believe it.

How is she giving off a version of Alpha waves? Is this part of her new power?

I can barely breathe through the need to be in her, and dive two fingers deep, living for her little whimper. Aeon growls and plants tongue-heavy kisses along her side, and even Veikko, one knee braced on the bed, is stroking along her spine.

Cyan's growl rockets out, loud and possessive, dangerously on edge. Aeon blasts another wave but I'm not sure it's having an effect. In fact, I think Cy's reacting to her energy, like it's a challenge.

Guys, I think we should—

I blink. Cy...muted the link? Or, is it broken? Maybe warring Alpha waves in the same pack cancel...things? I'm so confused and turned on and everything is out of control.

Reanne doesn't have a clue what's going on, either. She's getting wetter, and I can't stop fingering her until Cyan grabs her ass in both hands, claws forming. I withdraw and instead, nip at Cy's hip, my hand toying with his balls from behind. He rams his cock between her legs, gliding along her slit, and with the grip he has on her cheeks, his head is coming out the other side.

Aeon groans and quickly buries his face there, tongue out, lavishing Cy's cock when it appears. I'm about to come again just from watching.

"Fuck...fuck, yeah." Cy, back to himself for a moment, moans against Reanne's mouth, but that turns her on even more, and the energy flares, which triggers his beast again.

He picks up speed, aggressive, his claws cutting into her skin.

I'm worthless right now, because all I want to do is suck

Aeon's cock again, which bothers me, but I also can't stop myself.

I manage to twist onto my side, fitting between and under him a bit, and the second my mouth makes contact, he greedily thrusts in, like it's exactly what he wanted.

Why does this have to be so hot?

But the shock that sends me careening to the edge is when Veikko's huge hand lands on the back of my head, and he shoves me down farther, until Aeon's cock is choking me. I can barely breathe, and that has never, ever been my thing, in fact it's always scared me, but Aeon groans, rocking his hips, and there's so much Alpha energy in the air, and Vik's grip is firm, but forgiving, and I can tell he'd let me up if I needed it, and...that's it.

I'm not even touching myself, in fact no one is, but my muscles shudder, clenching in waves as I launch into another orgasm. Vik rumbles something I can't understand over my pounding pulse and lets me go. I gasp a breath at the same time Cyan roars through his own release, Reanne moaning from the friction, Aeon groaning at his fresh mouthful of Cy's cum. Weird jealousy bites at my heart. I seriously love the way Cy tastes, and Aeon keeps getting the lion's share of it.

Vik steps out of his shorts, grabs Reanne's hips and pulls her backward, right onto his cock. Her shocked gasps, the harsh sound of skin slapping against skin, and Vik's deep pleasured grunts set us all off again. Plus, and I'm not ashamed to admit this, he looks insanely hot pounding her like that, all giant muscles and big arms. The extra energy dampens, thankfully, all her attention on being railed by a mate. Cyan's Alpha waves skitter back to some sort of order, and he grabs Aeon and I by the scruff of our necks, tugging us up to our knees.

He pushes our faces together with his and the three of us make out. I attack Aeon first, stealing every bit of Cy's flavor from him. He's breathless when Cy takes control again, another victory point for me, and we alternate between kissing each other and twirling tongues. This is honestly nowhere close to how I planned this, but now our cocks are bumping, rubbing together and I think if I die now, that'd be okay.

"Yes, yes, yes!" Reanne screams through another orgasm, drawing moans from us all, and despite the fact Cy's energy is still on the fritz, he's happy, I can feel it. That's worth more to me than anything, really. And if he thinks he's sleeping with anyone other than me tonight, he's wrong. Except...maybe Aeon could come, too. As long as he stays on the other side of the bed.

Aeon's tongue dips into my mouth again, scrambling my brains, tasting like Cyan and himself and I get lost in it, groaning. Cy evidently likes what he sees and grabs my cock. He must grab Aeon's, too, because we both make the same needy sound, deep in our throats, eyes popping open as we break apart.

Cyan's energy has leveled. He's figured out how to balance and is stroking us both. I can feel what he's doing to me, and it's perfect, just the way I love it, but I can't look away from how he's so violent with Aeon's cock, or the sheer ecstasy on Aeon's contorted features as his head falls back, Cyan biting deep into his neck.

"Damn," I whisper, my hand finding its way to Aeon's nipple. I can't be rough, it's not my style at all, but teasing, that I can do. I brush my fingertips across one, then the other, lightly, Cyan's hand working magic on me.

"Oh, fuck," Aeon moans, trembling, gasping, as Cy's grip turns more violent, faster, harder, blood leaking from the wound. "Fuck!" He shouts, makes unexpected eye contact with me, sending fireworks through my body, and launches ropes of cum onto my stomach. It's so startling, so erotic I can't breathe. Aeon came on me. I...

Reanne moans loudly, and I whip my head around to find Vik still pounding her, but his arm is hooked around her hip, fingers working her clit. Her eyes are locked on mine, so hungry, but so satisfied it makes my heart jump.

I'd love to let Cyan finish me, but I really want to be the one to suck him off this time. I drop to my hands and knees and take him fully into my mouth. There's a bunch of movement behind me, and Reanne's hair tickles the inside of my legs as she scoots under me. Before I can process anything, she takes my cock in her mouth, moaning around it.

Holy...hell! I've never had my cock sucked while sucking someone else's. I try to twist to see what Vik is doing, but Cy thrusts deep into my mouth.

Maybe a good time to test the link.

Are you eating her out, Vik?

He sure fucking is, like a pro. Keep sucking, Neo.

Cyan's voice in the link is too much for me emotionally, especially after today. It was so empty while he was unconscious, and then he cut it off, and now he's back and fully in control, way more than he ever has been, and my dumb ass is tearing up, with his dick jammed in my throat. There's no doubt in my mind he's the best choice and why

Reanne doesn't throw herself at him right now boggles my mind. No, now is not the time to get sad about that or anything else, damn it.

Cy's fingers trail tenderly through my hair, along my earlobe, and down the side of my cheek. It's perfect, soothing just like I need, but I can hear Aeon's twisted rapture continuing, can smell the blood that hasn't stopped flowing from his neck, and for some reason, I hope he shoots all over me again. That thought has me panting, throbbing in Reanne's mouth.

I guess I've been completely broken by today. Or fixed. I dunno.

Reanne pulls off me with a pop, half-way stroking as she writhes and screams through another orgasm. Cyan groans, thrusts deep into my mouth, and leans up, molding my ass in his palm.

It makes me ache, and I wish it were just us, so he'd fuck me like normal, but this was my idea in the first place. I reach under myself and guide my cock back into Reanne's mouth, whose moaning turns to hums as she bobs and sucks and strokes. It feels so damn good.

I increase the speed on Cy's cock, side-eyeing his death grip on Aeon's cock. The scent of blood is gone, now, probably because Cy's getting close, his groans aimed at the ceiling again. He seizes, thrusting hard and stilling as he fills my mouth. I rock in Reanne's mouth, my orgasm following just behind Cy's.

I swear I hear a huff of disappointment from Aeon, irritation confirmed when his face is waiting for me as Cy pulls back, freeing himself. Aeon clutches my face, kissing me, growling, and I can't help grinning against his lips because I already swallowed. Another victory point for me.

But I think he misreads my smile, because his attack kiss stalls, panting breaths mingling with mine as he stares at me. My stomach swoops. Of the two of us, the one I least expect to close the distance first is me, but I do, slowly, gaze bouncing between his wet lips and his smoldering eyes. And when our mouths touch again, there's a rush of fire, curling in my chest. I clutch the back of his neck as our tongues dance.

"I could watch that all day," Cy murmurs. "I've got one left before I need a quick break, who wants it?"

I would scream "me", but I can't stop kissing Aeon. He's also not stopping, not bruising me anymore, either.

Reanne does.

Vik's voice cracks the thin glass dome of this weird moment with Aeon, bringing me back to the present. I pull away first, extricate myself from Reanne's hungry mouth, and sit back on my heels at the foot of the bed, rubbing my face, eyes closed.

I can't fuck her again yet, not until Korey gets his mark on her.

I exhale shakily and nod, not that I'll know if they see it. I refuse to look at anyone again. I have no idea who I am anymore. I've never felt anything for another guy. Cy's been it for me, and even that wasn't my first choice.

I'm with Cy because being wooed by an Alpha is almost better than sex. Plus, he's really hard to say no to, he needed another partner, wanted me, and that was pretty intoxicating, not going to lie. Still is. I get hard just thinking about the way he looks at me sometimes. But somewhere along the way I fell in love with him, and that's fine, too. No one would ever fault me for that, it's Cyan. I think we all love him, on some level.

But Aeon doesn't make any sense. I have a mate now. I'm an Alpha's plaything. Though, I guess he is too, really. Does he love Cyan? Damn it, maybe I'm seriously overthinking everything. Yeah, that's it. Heat of the moment, hot and sweaty, lots of Alpha waves blasting all over. Or...maybe he was also hurting because Cyan was unconscious. Yeah. Okay. I can deal with that. We're good. We can still just be friends.

What if there is a way, Alpha?

That gets my attention, and everyone else's, except Reanne's, who is still thoroughly enjoying Vik's evidently talented tongue. I really hope he's not about to tell Cyan the one thing she wanted to keep from him. This could be bad.

Then you better fuckin' tell me.

LAZAROS

Korey is, without a doubt, a spectacular specimen. As if staring at his body wasn't treat enough, he held my hand. Kissed it! Like I'm, like we're, I...I don't know what.

His cabin is so different than Cyan's. The walls are lined with shelves, full to brimming with things, but each in its place, organized and loved. Matching pairs, no matter what it is, little bird carvings, mugs, abstract sculptures, even rocks have a mate. I had no things, no space to keep them if I had. Part of why it was so easy to leave, nothing to miss.

But this place is evidence of a life enjoyed, or at the very least, experienced.

He has a large bed along the back wall, coverings aligned with precision. Here at the door is a small, round table with two chairs, similar to Cyan's, but Korey has another section further in with a sofa and a soft rug, facing a rustic fireplace. There's also a closed door, which leads to a bathroom, I assume.

I'm gawking shamefully, letting my feet lead me around the space, while he leans his hip against the table, watching me with a smile.

"You like it?"

"I do, I mean, how could I not? I absolutely adore it," I breathe, touching the shelf in front of two small rabbit figurines. "It's neat and tidy. Clean, but so very lived in. Full, but-but with so much room for more, warm, happy...I could stay here quite blissfully for the rest of my natural life and never tire of it."

"Sounds good to me."

"Ehkh?" I fully intended to make a word, but what comes out is a shocked, choking sound not unlike something that might be made by dragging a wildebeest around by a noose. Not my finest moment. He can't be serious, though. "What?"

He laughs and pushes away from the table, strolling over to me. "I said, sounds good to me." He stops in front of me and strokes that mind-altering finger down my cheek, leaning closer. "Little pup."

Damn, damn and double damn. Who knew I had such a ridiculous weakness? He does, clearly, that blasted sexy grin of his eating up his face.

I manage to find some courage from the bottom of my shoe and give a valiant final stand.

"B-but this is your home. Cyan said he'd build me my own, well he also said he'd, aha, nevermind, but I—you only just met—"

"You can still have your own place. Just also stay here. Primarily stay here. And Cy bounces around all over anyway, we're used to sharing our beds, so you'd see him practically the same amount."

That finger glides along my neck again, melting my kneecaps. How's a man supposed to do any rational thinking when all his blood is racing to his stupid cock? He's not, that's how. But it's a moderately terrifying prospect, to go from being so alone to living with someone who wants me in all the possible ways, and who doesn't have a problem sharing me with another someone who wants me. Dizzy doesn't quarter cover it.

Korey sees something in my eyes, just like before, and withdraws, leaning back, closing off. "Unless you don't like me like that."

"I like you...like that." I grab his hand. "I do. It...is a tad on the fast side."

He shrugs. "You'll need a place to stay while your cabin's being built. Besides. When you know, you know."

That is an excellent point. I'm more interested in the other comment, however and quirk a brow at him. "And you know."

"Oh yeah, little pup." He smiles again as my heart catapults into my ribs.

"What," I whisper, swallowing in my drying mouth, "do you know?"

His confidence is fully back, and I daresay it makes him even more attractive, like he needs any assistance in that category.

"Lots of things." He smirks, devouring the last bit of resistance in my body. "For starters, how badly I want to kiss you."

I hear that blasted squeak noise again, the one I'm still not sure is me. "I-I'd like that," I gasp out.

He doesn't descend on me the way Cyan did. Instead, he strokes the backs of his fingers down my cheek again, pushing the knee-wobble button I evidently had installed while I wasn't looking, and leans in slowly.

It's squirmingly intimate, but not in a bad way. When his mouth brushes against mine, there are definite sparks, no question. It's gentle, slow, fantastic. His beard and tongue...there's so much sensation. It also unlocks something fairly primal in me, something I didn't know I had.

I throw my arms around his neck and kiss him harder. He chuckles and circles my waist, lifting me so he can stand straight. Mercy, he's as hard as I am.

He breaks the kiss but doesn't set me down. "You're really great at that, for not having much experience."

"You're a fab kisser, too."

"Thanks." He grins again, planting a kiss on my neck. "So, want to know what else I know?"

I nod, clutching him tighter.

"I know," he runs his tongue along the space behind my ear, sending lighting all through me, "how much you want me to help you out of those clothes, how you want me to touch you and a whole lot more, isn't that right?"

"Yes!" I yelp as he nips my skin.

"Mm, damn that was nice." His tone dips to a magical level. "Felt that cock twitch, little pup."

Oh, I may actually die. That word from his mouth is like a lewd invitation to a devilishly dirty party for two.

He lets me slide down his body, keeping me close as he grabs the hem of my shirt, fingers grazing my skin as he tugs.

"Arms up."

Blimey, I didn't think he was serious about that part.

He's all smug grin and sexy voice where I'm naught but a useless sack of bones. Though, I do manage to make those specific bones work, and he inches my shirt up, following it with his gaze.

Shirt off, I'm even more conscious of how different we are, in every way. He lets it drop to the floor, jaw clenching as he studies me.

"Wow," he breathes, that grin still in place.

I'd rather he throw me across the room, or leave, than stare at me so intently, so lovingly. At least the former would be familiar territory.

"Good? Bad?" I cross my arms, fidgeting. "Bad most likely, I'll see myself out."

"Little pup," he growls with the slightest hint of annoyance, brow low, gaze holding mine, and I am completely unraveled. "Put those arms back down."

They fall, and I blink up at him. That commanding tone does exciting, scary things to my insides. He's silent as he undoes my pants and shoves them to the ground, no hesitation, no waiting, just pure, calm control.

My greedy cock springs free, already leaking. His deep breath, that hunger in his eyes as he sweeps my body...

If I hadn't already been nearing obsession with him, this would have tipped it that way. I appreciate the patience, and the concern, the caring kindness, more than he'll ever know. I'd thought that's what I'd get with him, something safe and welcome and warm, a type I needed desperately. But I want the other, too. To get both from the same person?

He hums and slides his wide, rough palms over my stomach, my arms, my back, soft at first, then firmer. He flicks my nipples, sending delicious twinges straight to my cock, which is already painfully hard. It bobs, and he smirks deeper, but he doesn't touch it, no, the bastard runs his hands down my thighs instead, then over my ass and up my back.

"You're so soft." It's a reverent whisper, like he's shocked by the fact. "And small, and gorgeous, and perfect. *Fuck.*" The last word is a guttural sound, a promise, and I lose all my breath.

He helps me step out of the pants and nudges them out of the way as he backs me up to the bed. Each step makes my chest tighten in anticipation. I don't know what he'll do, not really.

I find out the second my legs hit the blanket edge. He stops walking and hooks his thumbs in the waistband of his shorts, but, in what may well be the only granule of bravery ever to grace my bloodstream, I stop him.

"W-wait. Can...I?"

There's a deep rumble in his chest that turns me to goo as he gives me a single nod.

I'm too afraid to reach out, but, again, he somehow knows what I need, and gently grabs my hand, placing it on his lower stomach.

Fire races up my arm. His skin is hot, tight. And rather than what I asked to do, all I can do is study him the same way, gliding both hands along his stomach, up his muscular chest, his big arms.

"Is this payback, little pup?" He chuckles, breathy.

I cut my eyes up to his and get lost there a moment. But only a moment, because he takes one of my hands and plants it straight on his cock.

Bloody hell!

I only thought it looked big, it feels enormous, even through his shorts. I get so excited, claws spring out on my other hand, digging into his chest a little as I give him a testing stroke.

My mouth opens for an apology to tumble out, but he groans and grips the back of my neck, ducking to kiss me again.

One of his fingers trails over the tip of my cock, the sensation shocking me so much I jerk away. Save for his grip on my neck, I'd have fallen flat onto the bed.

"S-sorry!" I pant, but he only grins at me, sending another rush of blood through me.

"Lay back."

I blink. "On the, here, you want, I..."

He raises his brows, staring at me expectantly and I can't help but listen. Not breaking eye contact, I reach back, feeling for the mattress, and sit before leaning on my elbows.

By all the stars, this is so open, and he's just there, cock bulging in his shorts, while mine juts up to the sky. It's almost embarrassing, but his own excitement is leaking through the cloth, so he obviously likes what he sees.

My heart comes to a full stop when he braces on my thighs, pushing them apart, and drops to his knees in front of me.

Heat floods my face, and I can't decide if I want to hide it in a pillow or keep watching. I suppose at this point it goes without saying, no one has ever been in this position, even though I've dreamed about it endlessly.

"Another set of firsts," he rumbles, grinning at me, raking his fingers up the inside of my legs, ramping up my excitement ten-fold. I expect his mouth at any second, but he hesitates.

I tilt my head, detecting...ach, my heart! He's nervous! I send a Beta wave on reflex, and tension melts from his shoulders. His smile softens and he plants a kiss on my knee, thoroughly cementing himself on my soul.

"Aw, little pup. You didn't have to do that, but thanks."

"Speaking of-of things one doesn't, ah, have to—"

"I'm sucking this beautiful cock, that's not the problem."

Oh... The sheer level of arousal that blasts me is murderous. A dribble of pre-cum leaks out of me, and his gaze darkens. He leans in and chases it with his tongue, slow and firm, flicking that wide thing over the tip before sliding it down the whole length. A shocked moan escapes as my whole body tenses. He tongues my balls, licks back to the top, circles the head once and I can't take it. Fireworks lash through me, tiny explosions leading to one big one. I groan at a shameless volume as I shoot all over myself, panting. He dips the tip of his tongue into the leftover cum leaking down the side while I pant.

It felt better than I could have possibly imagined, and so different than I ever did.

He chuckles and eyes me again. "Was figuring out the right words. To warn you. It's okay if you come quick, you're not allowed to feel bad about that, because we're just getting started."

"Ah," I laugh, letting my head fall back as I rub my face. "I see. Blimey, that was phenomenal."

"Just wait," Korey chuckles, and takes my whole cock in his mouth, shocking the soul out of me. I jerk my head back level, and stare, mouth agape, body blazing back to life again. His tongue presses against me while the wet heat surrounds me, slight suction forming. My eyes bug. But it's when he flattens his palm to my lower stomach, my cock braced in the crook of his thumb and index finger that all life stops.

"*Shit!*" I almost whisper scream it, but I've never felt anything like this.

He slowly lifts his head, the tongue, the heat, the suction traveling up my length until he reaches the tip and sucks harder. My hips buck, another sharp groan blasting from my throat, and he plunges back down, repeating the sequence faster.

"Oh, hell," I whimper, clutching at the covers, bunching them in my fists, watching as my cock vanishes and reappears. "That—Oh...fuck!"

I thrust again, and Korey hums, pulling all the way off on the next ascent, catching my gaze with a smirk. "You've got a dirty mouth, little pup."

"Yes, sir, I guess I do," I say on a fast exhale, delirious, legs trembling.

His breath catches, and his eyes smolder. "Call me that again."

What? What did I say? Oh brain, please work. I finally remember, and more embarrassment than I've ever experienced pours over me. Why oh why did that come out?

But...I suppose, he liked it, and he, well, he is a...

"Sir?"

He growls, animalistic, and renews his spectacular assault on my body, faster, hungrier. I lose myself in a cacophony of sounds, tangling one hand in his hair, braced on the other elbow. I can feel another orgasm cresting, and expect him to pull away, but he doesn't. Surely, he must not know the signals yet.

"I-I'm...S-sir, you—"

He growls again, sucks harder, and I explode, moaning, destroyed completely as he drinks me down. The sight, the feel of it makes it last even longer than the first one, my body losing itself in the moment.

When he glides up the final time, grazing my head with his teeth, I'm quite certain I've ascended some other level of existence and flop back on the bed, arms wide.

"You taste," he pushes up to his feet by the mattress, "really damn good, little pup. That could be dangerous. For you. Hell, both of us," he chuckles.

I can't help my grin, breathless as I drape my arm over my eyes. Just fasten me to the wall and put me on tap, because life can't get better. It surely can't.

The moon accepts that challenge, and I hear a rustle of fabric, my body on full alert again. I hit the mattress and push up a little.

"Bloody...hell..." I say it in two long breaths, suddenly hungry and thirsty as I gaze at Korey's magnificent, fully nude body.

Soft, dark hair covers his meaty thighs, too, not that I assumed it wouldn't. I truly could stare at him forever, but the best part bobs under my stare, forcing me to gulp.

His cock is wide, rude, angry, and the hottest thing I've ever seen because his current state is due to me. Insignificant, worthless, overlooked Laz. Me, who's never meant a whit to anyone, has this huge, wonderful man, hard and leaking.

Like a starved fish to bait, I shove off the bed, ready to return favor, but he gathers me to him, instead.

With one of his rough fingers, he tilts my chin up and claims my mouth again. I mewl, surrendering in his embrace. I can't help it, this heat, this-this, well, it has to be love, it just has to be. And it's overwhelming.

He gives me a smaller parting kiss, before he rubs his nose on mine, effectively mashing my heart in his manly hand, marking me for etern...oh.

I blink up at him, and I know the second my blush forms because his gaze flicks to my cheek and his eyes crinkle. "How," he lowers his voice clutching me tighter, "did you get so damn adorable?"

I shrug, but it's more a full body shiver. He chuckles as he turns and sits on the bed. I quickly brace on his shoulders and sit on his lap, legs over his. Before I'm brave enough to do it, he grabs my hips and slides me forward until our cocks mash together.

His groan hits me in my bones, so deep. I have a guess of what comes next, and I'm not entirely sure how to, well, I know how, but how will I—

"Before you panic," he kisses my cheek, "we're not doing that tonight. There's no way you're ready for it, but we're far from done."

I pout. Full on, bottom lip jutting, pout. It's not something I've done before, obviously, but I'm comfortable with him, and dash it all, I was really hoping to have all the firsts tonight.

"Mmm, you asking me to bite that, little pup?" He clacks his teeth and I squeal, prompting his delicious laugh.

My insides swirl, sparks and fires and arrows shooting through me as I gaze into his glittering eyes.

"Korey," I whisper, swallowing, "sir."

Oh, I'm dead. That name is his trigger like his damned cheek stroke is mine. His chest rumbles, and his hand wraps around both our cocks, stroking slow as he licks my shoulder.

My question vanishes in the sensation, I can't look anywhere but down. Until he wraps an arm around my waist, and shifts us backward a bit before flipping us. I'm on my back again, looking up into his gorgeous furry face, his wide body consuming my vision as I plummet into scary, lovely feelings. I nearly ask my question, but he rolls his hips, grinding his cock along mine in slow waves, his balls swaying against mine, and I'm rendered stupid.

"Ah, oh, what...unhh...that feels..." I moan, covering my face, because this is seventy-two times more intimate than having his mouth on me. He's using my body for both our pleasure in a way I never imagined.

"Little pup," he growls, low and gooseflesh covers my skin. "Hands down."

"Sirrr," I whine, but slowly comply. The furrowed brow that meets my seeking gaze pumps heat through my system.

"Better. Don't hide yourself from me."

He winks, attacking my emotions again, and picks up speed, groaning for each of my moans. I clutch at his waist, my hips matching his rhythm on their own, chasing the feeling he's giving me, like he'll take it away any second. It's so wonderful, soft skin over hard flesh, sliding along mine.

He leans down and nips my jaw, flooding me with need.

"You're so hot, little pup," he rumbles, nuzzling my ear.

I grind faster, so close, so lost in it all that my wicked thought escapes before I can stop it.

"Mate me," I gasp.

He stills, panting and catches my gaze. "What?"

Damn all the stars and all the trees and every damned, blasted, bleeding thing on this rotten, miserable—

"Mate you?"

I blink as his eyes light up, a tentative smile forming.

"Did...did I hear you wrong?"

He drops down to his elbows, caging me in, hands on my face, pushing his nose against mine. "You want to be my mate, little pup?" He whispers it, so full of joy and hope that tears spring up in my eyes as I nod.

"Are you sure?" He kisses me, and I nod again. "It's not too soon?" Another kiss, and I shake my head, smiling. "You're absolutely certain, I'd get to have you as my little pup forever?"

"Yes," I laugh when he scrubs his beard along my neck. "And you'll be my, ah, sir. Forever."

"Mmm," his tone changes in a heartbeat, heat filling the room again as he runs his tongue along my ear lobe. Chills sprout up, my cock twitching against his.

"That sounds damn good to me," he growls in my ear. "Where do you want the mark?"

Oh. Well, now. That's an exceptionally good question. But he's grinding again, and the handful of brain cells that were active have now gone on vacation to erection-ville.

"Unh," is all I manage, which could mean my neck, my arm, that statue, a frog in the creek, or any number of things.

NATALIA PRIM

He chuckles, and I'm beyond lucky he finds me amusing, because I already adore that sound.

"Okay, how about here," his breath is hot on my skin as he sucks at the tender flesh where my neck meets my left shoulder. I wouldn't mind a visible mark there, but how will I know if that's the best place for it?

It feels nice when he licks, good when he nibbles, and absolutely fucking brilliant when his teeth threaten to sink in.

I gasp, "Yes, there!"

He hums against me, his cock gliding along mine again, only this time he takes my hand and maneuvers it between us, making me fist us both.

The grinding and gliding doesn't stop, and with me helping things along faster, we're both moaning and panting in a minute flat. I can't get enough of how we feel together, and I mix our pre-cum with my thumb, rubbing across both of us. Korey groans loud, vibrating against my skin, and thrusts harder. Tension thunders through my body, pressure building.

"Sir," I pant, "I'm—"

With a deep, monstrous growl, his teeth elongate and pierce my skin. I yowl in pain, in euphoria as my orgasm breaks. A searing line of fire spreads from the tingling mark, and I can feel him, meshing with me, threading his bits in with mine. I feel his heart, his soul, his utter and complete happiness at being chosen by me, how he wanted to ask me, but thought it would scare me, how he meant every word he's uttered since he met me, and how he'd do anything in this life and the next eighty, just to make sure I'm happy, cared for, protected, and loved.

298

I didn't know anything this pure and special existed, but it does, and its name is Korey, and I have him, he's mine forever.

He takes over pumping, because I'm a sob-laughing lump of useless. He paints my stomach with a gloriously loud roar, muffled slightly by my shoulder, and stills, breathing heavily, smoothing his hand over our combined seed, smearing it on my stomach.

I can't believe the audacity of my cock to twitch again at a time like this, but it actually whacks Korey's hip. He chuckles and unlatches, giving me long, slow, nurturing licks as the wound closes. Little zips of energy skitter through me with each one. It's amazing. No wonder everyone's so keen on mating all the time.

"I bloody well loved that," I rasp, grabbing his face when he's mostly done. I kiss him over and over, smooth my cheek along his beard, rub my nose on his, and finally collapse back on the bed. I haven't been this comfortable with anyone my whole life. It's something I didn't even know to miss.

"So did I," he murmurs, kissing along my collarbone. "Still want your own cabin?"

An amused scoff bursts out of me. "Sod off, I'd crawl under your skin and live there if I could. My own cabin."

Korey laughs, deep in his chest, warming me to my toes.

But then I think better of it and wince. "Actually..."

He pulls back and tilts his head. I see the moment it dawns on him.

"Oh...shit."

I nod. "Shit indeed. Cyan."

30

VEIKKO

Cyan's expectant gaze keeps drifting from me to my writhing mate, until he can't help himself and leans over, claiming her mouth.

Her pleasure doubles, spreading through the room like a summer breeze. When he hooks his hand around her throat and squeezes, she shatters, screaming into his mouth, bucking against my tongue and fingers.

It's an incredibly arousing scenario.

All of this has been. Had I known the pleasures that awaited if I simply gave in to the pack bond, I might have considered it earlier. Though, perhaps not.

The energy between Neo and Aeon has been interesting as well. I couldn't say what possessed me to shove his head down, other than I was enjoying their enjoyment of each other.

I could never be that rough with Reanne, though. I'm too strong, the risk of injury is too great. While we believe she's aiding in our healing, that doesn't mean she's able to heal herself from a potentially mortal wound.

Start talking, Vik.

Cy cuts his gaze at me as he frees her neck and shoves two fingers in her mouth, which she sucks with fervor.

My cock throbs at the sight, longs to be in her again, but I suppose that will have to wait.

I glance at Neo, whose eyes are wide, brows up and mashed together. Aeon's face is less concerned, though still curious.

They worry needlessly. Yes, Cyan is the only logical choice, one Reanne knows in her heart. I can see it in her reactions to him, feel it in the air around us.

But I will not force anything upon her via trickery or coercion. I am not a monster. Anymore.

I place kisses along her soft inner thigh before standing.

You can use Aeon as a bite surrogate. He enjoys the pain.

Aeon's eyes widen, but he doesn't deny it. It would be foolish to do so. Cyan blinks at me, hand stalling mid stroke and takes his fingers back from her mouth.

Reanne sighs happily and pushes up to her elbows, but once she catches our expressions, her smile falls. "Are you guys talking in the link again? What about? Wait, not about me, right?"

Cyan's gaze narrows. *My beast is horny, not stupid. No. It's a bad idea. Korey just needs to hurry the fuck up. I'm sick of waiting.*

"Hi." Reanne waves her hands in front of my face, smiling, now on her knees. "You know what, okay. We'll do it my way then."

Before I can do anything, she presses her forehead to mine.

It is impossible not to think about her proximity, her

scent, her softness when she's mashed against me. I love her so.

Her mouth curls into a smile. "Well, what you're thinking about is pretty straight forward. I love you, too." She gives me a sweet kiss and faces Cyan. His eyes no longer hold heat, there's jealousy there, unless I'm wrong.

"Do I need to get into your head too? Or are you guys going to share?"

Cyan quirks a brow, energy snapping in the room like a snare line, and grabs a handful of her hair, craning her head back. She gasps, but it's not in pain, no, I've learned my mates sounds. He tugs her close and bites her chin before dragging his nose down her neck.

"Nobody gets in my head without permission. And you'll know what I want you to know."

"Sorry," she whimpers, shuffling closer. "I just hate being left out."

"Funny, so do I."

"W-what do you mean?"

Cyan's mood darkens further, his beast shimmering closer to the surface.

"We should keep her more in the loop. There's no reason not to." Aeon's tone is too sharp. Too commanding.

Cyan growls, low, running his nose along her shoulder now in warning. Aeon doesn't care, or doesn't notice, recklessly endangering her either way.

Aeon...

My attempt falls on deaf ears. Reanne's energy has changed too, whether in relation to Cyan's or the room in general, her instincts have taken over, the Aruna side now in control. She's still as a stone, doing her best to not attract attention. I fear it's too late for that. At least she's in the proper mindset for what might occur. It will be less...devastating.

"I'm serious. She's smart and if things concern her, I think—"

Without additional warning, what I excepted comes to pass, and Cyan clamps down on Reanne's shoulder—Aeon's mark—slicing into their bond. She cries out in genuine pain, and Aeon grunts in shock, clutching his chest, tears hovering in his eyes. Neo panics, unsure who to go to, while I simply wait, despite the bitter ache in my soul.

I've seen this display in the past. At times, an Alpha must remind the mates who is truly in charge. Especially when the mate claim threatens the hierarchy. It isn't enjoyable, but is necessary. Ours is an even more precarious situation, because Cyan isn't her mate yet, and if Aeon wasn't so bonded to the pack, to his Alpha, he could lose control, attack Cy for hurting her. Even I can't deny the impulse to protect her.

But still, I simply wait.

Because Cyan isn't an ordinary Alpha, Reanne isn't an ordinary Aruna, and I have a uniquely renewed sense of faith in what they can be together, what they will gift werewolf kind with their union. I've fought it long enough.

The loss of any of us along the way would be inconsequential to them reaching their true heights, their true purpose. Perhaps mating has turned me into a new version of myself, one too full of hope for my own good. Or perhaps I was born to be a zealot of any cause, but I much prefer this one, where I get to be happy, where packs can flourish, and love could truly conquer all.

The energy in the room changes, dimming slightly, and Neo ultimately stays put, though he vibrates with uncertainty. After leveling a chillingly heavy stare at Aeon and a slow examining sweep around the room, his point well made, Cyan unlatches. Aeon sucks in a deep breath and stumbles off the end of the bed, shock painting his face.

Reanne is worse by far. Her tears hurt me, they hurt all of us, and as much as I want to hold her, only the Alpha can soothe this pain, if he chooses to. He could leave her suffering as further show. He could go so far as to let the bite fester, leaving the bond weakened, the two of them vulnerable and inconsolably heartsick.

His father did that and worse on many occasions to keep the BriarMaw in line.

But I know Cyan, and he is not his father.

Slowly, cautiously, he loosens his hold on her hair. He moves that hand to the back of her neck and wraps his other arm around her waist, cinching her against his body. Blood trickles down from the unloved wound on her shoulder as he sits back and cradles her pliant form across his lap.

He grips her chin and presses his forehead to hers, closing his eyes. She cries harder at first, but slowly calms, tears stalling before drying completely, yet they stay locked in their positions.

Neo glances around the room, trying to catch my attention, but I'm too focused on Reanne's shoulder.

Despite knowing order has been restored, anxiety flits through me at the still bleeding mark. Her system should have slowed the flow at this point. Perhaps mate bites are beyond her healing ability. Or I've interfered just as I feared.

Finally, Cyan breaks their connection, tucks her head on

his shoulder, and laps at the wound. A shiver ripples her muscles, a stuttered breath in her lungs as she relaxes. He's tender and slow, long licks combined with soothing strokes on her hip as he cleans and heals with so much love it makes my own heart react.

It's a charged encounter, to be sure. Threat, punishment, promise and forgiveness, all done to show stability and control.

Aeon doesn't appear to be handling any of it well. But, he is not my primary concern. She is, and at present, Cyan's attention is heating her skin, stoking her fire back to life. I can only assume he mentally explained why he had to do it, but that's not my place to know or question.

My place is at their side in whatever capacity they see fit, but I will also keep my primary goal in mind. Reanne must not choose Mishka, under any circumstances.

Aeon

I can't believe he **did that**. Why would he hurt both of us just because of my stupid mouth? He could have done like last time, or punched me, or I...I don't know, anything other than use our bond.

My chest burns, ReeRee's pain compounding mine with each of her heartbeats. At least he's tending the bite now.

But he's leaving me here, ignoring me completely, while he heals her. What kind of dick move is that? You think he'd care about me at least a little, after everything we've been through, what we all just did together, I mean, I'm his partner, his Beta for fuck's...

Oh. It all makes sense now.

This pit of hurt he left in me sours, sending daggers through my limbs.

He really does plan to replace me with Laz, and he's forcing a wedge between us, hoping it won't hurt as bad when he finally kicks me to the tree line. It's the only reason I can come up with for such a randomly harsh punishment.

I can't enjoy Reanne's renewing excitement, because I still feel like I'm being scalded. A heavy dose of Alpha waves fan out, and even though none of us want to, we're all compelled to leave. I can't even turn around to see if she's okay.

We're all the way to the fire pit before I can control my feet. Funny, because control is actually the last thing I have right now.

I stare at the flames, fists clenching, this pain boiling me. "He's gone too far."

"That was weird, wasn't it?"

My skin tingles. Neo is too close. I don't need his energy right now. I don't want to feel anything good and pure and soft. I need to hurt something.

"Sonofa...I forgot about the stew. Again."

He moves off to my left, grabs the giant pot with a huff, and trudges to the bramble pile near Vik's clearing, taking his irritatingly beautiful energy with him. I watch him walk, watch his muscles flex and jump until he's out of the fire's glow, then I close my eyes and rub my temples.

If Cyan wanted to bump me down, there were easier ways to do it. He could have just told me, for starters. 'Hey, don't want you as my Beta anymore.' That wouldn't have been hard.

I wince, gnashing my jaw as the pain spreads.

"He should have tended you," Vik rumbles off to my right as he sits on a stump.

"Yeah, no shit." I hate that my voice catches, my vision blurring.

"I...could try."

I spin to face his perfectly sincere expression. "Huh? How?"

Maybe he means with his medicines or something.

He stares at me, tongue in his cheek like he's sizing me up. "Can we trust each other, Aeon?"

"If you're asking me to keep something from Cy then the answer is hell yes."

"I am asking...if you will continue to keep it from him when you are no longer angry." He stands, looming above me, underlit by crackling flames. "I am asking, if you will keep it from Neo. From everyone."

Neo. Why is everything about him all of a sudden? Why does thinking about that kiss completely destroy my brain? I don't want to be with him. Ever. It would be awful, we aren't the least bit compatible. That's final. Which means I have no problem keeping a secret from him.

I shrug with a nod. "Sure."

Veikko scans the area before focusing on me again. "I have Alpha blood."

"Wow. Seriously? That's crazy!" Wait... My eyes bulge. "Oh. Oh, damn. You mated Reanne, but if you—he would have never let—"

He holds up his hand. "I am not a seated Alpha, Aeon. And I have no intention of breaking pack, stealing her away like a thief in the night. I believe in Cyan. He is a good Alpha."

Yeah, I thought so too. Once. My lungs deflate, but I hold my tongue. It explains why she's so extra drawn to Vik, though. And that weird energy while we were all having sex. And why he stayed on the outskirts, here and when we were in BriarMaw. I can't believe we didn't notice. I guess, though, he was holed up with Fen and Agnar most of the time. And his size makes sense now, he must be really old. Way older than we thought. I wondered why he was so damn big, but never asked. Not that he ever talked. Cyan might not get that big, but he will grow more with time. Fucking Cyan.

I stare up at Veikko again, with new eyes. An Alpha. I could follow him if he did start his own pack. I know he doesn't want to, but it's an option maybe. I bet he wouldn't replace me. Well, assuming he wants a sub-standard Beta. And if I went, maybe Neo could come too, and we could— what in the fuck is *wrong with me!*

I scrub my face over and over, hoping to clean the thoughts from my brain.

Another wave of pain hits, and I whimper with the most injured sound possible, because I am injured. If I were a woodland creature, predators would be swarming.

"The alternative is to hurt until he allows us to return. Then ask him to assist."

"Fuck no," I grit out. "No, you do it. Uh, please."

"It could damage your bond with Cyan."

"That's his whole plan anyway." I slap the tear off my cheek.

"Why do you think that?"

"It doesn't matter." I wince again, my whole torso stinging like I'm being sliced with thorns over and over. "Please."

He exhales heavily through his nose and grips my arms. "Your mark is on her left shoulder?"

"Mmhm." My lips are mashed together to keep from crying out in pain, my muscles quaking.

He steps behind me. "I will try to be careful, but I have never done this. I need to cut you. It is best to keep quiet."

I nod once.

I know what Cy's healing energy feels like, all too well. But I don't know what to expect from Vik, and I should be more nervous than I am, given how old and probably powerful he is, but this is too much.

My breath catches, a shout lodging in my throat as a claw slices into my upper back, behind where Reanne is marked. He drags a crescent shape, blood draining out. Strange, jagged energy seeps into my body from his hands, thick, heavy, nearly choking. An attack on my system by a foreign Alpha.

He quickly runs his tongue along the wound, and I suck in a deep breath, dizzy from relief. It's gone. I almost laugh from joy. Now, I can tell I'm still connected to Reanne, she's still my ReeRee, and she's not hurting at all. Everything is fine. I could die happy compared to before.

"Thank—"

He licks again and my teeth buzz. That energy curls through me, plucking away, beckoning me, promising me, asking for my loyalty, my allegiance, my body, my life.

It's tempting, even though I know he's not really asking. He's so powerful the call is probably tied directly to his energy at this point. Damn. That's dangerous. It's also hard to...deny. It sweeps over me, caressing my skin now, like ten hands at once. I lean into him, pushing my spine against his stomach, needing more contact, more energy. I don't mean to tilt my head to the side, baring my neck, and I sure as hell don't mean to whine, to keen.

He lets out a scarily soft, slow, deep growl, tightening his hands, because I'm submitting so hard right now it's ridiculous. Even if he doesn't want me, this, a pack, none of it, he's still an Alpha, and my energy is still begging to be his.

The only thing that stops me from severing the bond with Cy right here, right now, is Neo, clearing his throat in front of me.

My eyes pop open, and Vik straightens, letting his hands fall away. It's a nearly violent loss to my body, but I keep myself standing.

I can't read Neo's expression, but the flickering shadows across his face make him seem angry and sad, in alternating patterns.

"Starting again without me?" It's a joke, but there's no humor in his smile or his eyes, eyes he casts down at my— oh, hell.

I cover myself, which is frankly, the stupidest thing I could have done and makes this seem like some...affair. Doubly stupid, because we're all naked most of the time and erections are a thing that happen a lot. Like, a lot a lot. Especially if you're being wooed by an Alpha.

But I can't explain that. Shit. Whatever. I'm so tired of this man messing with my mind.

His brows launch up, a soft laugh escaping through his nose as he flails a hand. "Don't stop on my account."

"It's not like that." Oh, my fucking—my mouth needs to stop. Immediately.

"Why would I care what it's like?" He tilts his head, genuine curiosity in his gaze and I couldn't feel more idiotic. He doesn't like me either. That's a good thing. A great thing. That means there is no thing. I didn't want a thing anyway. So, no explanation is necessary.

He sets his pot down on his prep station with an extra

loud clang and rubs his face. "When do you think he'll let us back in?"

Yes, that's what I keep forgetting. He's madly in love with Cyan, and that's another great thing. The favorite toy. The soft one, who gets all the gentle affection Cy has without having to be hurt first. Which is great, and I'm not jealous at all. I don't like that stuff anyway, not from Cy.

I scream-grunt into my palms and drop down on a stump. I can't stay here. I can't think about Cyan, I don't want to be replaced, and I obviously can't stop thinking about Neo with him in my damn face all the time. But I love Reanne, and I need to be with her. I need to hold her again, kiss her, that would help tremendously. None of which can happen without being near Cyan again.

"Soon," I sigh forcefully. "I hope."

32

REANNE

He's being careful and quiet this time, but I knew the moment Cy and Mishka swapped, while Cy was still attached. It's so bizarre how, even though it's still Cyan's body, everything changes, from the pressure of his touch to the way he breathes. I'm still on his lap, pretending I haven't noticed anything.

But this means it's Mishka who unlatched and healed me. Mishka comforting me, soothing me. Mishka, pretending to be my Alpha, inching his fingers closer to my core with each stroke along my hip. And I kind of hate my body for enjoying his affection, but I still don't feel that violent need that Cyan gives me. Mishka's energy just isn't the same. At least...not in someone else's body.

His thoughts were a racing jumble. He doesn't know I can read those, so he was just connecting, being gentle. Playing the part. And plotting.

He's angry that Cy had hurt me and was consumed with fixing it. Frustrated that his plan to kill Cy didn't work, confused at how he's still alive. He pictured all the ways he would worship me, figuratively and literally. Tons of servants at my command, a huge throne, feasts, a beautiful bedroom.

Then the thoughts turned dirty, those same servants bringing me to new heights of pleasure, he and I doing all sorts of things on that throne, food served to him on my body before more sex, and that bedroom defiled in every conceivable way.

After that, they turned dark and calculating. He wanted to be patient, wanted to wait, wanted me to come to him. But he knows I have three mates, now, and he's coming for me instead, before Cyan has a chance to claim me. Which means I was right in guessing Cy is the other High Alpha.

When Mishka gets here, he'll kill anyone who stands in his way without remorse. Even my mates, even though that would destroy my heart and make me hate him forever. He's prepared for that.

I can't let that happen.

The way I see it, I have two choices. I can pick Cyan as soon as he and Mishka swap back, or...I can go with Mishka to keep him from hurting the ones I love, and hopefully buy myself a little more time.

Because I'm still scared as hell of this power, the position, all of it. I haven't suddenly decided I'm okay with it, I killed a man for God's sake, with my mind! Was it a one-time accident? Is this a thing I do now? Will it get worse? And I know we haven't had time to really chat about it, but no one here seems to be able to tell me what it means, or how to control it. What if Mishka can? What if he has books or people who've studied this, people who can help me?

Worse, what if I do pick Cyan? They'll want to kill Mishka, there might still be a battle and my mates could be hurt or killed, and if they succeed in killing Mishka I'll never learn what he knows. Hell, I might accidentally end up killing my mates because I get mad about something stupid. What if my next bout with PMS wipes out all the werewolves and I'm left completely alone?!

Okay, calm down. Calm down. I still need to pretend, I still have a little time.

Mishka's fingers graze my overly sensitive flesh, and I can't help my small gasp. It's Cyan's skin but colder, and I'm so distraught. His mouth slowly curves in triumph against my shoulder.

A blast wave of Alpha energy circles the room, and my mates file out, silently. My heart hadn't stopped hammering, but now it thunders. We're alone.

"What gave me away, precious dove?" He whispers in my ear, sending chills parading down my arm.

I try to sit up, but his grip turns painful. "Ah, ah. Be still. I have far less control over this body when it's in such an aroused state. The beast is just there, waiting for the slightest provocation. There's no telling what it might do without its proper master. What I might let it do."

I open my mouth, but he claims it before I can speak, and again, even though this is fully Cyan's body, this isn't his kiss at all.

It's solid, rhythmic, and steady like the ocean. Almost mesmerizing. He cups my face and dives deeper, tasting me, and I can't help but return it, breathing harder as his other hand slips along my leg again.

But it's wrong, it's all wrong. The energies in here are twisted, my mates are confused, hurting, but they can't get back in, and Cyan is who knows where, probably worried. I have to end this, one way or another.

"Stop," I gasp, breaking free and grab his hand now on the inside of my thigh. "Not...not in his body."

He stares at me, searching my eyes for something. "Do you know I'm coming for you?"

I nod, stuttering a breath, holding his gaze, pretending to be some stronger version of myself.

"I'll win, sweet dove, even if you fight me. Whatever plan, whatever plot you think will grant you victory, I assure you, I've prepared for it. I will have you."

I nod again, tightening my grip on his wrist.

He spreads his fingers and presses them into my flesh, gaze dipping before he brushes his lips against mine, his warm breath tickling my skin. "Are you going to fight?"

"N-no," I murmur, releasing his wrist and placing my trembling hand on his face. "But only if you promise not to mate me right away. I need time. And you can't hurt anyone else. No poison or anything like that."

He chuckles and slides his hand the rest of the way, grazing my outer lips with the backs of his fingers before sliding two inside. I suck in a breath while his whooshes out in a low groan, his mouth barely touching mine.

"Why would I promise anything of the sort?"

He eases his wet fingers out and back in slowly, teasing my body to a frenzy. I don't want to enjoy it, but they're Cy's fingers and all of my cells cry out for his.

"Because...if you...do...ohh."

He's picked up the pace, his smile curling up again. "I'm listening. Do hurry, though."

I whimper and force the thought out in a rush. "If you kill my mates, I'll never be the same...*ahhh*...won't be able to love you, like you want. Just give me the chance to learn. I'll go with you, meet your pack, get to know you, just please, please don't hurt them."

He stills, and I'm a tangle of reactions. I need the release, my skin burns, every part of me aching, desperate for the contact and hyper-focused on the air we're sharing.

I bite into my tongue to keep from begging him to finish. He eases his fingers out, and gives me a soft kiss, but instead of removing his hand entirely, his fingertips trace up my stomach, stalling in the center of my chest.

"Very well. If you do as you've said, then I'll do as you've asked. They'll be spared."

Tears spring up in my eyes, spilling over before I can wipe them away. "Thank you." It's watery and weak, but it's full of as much gratitude as I have in my soul.

"You even cry like a goddess," he murmurs, kissing each of my cheeks before leaning back. "I'll have you know, I only used what was available. Someone here had plans of their own. And it would have been foolish of me not to take advantage of such an obvious gift. Removing one's competition is the most expedient way to get what one wants. Now, no more tears." He sends another wave of his energy, and I swap from relieved to overheated like he flipped a switch.

"Tell me whose mark this is," he lazily traces the side of my breast, leaving a trail of my wetness and setting me on fire.

There's not enough oxygen in this room. I can't hold out much longer, but I dig my nails into my palms.

"Neo's," I whisper.

"Mm. The feisty little Zed. And this one?" He continues

the path up to my neck, leaving another lazy trail along Vik's bite.

"V-Veikko." Don't beg him, don't beg him. When he's gone someone else can help me.

His gaze collides with mine like a ship crashing into a glacier. "The Sentinel...mated you."

I nod, but me confirming doesn't seem to make him any happier, despite his growing smile. In fact, the glacier turns into an ice storm, threatening to slice me to shreds. "How clever." He pulls back all the way, eyeing me. "Very clever indeed. I told him you were smart, but it seems I didn't give him enough credit."

I'm too keyed up to keep my emotions in check, everything too much. "There wasn't some master plan, I love him. He loves me!"

"Of course you do." Mishka chuckles again and thumbs my nipple, sending a violent shockwave of desire all the way to my toes. "You know, this used to be my favorite game," he purrs, "with our previous Aruna. Tease her until she couldn't take it, then pleasure her until even that was too much. I feared I'd never find anyone else so...aware. Yet here you are, half again as sensitive as she was. It's rare, you know. One more way you're special."

There's an unexpected sadness in his gaze and permeating the air around him. I get the idea he truly loved her, whoever she was, with his whole heart. And he's suffered without her. But that doesn't excuse, or...or change anything.

He repeats the action, and tremors rock my frame as I force my shaky breathing to even out. I can't...I can't.

"Not only stunningly beautiful, but also powerful, and

finally soon to be mine. A glorious life of extremes awaits you, sweet dove."

He hovers his hand above my breast, each of my labored breaths putting it millimeters from contact, and I know, beyond the shadow of a doubt, if he touches me again, I won't be able to control myself. His eyes hold mine, softening.

"I look forward to meeting you, Reanne. In the flesh."

He hasn't moved, but the heat radiating from his palm pricks my skin, commanding all my focus. I can't help but wonder how long he played his games before, how much I could take, how I'd compare.

"And tell your Alpha," he brushes my lips with his again, but there's a static pop, an explosion of all the right energy as Cyan jerks back and pushes me off his lap, glancing around with terrified eyes. He studies my shoulder, like he's locked in a nightmare. It only takes him another second to reorient, but when he does, he's angrier than I've ever seen, ever felt.

"Fucking piece of shit," he roars. "I'm gonna rip his arms off and beat him to death with them when I see him. Stay put. I have to find Korey."

I don't even get a chance to reply, the door cracking behind him, as my heart races.

There's only one reason I can think of that he needs Korey. And I'm not ready to mate yet, I don't want the power yet. It's too soon!

All I can do is run. I scramble off the bed and fling open the door, only to be met by three sets of concerned eyes.

Aeon's arms are around me first, so tight I can barely breathe, and I want to cry and cling to him and hear him promise me everything will be fine, but it won't be. "Put me down, please. I have to go!"

"Go? What? Where?"

Veikko grips my shoulder, trying to get me to look at him, but I refuse, kicking and struggling harder.

"I can't stay here, Cyan wants to mate me now, and if I do that, Mishka will kill you all, he was just here, talking to me, so please let me go!"

"He could try," Veikko rumbles, a dark tone in his voice I didn't know he was capable of. I wish I shared his optimism, but the things I saw in Mishka's mind were not untested plans. There's a wave of energy from Aeon, and my heart slows, closer to normal speed.

"I knew something was up when he shoved us out the door." Neo frowns behind Aeon. "But baby bird, you can't go racing into the forest alone at night."

"Then come with me, but I can't be here when he gets back. Please, I'm not ready. I don't want the power yet, I don't want things to change, I don't want you guys hurt, I love you too much."

"Leave?" Neo's eyes widen. "Us?"

"I'll take you," Aeon growls against my shoulder. "I'll go with you."

He sets me down and I stare up into his soulful eyes, nodding.

"Oh, this is such a bad idea." Neo whines. "You're his Beta, you don't think he'll notice?"

"Nope. I think he'll be just fine." Aeon's face is a mask of pain.

Veikko sighs, eying Aeon weirdly. "My cabin—"

"No, wait!" Neo plugs his ears, "Don't let me hear it." He hums and squeezes his eyes closed.

"—Two hundred miles northeast, between MoonMare Cavern and the Lake of Tears. Go."

The sudden blip of Alpha energy makes panic well in my chest. Cyan must be on his way back. "We have to hurry."

Vik taps Neo's shoulder and nods as he lowers his hands. "They are leaving now."

"Okay, but..." Neo whispers it, glancing between the two of us. He and Aeon lock gazes for the longest, a heavy pause in the air. "Will you come back?"

Aeon takes a half step toward Neo but stops, instead thrusting out his hand. Neo glares at it like it's the single most confusing thing he's ever seen, but he twists his mouth to the side and firmly grasps it. They stare at each other, and I don't know if they're talking in link or too afraid to say anything at all. But finally, Neo gives it a single pump before jerking his hand back and crossing his arms tightly, his focus now completely on me, despite Aeon's unbroken stare.

"Are you sure you want to do this? How long will you be gone?"

"I don't want to," I sniffle, "I have to. And I don't know, I just need a bit more time." I hug his neck, forcing him to lose his closed off posture.

He squeezes me to his chest and kisses me firmly. "I love you, be careful. Come back."

Not soon, not in one piece, not someday, just come back at all. He's worried this is the last time he'll see me. It won't be. It can't be.

Veikko tucks Laz's coat around my shoulders and spins

me to face him. "When you are ready, Cyan is the best choice. The only choice. His heart is pure, his motives are pure, and he loves you, even if he does not know how to show it."

Damn my eyes, leaking again. I know he loves me, that's not what this is about. But I nod and leap up, wrapping my arms around his neck. "I love you, I'm sorry."

He nods, kissing me deeply before setting me down. My hands don't want to let go. I wish it was Vik coming with me instead, but Aeon grabs my hand and pulls me through the door so quickly all I have time for is a single glance back as it closes.

The next breath, his form erupts into a massive brown werewolf, and he scoops me up with no effort, so careful with his clawed hands. The adorable cabins, the fire, Neo's prep station, Veikko's clearing, the river, it all shrinks behind me as we race through the forest, until there's nothing to look at but trees.

That's when I let the tears come. And they come in sheets, in chest punching sobs. Cyan is going to be so sad. So angry. Because of me. That's what hurts the most. The farther we get from his energy, the emptier I feel. There's a void inside me, now. Aeon clutches me tighter against his furry body, but even his warmth can't chase this bone-deep chill away.

It's all happening so fast. I just wanted to be happy. I want everyone to be happy. I'm not sure I'll ever be ready, really, but I know I'm not ready today, and I know I won't be able to wait much longer.

I can only hope this is the right decision to buy myself a little time.

CYAN

I'm already so tired of that asshole jumping into my body I could puke, and it's only been twice. Closing my eyes in my house and opening them in some weird, dimly lit cavern is too fucking much.

There wasn't anyone to pretend in front of this time, at least. But I did check out the place, and it's a damn good thing.

I burst through the door to Korey's cabin, to find he and Laz cuddled up on the bed. They sit up, and Laz flushes from head to toe, quickly covering himself with a pillow. Fucking adorable, but no time to deal with that.

"He has Suzette," I growl.

Korey leaps to his feet, eyes wide. "What? No. She...she died."

"She's alive as hell, Kor."

He's not listening to me, gaze distant. "She wandered too close to the border. Or got injured and we couldn't find her. She's dead."

"Korey. He has her. Or he knows where she is. In a cell. She's not dead."

Something like recognition hits him and he focuses on me. "Who? Who has her?"

"Mishka."

All his color drains away, and he races to me, gripping my arms.

"Are you sure?"

I nod. "Dead ass positive. I saw her with my own—well, fuck, I guess his eyes. She looks different, obviously, but I'd know that silver hair and frown anywhere. She's probably been there this whole fucking time."

"Mishka...was here? You-you swapped again?" Laz's voice is a trembling whisper.

"Yeah, but it was quick. Just long enough to know that bastard is going down."

"Suzette..." Korey drops to his knees, hands over his mouth, shaking with fear, with excitement. Laz slinks off the bed and curls against his back, hugging his neck as Korey holds his arms like he's a lifeline.

I crouch in front of him and grip the back of his head. "We'll get her. I dunno how, or when, but I swear to you, as your Alpha, as your friend, we'll get your daughter back."

He nods, letting out a shaky breath.

"You gotta tell Reanne, too. I could, but it ain't my story. What kind of slimy stain steals kids?"

"Ah, well, that does seem to be his-his method. It's how I came to be, er, his. To start with. His collection, he called us sometimes. I know of that Nikta. We never spoke, you see, as I wasn't allowed—no matter, she seemed...lovely."

She was the cutest pup in BriarMaw. With her huge purple eyes, bright silvery-white hair, and dark skin, just like her mom. A complete accident, too. Luce, her mom, was visiting for some reason I can't remember, and she and Korey hit it off. Luce got pregnant that night, stayed until she died giving birth, like they almost always do.

Which left all of us caring for that furry terror. We loved her, and Korey was so proud of her, because having a Nikta when you're not an Alpha is unheard of. Non-Alpha breedings are always male. But Suzette obviously didn't give one shit about that rule, and that attitude never changed. Right up until she vanished.

Now, that bratty little nightmare is all grown up, living in some kind of prison slash zoo.

"A daughter," Laz chuckles softly. "Was afraid she was a long-lost lover."

Korey glances up over his shoulder and brushes his lips across Laz's. "There's only you, little pup," he murmurs before they remember I'm here, then they both manage to look sorry and not sorry at all.

If I thought the difference between Vik and Reanne was hot, I swear on my dick the way Korey and Laz look together is the sexiest fucking—this is a sandwich I need to be slap in the middle of, the first damn second I can.

He clutches Laz's hands tighter, leaning his head against his, and that's when I see it.

"Lazzy boy."

His eyes snap to mine, widening by the second. "Y-y-yes?"

"Is that what I think it is?"

His hand flies to his neck, and Korey straightens, all fluffed out like he's big and bad. Like he could stop me from doing a damn thing I wanted to.

"Whose is it?" As if I don't know.

"Ah, well, you see—"

"Mine. Laz is my mate." Korey stands, blocking Laz from my line of sight completely, sending out protective vibes.

It takes all I have not to laugh. "You coulda waited for me."

He nods, jaw tense. "I'm sorry. We sort of got carried away."

"Did he get hurt?"

"N-no, no it was...wonderful." Laz mumbles into Korey's back.

Why the hell they think I'll be mad, I have no idea. This is the greatest fucking news ever.

Joining Laz to the pack will be a breeze now. But best of all, Reanne and I don't have to wait anymore. Will it be sketchier with only three mates to help out? Probably, but she's strong and with Laz around to help Aeon keep things calm, I'm not worried at all.

Oh, shit. Aeon. Mishka hijacked me before I could tend to him. I doubt he took care of him, even though I noticed Reanne's shoulder was healed. Shit, shit.

I slap Korey's shoulder. "Good job."

Laz peeks around his arm as Korey blinks at me. "Uh. Thank you."

"We'll make up for my absence later." I toss a wink to Laz, who blushes like it's his job. "I need to check on Aeon."

"What happened to—"

I'm already out the door, trotting toward the fire pit, but they aren't out there. My door is open though. Good, they're checking on Reanne.

I slow a bit, weirdly nervous about this whole thing. I can't wait to mate her, no question, but I still can't shake the damn shadow of my dad. I'll probably always worry about hurting her, but maybe that's the one thing that'll keep me from becoming him.

Look at me, growing and shit. I snort and stroll through my door. "Can't fucking wait to tell you guys my..."

Neo stares at me from the edge of the bed, wet eyes, tense posture. Veikko's giving off really weird, muted energy, but he's also tense, clutching the back of one of my chairs.

And...that's it. There's no one else in here. Maybe they're walking?

This black hole forming in my chest tells me that's a damn lie and I know it. I can't feel either of them here.

Korey and Laz come in behind me. "Oh, w-where is he?"

I can't breathe. The room narrows, twists. Thankfully, Laz rests his hand on my arm and blasts the whole cabin with Beta energy. I force my lungs open, but what comes out after that, I have no control over.

"Where...?" It's more growl than word, my beast clawing at the underside of my skin, Laz the only reason I'm not in full were mode, destroying this entire village.

"Gone, Alpha." Veikko lets his gaze fall to the floor.

There are tears on my face despite the rage eating away at my sanity. "Why?"

"She wasn't ready," Neo whispers, unable to meet my glare. "Wanted more time. So...Aeon took her...somewhere. Mishka has her scared. I guess he said things to her."

Fuck. I should have checked on her first. When I came back and she was in my lap, instead of wigging out, I should have made sure he hadn't hurt her, but Suzette is alive, I had to tell Korey.

"That fucking—" I grab the empty chair and fling it through the door with a wail. "She didn't have to leave! I would have given her time!"

"Would you?" Vik's tone is way too calm for this fucking nightmare situation.

I can't think about the honest answer to that question. I told her I'd take whatever I wanted, when I wanted, and that wasn't a lie. But I only want her. I thought she wanted me, too. Maybe I was too harsh, but fuck, I don't know how else to be! I would have tried for her, though. I still will, if that's what she wants.

It's Aeon's betrayal that digs at me hardest, though. To leave without word fucking one to me, to take our Aruna, take Neo and Veikko's mate, knowing that's going to cause them pain. Plus, I'm worried as hell that he's out there, hurting, because of this stupid shit with Mishka. And damn the moon, I already miss them.

"Mishka threatened our lives. She felt she had no choice."

"I'll show him threatening." I dig my claws into the back of my neck as I pace. The Beta energy in the air is helping less and less, either because I'm losing it, or because Laz isn't bonded to the pack fully, I don't know. And even if Laz was pack, I wouldn't replace Aeon. I love that mouthy fucker.

What am I gonna do without her? Without him? I send out a wave on reflex, testing my links, their energies, and the absence of his Beta response is the most violent thing I've ever felt.

I stumble through the door and arch back, roaring with what little air I have left.

Laz's energy doesn't touch me at all now. The pain is too fucking deep. They're gone.

I roar again, but this time it's a promise and a threat. I'll find them. I'll bring them home. I'll fix this. Then, I'll eat that body-jacking bastard's heart, right out of his chest.

Nobody messes with my family.

THE END!

Just kidding ;)

*To Be Continued in book two: **Hunted for the Pack***
Pre-order now!

Flip ahead for Hunted's blurb and a super helpful Guide to The Glade!

**The release date is set way in the future, just to give myself breathing room. Don't worry, it WILL be released sooner than the date you see, so make sure to join my group or my newsletter to stay up to date!

HUNTED FOR THE PACK BLURB

New bonds form while old ones are tested, another mate proves himself in more ways than one, and a certain secret may be the key to solving the worst puzzle they've encountered.

Reanne's choice tries to consume her, while the answers she seeks could come from deep below—and high above.

Cyan's race to repair his crumbling family is met with as many heated moments as heartbreaking ones, and our contender for High Alpha learns more truths than he ever wanted to know.

But nothing is as it seems in The Glade, and the moon is always watching.

Buy it now!

READ MORE OF
PRIM'S BOOKS

You can see current books & their content alerts on my website:

www.nataliaprim.com

MATES OF ARTRIZIKAS

Kali and the King

Gilly and the General

& many more coming!

THE GODLESS GALAXY

Talini's Ship Mate

Victoria's Nightmare Mate

& more soon

CELESTIAL CLAIM SERIES:

Dark PNR Werewolf Poly/Reverse Harem

Abducted for the Pack

Hunted for the Pack

Protected for the Pack

VIE DE MORT SERIES: Cowritten with Helena Novak

Dark Contemporary MF Erotica

His Innocent Muse

His Christmas Muse

His Insatiable Muse

& more

One offs: Jupiter's Fantasy

Natalia Prim has been fascinated with the broken and less-than-beautiful since she was a small girl. Now, not much bigger but definitely older, she writes s3xy stories where the rejected, misunderstood, or even downright evil get their happy endings and then some.

Sign up for my newsletter right on my website, or here:
Click here to join my email list!

Want more content? Check out my Patreon!
www.patreon.com/NataliaPrim

EVEN MORE?! Pop over to my discord server:
www.nataliaprim.com/discord

Click here to follow me on le Zon for release alerts.

For more k^nky shenanigans, hop into my reader's group: Prim's Pack
I do giveaways, write custom shorts, and am just generally goofy, so come hang out!
And follow me everywhere else by tapping the icons below!

facebook.com/NataliaPrimAuthor

twitter.com/AuthorNataliaP

instagram.com/author_nataliaprim

bookbub.com/authors/natalia-prim

goodreads.com/nataliaprim

tiktok.com/@author_nataliaprim

amazon.com/Natalia-Prim/e/B08VV7TSZY

A Zealot's Guide to
The Glade

Packs Thus Far & Characters
Met or Mentioned

SteelTooth — *Cyan, Aeon, Neo, Korey, Veikko, Agnar*
BriarMaw — *Yuli, ~~Fen~~, ~~Bertram~~*
GrimBite — *Mishka, ~~Silvin~~, Lazaros, Suzette*

~

Terms
(As have been revealed & are currently understood by the characters)

Alpha — *Leader and protector of a pack. Receives the right to lead by eliminating his father and taking the Alpha energy into himself. Done during an official 'Challenge'. Can choose not to form a pack of his own, thereby not fully activating the Alpha energy.*

Aruna — *Uncommon. A female, either human or werewolf, who is able to bond to all pack members, sate the Alpha urges, and if they survive mating the Alpha, they can produce offspring without dying.*

Aruna Rigdis — *According to prophecy, the one capable of ascending and ruling all werewolves as their Queen.*

Beta— *Any werewolf whom the Alpha chooses. Tasked with releasing Beta energy to keep emotions and pain at a reasonable level.*

Born Beta— *Extremely rare. Werewolf who can produce Beta energy without an Alpha present.*

Full moon freedom — *The one night a month werewolves can cross to the human world.*

High Alpha — *According to prophecy, the mate of the Aruna Rigdis, and therefore potential King of the werewolves*

Lake of Tears — *According to legend, where the moon goddess met the first Alpha.*

MoonMare Cavern — *According to legend, a place often visited by the moon goddess.*

Nikta— *Rare. A female werewolf. Typically dies giving birth. Born to Alpha pairings only.*

Seated Alpha— *When an Alpha takes his first pack member, typically a Beta, thereby fully activating the Alpha energy he obtained through Challenge.*

The Glade— *The protected realm where werewolves live. It weakens once a month, when the moon is full.*

Zed— *An Alpha's partner who has no other purpose in the pack. Sometimes used as a derogatory term.*

DON'T FORGET TO ORDER BOOK 2,
HUNTED FOR THE PACK!
http://www.smarturl.it/BuyHunted

BTW: There are teasers and more in my facebook group, so come join the fun! fb.com/groups/PrimsPack

Printed in Great Britain
by Amazon

15729984R00194